MQ WEBB

How to Spot a Psychopath

An Oscar de la Nuit Psychological Thriller

TBR
PRESS

First published by TBR 2022

First edition

ISBN: 978-0-6453520-1-6

This book was professionally typeset on Reedsy.
Find out more at reedsy.com

For Donald

Straw Man Argument

An argument and informal fallacy based on giving the impression of refuting an opponent's argument when really refuting an argument not presented by that opponent.

Chapter 1

Now

She'd caught Oscar's attention as soon as he saw her. Jessica Green, fingers laced together under her chin like a locked puzzle. She didn't fit the typical killer profile. Suburban journalist with a four-year-old and a husband.

Oscar's anxiety had subsided until it felt like he could breathe again. He was a forensic psychiatrist—reading people was what he did, and Jessica was interesting.

Whitner Psychiatric Hospital often saw people who were impacted by crime, but the media had painted Jessica as the perpetrator, and the police had placed her in remand. It looked like they were right, but she wouldn't tell anyone what had happened.

Oscar became fixated on her refusal to talk. There must be a reason for her silence, and he wanted to find out what it was. When the reporters asked their questions, pressing to find out whether she killed Mia Edwards, she averted her eyes, silently confirming their suspicions.

The journalists spinning stories about Jessica were her

colleagues. Did she feel betrayed by their willingness to turn her into an entertainment headline, using what they already knew about her to paint a picture of a woman who slowly unraveled?

Using the information from Jessica's remand center report and his own observations, Oscar had devised theories about what happened in the lead up to Mia's disappearance. Could a little girl just vanish on a play date without anyone noticing?

Oscar turned off the computer and walked down the hall of Whitner Psychiatric Hospital, slowing to watch the rain as it pelted the glass overlooking the courtyard. Maybe he'd brave the wet and take a walk—he needed one today.

Staying busy stopped his darkest thoughts from settling, and the soaking rain might be the distraction he needed tonight.

Popular opinion was that Jess knew what happened to Mia. Many thought that Jess had kidnapped or killed Mia. It was right there in the words the reporters used, their accounts laced with concealed accusations, but Oscar wasn't so sure.

He had watched uneasily as the case unfolded, listening as the police guessed what happened to four-year-old Mia. The first forty-eight hours were critical, but Mia had been missing for weeks. Despite their theories, the police hadn't found her and the remand report had suggested their counselors had all but given up on getting Jessica to speak to them.

But Oscar couldn't help thinking Mia had to be somewhere. Someone must have seen something that could help the police find her. Maybe someone knew what happened to her but didn't know how to say it, or they didn't even realize what they'd witnessed.

When Jessica was asked if Mia was alive, she hadn't answered.

Oscar had encountered missing person cases before, and he wasn't convinced that Jess had hurt Mia. He wouldn't make an assumption until he'd spoken to her. Right now, he knew that she didn't have a history of violence, except for the police report detailing the attack on her husband months before. She had a recent history of anxiety, but that didn't explain a leap to kidnapping and killing. There was no proof she'd hurt Mia, but they had pinned this on her and kept her in preventive detention until they found the proof they expected to find.

Mia.

Of course, the official line was that holding Jessica Green would prevent her from harming another child.

Oscar asked himself what Jessica's motive could be. He pored through reports, interviews, and details of Jessica's life, searching for something that would lead him to Mia.

Mia had attended the same kindergarten as Jess's daughter, Zoe, which only made Oscar question Jessica's guilt further.

Why would she kidnap a child when she had a daughter of her own?

Why give up little arms wrapping around her every morning, trading her family in for blank walls and prison regulations?

Why leave her own daughter without a mother?

Oscar pulled his attention from the raindrops, which ripped scars down the window. His briefcase sat against the wall below, inviting him to re-read Jess's notes one last time.

She'll be here tomorrow, Oscar reminded himself. *You can talk to her then.*

He'd spent all afternoon poring over Jess's remand center notes, preparing for her arrival. The reports all mentioned the same things. *Not responsive. Replies only when prompted.*

It was possible that Jessica had seen something that was too traumatic to remember. If there was any hope of Oscar helping her, he would have to get their first meeting right, or risk becoming another person she couldn't talk to. He needed to find out what she had seen, and if it turned out that she had kidnapped Mia, at least there would be some closure.

He was going to need that walk if he was going to get rid of his restless energy and get any sleep that night.

"Hey," said a friendly voice behind him. Oscar had locked himself in his office all day, reading over files, jotting notes and reviewing plans and catching up on emails, intentionally making sure he had no consultations scheduled. It was the first time he'd spoken to another human in hours.

"Oscar? Are you okay? Why are you standing in the hall?" asked Hayley Manning. She was somewhere around Oscar's age, also a psychiatrist, and someone whose professional opinion Oscar sought regularly. Hayley had a way with her patients, and could achieve a lot, even with a short stay. After a conversation with Hayley, you walked away feeling like you could achieve things you didn't know were possible.

"I was just watching the rain," said Oscar. "I thought everyone except the night staff had gone home." This part of the wing was peppered with offices, separated from the nurses and patient in-stay by a closed doorway to keep the noise of the ward from interrupting session consults and external meetings hosted in the building.

"Yeah, me too." She smiled and locked the door behind her, wrestling a satchel that was slipping from her shoulder.

"What kept you so late?" asked Oscar.

"Just staying on top of things... and avoiding laundry. How about you?"

Oscar shrugged. "New arrival tomorrow."

"Oh, that's right. Jessica Green. She kidnapped that little girl."

Oscar stood taller, tensing at Hayley's unexpected judgment. It seemed like everyone thought Jess was guilty, but Oscar hadn't expected it from Hayley, who usually asked questions before drawing conclusions, sometimes to the point of seeming like she was questioning Oscar's decisions.

What if bringing Jessica here was the wrong thing to do? He'd put in the transfer request assuming she might be refusing to talk because she was in a horrible environment, being held in detention and treated like a criminal without any proof, but what if he was wrong?

What if she didn't want to talk to him?

"What do you think she did with her?" asked Hayley.

"Excuse me?" said Oscar, uncomfortably.

"The little girl. Do you think they'll find her?"

Oscar sighed. "I don't know. I don't know that Jessica knows what happened to her."

Hayley seemed surprised. "She went missing from Jessica's house, didn't she?"

"Yeah. Jess was in the bathroom. According to the reports, she said Mia may have wandered outside and gotten lost. Anything could have happened. Maybe she got into a car—"

Oscar heard himself defending Jess and stopped. He didn't know what he believed, but it seemed unfair to decide without talking to her.

"If she didn't do it, why isn't she talking? I'd be telling anyone who'd listen that I didn't do it if I was accused of something like that."

"I don't know. It doesn't quite add up to me. I've been trying to figure it out." The truth was, he had spent too much of his time going over what happened, until finally, he realized there would be no further answers without talking to Jess. What he really wanted to know was why she wouldn't talk about what happened.

"Well, isn't that why you want her here?"

Oscar balked. He hadn't told anyone he'd made the transfer request, because he didn't want to draw attention to her arrival and cause speculation about transferring Jess to Whitner.

"What?"

"She's coming to Whitner so that you can figure it out, right?"

He breathed in, loosened his shoulders. Hayley didn't know about the transfer. She was speaking in general terms. He needed to calm down. He was acting too nervous, because he was afraid he mightn't be able to help her.

"Let's hope we find Mia alive and well."

"Listen, I haven't eaten since breakfast. I'm starving. Do you want to grab a burger?"

It had been a long time since Oscar had dined somewhere other than in his living room. "I should get home. It's late and I've got a busy day tomorrow."

Hayley's smile widened. "Come on. Still gotta eat, right? Can't run this place on an empty stomach, and I bet you haven't eaten since breakfast either."

She was right. He'd upended the oatmeal in his cupboard before leaving that morning, even the powdery bits at the bottom. He only shopped if he couldn't avoid it, keeping his distance from parents shopping with their kids, something he would never do again with his son.

"We can get burgers, maybe a side of fries, and I promise I

won't keep you out late. Kinda like after-work drinks, but with something more substantial. I have a question I wanted to run by you anyway, about a patient I'm treating for antisocial personality."

"Okay. Sure."

Oscar knew which patient she was referring to, but they didn't usually mention names outside of the office, and they tried to keep professional conversations as general as possible to protect the privacy of their clients.

"Meet you at Carnivals in fifteen?"

He knew Carnivals, it wasn't far from his place. It always smelled delicious when he walked past, the smoky scent of grilled onion wafting out of the doorway as people entered, but he never went in.

His stomach grumbled.

"See you there," said Hayley, smiling toward his growling stomach as if it had spoken for him.

Chapter 2

Now

Oscar arrived at Carnivals before Hayley, looking around at the blissfully unaware diners, smiling and laughing as if they were untouchable, immune to the horrible things that could happen without warning—the kind of things that could rip you from your family and put you in a remand center, accused of murdering a child.

Like Jessica.

Becoming a psychiatrist had sharpened Oscar's senses so that he noticed things about people that they didn't know about themselves. It was a curse, to know things people weren't ready to know, to see. Oscar had seen horrible things. He knew when someone was lying or being lied to, his senses primed by his own experiences, so that he could recognize the patterns that people followed when they were happy, sad, lying, or afraid. His subconscious worked over-time, sending him cues, telling him what to expect—even when he didn't want to know.

Busy attendants bustled between tables in black t-shirts

with vibrant lettering, bringing stacked burgers to hungry customers. Oscar eyed the food, trying to find the tastiest burger. His theory was, the more people who ordered something, the better it was likely to be.

An attendant with bright red pig-tails stopped in front of him, assessing his gray vest and matching pants. He probably looked uptight and serious compared to her flamboyance, but when he was at work, calm, neutral tones helped clients to focus, especially if they had a visual sensory processing disorder.

"Can I help you?" she said in a voice matching the vibrancy of her hair.

"Yeah. A table for two'd be great. Thanks."

"Alright," she said, her Doc Marten's moving toward a freshly vacated table. "We're pretty busy, but since there's only two of you, follow me."

She scouted the table for tips and wiped it down with a cloth from her apron pocket.

Did this many people really go out on a Tuesday night?

There were groups of two, three, four. A few had five or more. When he walked in the evenings, Oscar avoided this end of the street, where a bunch of pop-up cafes had sprung up overnight. It wasn't so much the cafés he avoided—it was the loud, buzzing voices coming from every direction. It was distracting and stopped him from thinking clearly.

Sometimes he waited until the lights went out in the sky. The darkness felt forgiving, like the past didn't exist, and the future was just an idea. At night he existed in the moment, without the stress of the day overshadowing him.

The attendant threw two menus onto a rectangular wooden table. "When you know what you want, you can order at the counter."

"Okay. Thanks."

Oscar pulled out a seat, the legs scratching at the floor. He sat and waited for Hayley.

He spotted her as she walked in, lips shining with color that wasn't there before. She waved and apologetically broke through the line at the counter, making her way to their table.

Was Oscar supposed to stand? It wasn't a date, but he couldn't remember how you were supposed to act in general.

"Hi," he said, offering a menu across the table as Hayley threw her coat over the chair.

She smiled and sat across from him, resting her hands on the menu. "Hey."

"When we know what we're eating, we order at the counter," said Oscar, looking around, regretting agreeing to dinner.

"Okay. I think I'll have the vegan burger," said Hayley, menu still closed. "Do you know what you want?"

"Vegan burger?"

"Yeah. Plant-based protein. You can't even tell it's not real meat."

"So, you're vegan?"

"Not really. I stick to a plant-based diet as much as possible, but sometimes I slip."

Oscar smiled. "Okay. I'll have the vegan burger too."

"Really?"

"Yeah. Now that you've said you can't tell that it's not real meat, I need to find out if you're lying to get me to try it."

"If it was a lie, it worked," said Hayley, pushing back her chair.

They made small talk about work as they waited for their food to arrive, from the mysterious buzzing in the lunchroom, and the many reasons to wear sunscreen even if you're just traveling to work, until Hayley said, "I have to ask—why did you approve Jessica Green's transfer?"

Oscar slicked back his dark hair, suddenly aware that he needed a haircut.

"You don't have to answer—"

"I thought she might need a new environment. She's not talking at the remand center."

Hayley studied him with the same focus she used when reading a patient. "Do you think? People have been trying to get her to talk since it happened. She didn't really talk to the police either. Maybe she doesn't want to say what happened?"

Oscar shrugged. "Maybe, but it's worth finding out."

Their burgers arrived hot, with a side of crunchy fries. Drinks followed shortly after, the attendant placing them on the table while their mouths were stuffed with fries. Oscar gave a *thankyou* gesture and eyed the burger patty. It smelled like barbecued onions and looked like meat—so far, so good.

"Some people in the team think this could put too much pressure on Whitner," said Hayley.

"Do they? What do you think?"

She wiped her mouth with a napkin, her gloss leaving a pink stain. "I think we should be careful. Jessica Green could get us a lot of unwanted attention." She looked sympathetic. "Mia went missing weeks ago. If they couldn't find her, what hope do we have?"

"Mia's disappearance is awful, and I hope they find her, but our job is to help Jessica. Imagine what it's like for her with everyone expecting answers. Maybe she doesn't know what happened to Mia. And if she does, we need to find out why she's not talking."

Hayley nodded and gripped her burger with both hands. She took a bite without making a face—good sign.

Eyeing the patty—not a vegetable in sight—he did the same, surprised at the deep barbecue flavor and juicy texture.

"What do you think?" asked Hayley avoiding a dollop of mayonnaise from her burger.

"It's good," said Oscar through a mouthful. It wasn't the real thing, but it was edible.

Hayley waited, and Oscar realized he'd answered the wrong question.

"Maybe I made a mistake having Jess transferred here, but I need to find out."

"If she could save Mia's family the pain of not knowing, why wouldn't she say something? She's had long enough. The kid's parents must be frantic. Jessica's a mother. She should understand."

Oscar set his burger on the plate. "I know it looks bad. Maybe she *should* know, but this makes no sense. I've seen a lot as a therapist, but this is new."

"So have I," said Hayley, matching his tone. "Enough to know that people do things you don't expect. Maybe Jessica did a horrible thing."

Wiping his mouth, Oscar scrunched his napkin and threw it onto the table.

"You don't agree?" asked Hayley.

"I think we should talk to Jessica first."

Hayley ate her burger in silence while Oscar picked at his fries.

"So, what did you want to ask me about treatment?"

"I lied. I didn't have a question about treatment."

"Oh?"

"I didn't want to talk where someone might overhear."

Oscar threw a snapped fry back onto his plate.

"Why did you fight so hard to get Jessica transferred here? Was it the publicity?"

"What do you mean?"

"I saw the request. I didn't read it, but I saw enough to know what it was about."

"Why were you in my office?"

"You wanted me to brief you on Lewis. When I got to your office, I knocked, but you didn't answer. I figured you had headphones in or something and the door was unlocked, so I went in."

"Shit."

"It was open on the screen," she said sheepishly.

"Okay." Oscar didn't remember leaving the email open.

What could he tell Hayley about the transfer request? He couldn't tell her the truth.

"It wasn't just a publicity stunt to build Whitner's profile, was it?" asked Hayley.

He checked the time. If he knew he was walking into an inquisition, he wouldn't have agreed to burgers. At work, he could escape to his office, but here there were eyes everywhere.

"I'm sorry, that came out wrong. I just couldn't figure out why you didn't mention it."

She was right. People would assume he wanted a high-profile case to show what a superstar he was when the infamous Jessica Green confessed to killing Mia Edwards.

"Who else knows?"

"No one," said Hayley. "I figured you had a good reason, so I didn't mention it."

Oscar nodded, trying to block the ambient noise. "I wanted

a chance to talk to Jess."

"She hasn't even talked to her family and friends."

"Maybe they asked the wrong questions."

"It's possible. But you're talking about a woman who attacked her husband with a kitchen tool that's used to pound meat. Maybe she's unwell, Oscar."

"Maybe, but what if she saw something traumatic? She might not remember what happened. And why Mia? We could go around in circles with this, but I'd prefer to ask Jess."

"All I'm saying is you might never know. Can you accept that?"

"Shouldn't we still try? What if Mia's out there, waiting for someone to find her?"

"Don't get your hopes up. Even if they find Mia, it's probably not good news after this long."

He nodded absently. "The transfer will probably stir the media. Maybe someone will come forward with new information."

Hayley looked skeptical. "And if not, get her to talk."

Chapter 3

Now

Oscar left with a full stomach, thinking about his ex-wife. Why was he thinking about Prisha now, when he'd just had a great dinner with Hayley? Prisha was the kind of person who didn't believe in second chances, especially when it came to Oscar—she'd tell Hayley not to date him.

Was it a date? It had felt like it. He wanted to kiss her goodnight, but didn't want to screw it up if she just wanted to be friends. Her shiny lips looked like they tasted of strawberries. Maybe he'd kiss her next time.

He walked her out to her car. They lingered, neither of them keen to say goodnight, but Oscar had to be alert the next day. Reluctantly, he closed her door and waved her off.

Prisha would've assumed Jess's silence made her guilty too. She'd agree with Hayley—an innocent person would want everyone to know they were innocent. They'd be angry at being accused of something so horrible.

Oscar wished he had the kind of assurance that came with fitting everything neatly inside of a box, but he knew that horrible things happened.

When Mia went missing, Avenue News had asked Jess for an exclusive, thinking that, as a former employee, she would tell them everything. They'd used the angle of her former employment to make her seem uncooperative when she'd told them the same as everyone else—that there was nothing to tell.

Other newspapers said there was evidence suggesting she'd killed Mia, but they couldn't say what the apparent evidence was. They claimed that her silence was a sign of arrogance, that she stayed silent because they'd never know what really happened.

They distorted her words for their headlines.

Nothing to see, nothing to tell: Jessica Green keeps her silence.

The search for Mia no longer had the urgency of the first days, when everyone had hoped she was hidden somewhere. Alive. The police had watched Jess, hoping she'd take food to Mia. When she didn't, they had assumed the worst.

Oscar knew what it was like to be accused of something horrific, to live with the guilt of ruining your life and the lives of everyone around you. It stopped you from forgiving yourself.

Was Jess punishing herself because she couldn't save Mia?

Maybe Jess's husband was like Prisha, pushing her buttons, pointing out everything she did wrong.

Attacked with a meat tenderizer.

No, the attack was before Mia disappeared. There had to be another reason. Was Clay a domestic violence survivor? There was nothing in her file about a conviction, but maybe he didn't report it.

What had Mia's disappearance cost Jessica? Her life would never be the same—people assumed she was guilty before she even had a trial.

Jessica's four-year-old, Zoe, wasn't likely to forget what happened. She'd lost her friend, and then her mother.

Oscar felt for the kid.

Prisha had never let Oscar forget their loss. Her need to express her pain had been greater than anything he'd felt.

What had happened to their family was his fault, and Prisha's anger was nothing compared to his own self-loathing.

He hadn't waited for her forgiveness. He couldn't forgive himself, and he wouldn't ask someone else to. It had cost them their marriage. It almost cost him his career. What hope could he offer when he had none? He was an imposter, asking people to share their pain, show their broken strings and still play in tune with the orchestra. He was the sheet music, demanding perfection without ever making a sound.

Years later, the same internal critic still told him he was a fraud. He'd learned to numb the criticism. Sometimes naturally, sometimes with the help of a whiskey or two after work. Over time, he got home later and drank them down faster before trying to sleep. He used to use something stronger, but now he only took the pills when his leg was at its worst.

And then he saw Jess.

Under the careful mask was the same self-loathing. He needed to understand where it came from because something told him the media got her story wrong. They wouldn't understand why Jessica couldn't talk about Mia. They wouldn't recognize the truth, even if she told them.

What had she done that she couldn't forgive herself for?

Chapter 4

Now

Jess was arriving soon, and Oscar waited in the common area, seated in an armchair.

"Get up," said a woman in her mid-fifties, wearing a rabbit onesie. "That's my seat."

"Sorry Chrissie. I didn't realize," said Oscar. "Is this yours all day today?" He pointed to the chair.

"I always sit there. Always."

"She always does," said a wiry man in a baseball cap, walking a few paces behind.

"Okay, I'll move somewhere else." Chrissie's chair would probably change again the following day, but Oscar moved.

With her chair safe, Chrissie moved towards the kitchen, hovering in the doorway.

Oscar sat on the sofa. "Is it okay if I sit here, Lewis?" he asked the man in the baseball cap.

Lewis shrugged. "I don't care where you sit. Long as you don't sit in Chrissie's chair, you should be fine."

"Okay, thanks. How have you been?"

"What does it matter? You're not my doctor anymore," said

Lewis.

"Give Hayley a chance. She might surprise you."

"I'm just a number to you people. Another crazy guy. Why do you give a shit how I am?"

"I'm not treating you anymore, but that doesn't mean I don't care how you're doing."

Lewis straightened his baseball cap and swung his legs over the side of the couch, off the armrest. "Well, I'm still here, aren't I?" he mumbled, before escaping to his room.

That was two for two, but Oscar had learned not to take it personally. Lewis was having a rough day and probably needed some space.

Hayley walked by, notes in one hand, coffee in the other. Oscar flinched, glad she didn't see him. He was avoiding her, which was completely unfair. What was he supposed to say? Great date last night? Thanks for having drinks with me, buddy? There had to be something better.

"Dr. Manning," he said, catching her by surprise as she passed.

"Oscar! You scared me." She smiled, her face lighting up.

The regret struck him hard. *I should've kissed her.* For a moment he considered kissing her right there in the middle of the ward.

The moment passed and he regained his composure. "Lewis seems down today."

"His sister was going to visit, but she cancelled. It's the second time this month."

"That's a shame."

"Yeah."

They shared a look. Some patients rarely had visitors, but Lewis's sister came regularly.

Hayley swept the room quickly, making sure no one could overhear them. "Listen, about yesterday—I wasn't trying to accuse you. I was curious that's all. It seemed like you went to a lot of trouble to get Jessica here."

"It's fine," said Oscar. He didn't have time to worry about that now. Jessica was arriving any minute.

"I hope you're not scared of vegan food anymore," said Hayley.

Oscar made a 'sort of' gesture with his hand.

"Science suggests it takes a few tries. I might need to take you back for another round," said Hayley.

He repeated the gesture and smiled to show he was joking.

She breezed past Oscar to the reception desk, her floral perfume trailing.

The front door buzzed, and someone behind the desk hit the button to open it. A man wearing blue jeans and a Carlson Remand Center ID around his neck wandered in.

David, Whitner's administrator, watched from the window of his office.

He glanced at Oscar, surprised to see him relaxing in the common area. "Do you want to take this?"

"Go ahead, David. Pretend I'm not here," said Oscar.

Hayley watched from the front desk, sipping coffee—apparently Oscar wasn't the only curious one.

A man stepped through wearing blue coveralls and a belt equipped with various gadgets. "Hi. My name's Tom. I'm the patient transfer for Jessica Green."

The automatic doors opened again and Jess walked in, escorted by a woman dressed in a uniform similar to Tom's.

"She's sedated," said Tom, "so rest her up today. She doesn't talk much on a good day though, so—"

Jess held her wrists in front of her, hands clenched, as if she was wearing invisible cuffs. Her dark hair wrestled against a ponytail band for freedom, her piercing blue eyes stared ahead, unaffected by the goings on around her. She had slimmed down to almost nothing since Mia's disappearance, her face wan, the roundness in her cheeks drained. Oscar made a mental note to test her vitamin levels—sedation didn't explain the weight loss and pale skin.

"Welcome to Whitner, Jessica," said David warmly. "We're looking forward to having you stay with us."

She didn't respond, seemingly uninterested in her new surroundings.

"We recently had a couple of residents leave, and we thought you might like your own room to help you get settled in. Does that suit you?"

Jess stared intently at a spot on the far wall.

Oscar leaned forward in his seat, watching Jessica twirl her wrist back and forth.

The corner of her eye caught Oscar. She stared right at him, like she was trying to place his face. Did she remember him?

You can see me. You know I'm here. What's going on in there, Jess? Why won't you talk?

She shuffled forward, spurred by her escort. "Come on, let's get you settled."

On her way through, Jess brushed past the chair Oscar had vacated earlier.

"That's my seat," screeched Chrissie, blocking Jessica's path.

Jessica averted her eyes and pulled her arms in close, as if by willing it, she could make herself small enough to go unnoticed.

Chrissie moved in, spitting words that Oscar couldn't hear into Jess's ear.

Oscar shot up from the couch as Jessica's face changed, but he was too late.

Chrissie's teeth latched onto Jessica's ear, biting down hard.

Twisting around, Jess's fist connected with Chrissie's nose.

Tom and David scrabbled to separate them as Oscar tried to calm Chrissie, as she screamed incoherently at Jessica.

"Chrissie! It's okay."

Tom pulled Jess away as David moved Chrissie in the opposite direction.

Oscar went to Jess. "Jess, my name's Oscar. Can I take a quick look at your ear?"

Jess watched him, forming an opinion.

He lifted his hand slowly and turned her head to assess the tear in her ear. "This might need stitches," he said gently, but Jessica didn't seem to notice the blood or the pain, her eyes still studying Oscar.

"Are you okay?" he asked.

"I know you," she whispered, so low he wondered whether he imagined it.

Chapter 5

Now

Oscar asked Jess how she knew him, but a nurse whisked her away to clean up her torn ear before she could answer.

After, Oscar postponed their first session, until she got settled in at Whitner. He'd paid her a few unofficial visits to see how she was, but she didn't answer. She usually listened politely as he spoke. Once, he thought the corners of her mouth twitched at a joke he made, but it might've been a grimace.

Now she was ready, and he'd turned up the thermostat to make her more comfortable. He kept his office cold. The brisk air sharpened his nerves and helped him to think. When it got cold enough, the prickling sensation on his forearms forced him to dig deep and ask questions that were too polarizing for a warm, cozy office.

Is she a murderer?

Oscar flicked through Jess's file to the part about Clayton Green. He'd been attacked with a meat tenderizer but Jess denied any responsibility. Eventually, Clay had dropped the charges. Given the weapon of choice, he was lucky his attacker hadn't checked for a pulse, or they might've succeeded.

What made her snap? In fifteen years, Oscar hadn't seen that kind of violence without a trigger. Maybe Jess didn't remember pulling the weapon from the draw—Dissociative Amnesia wasn't a popular defense in court though, so unless there was substantial evidence, a lawyer wouldn't use it as a defense.

Oscar flicked forward, looking for something he might've missed. There was nothing from the assessing psychiatrist to suggest that Jess had Dissociative Amnesia, but there was plenty about her unwillingness to talk and a few pages about possible social disorders. According to the notes, the psychiatrist didn't think Jessica's silence was a trauma response.

Jess had never denied kidnapping Mia. She hadn't said anything, but Oscar knew she could speak because he'd seen it. *I know you.* It was more than she had said since she had been accused of Mia's disappearance.

Skimming the pages, Oscar jumped past Sarah's interpretation of Jess's police interviews about Clay and Mia, searching for Malingered Amnesia. If the report said that Jess was faking memory loss, then she might be doing the same thing with Mia.

A knock at the door broke Oscar's concentration.

"Come in," he called.

Jessica stood in the doorway to his office, hands still tucked high against her ribs. Without the sedative she seemed more anxious, but her ponytail was neat today, like someone had taken the time to get it right. Her ear drew his attention, strapped up with medical tape that outlined the knuckles of the stitches underneath.

A nurse stood behind Jess. "I have Jessica here for her first session."

"Thanks, Chloe."

"I'll be back in an hour to show you to your room, Jessica."

Jess nodded slightly, acknowledging that she'd heard. Somehow, she made the gesture seem like a thank you.

Oscar gestured towards the sofas and armchairs placed around the wooden coffee table. "Take your pick."

Jess looked around the room until she saw a framed picture of Oscar holding a baby wrapped in a fluffy blue blanket. The photo wasn't usually out for anyone to see, but Oscar had forgotten to put it away.

Walking past the photograph of Oscar and Riley, Jess chose the window seat. She rubbed her shoulders, creating warmth against the cold air.

"I can turn the heating up some more if you like?"

She studied Oscar as he took a seat opposite her, shaking her head slightly at his offer. "I know you," she said, this time with more certainty.

He hadn't expected her to talk. Her voice was crackly, as if waking up from sleep, but she was initiating conversation.

"Do you?"

He turned up the thermostat. His mind would grow sleepy with the warmth, but Jess should be comfortable.

"You came to the remand center but they wouldn't let you talk to me."

"You remember that?"

"Yeah."

"A lot of people wanted to see how you were," he said.

Jess shrugged. "They just wanted an exclusive on why I

killed Mia."

Why I killed Mia.

Oscar shifted in his seat, eyes on Jess. "Would you have talked to me if they'd let you?"

"Yes."

It wasn't the answer he was expecting.

"Why?"

She looked out the window at something he couldn't see. "You said you wanted to see if I was okay. It was the first time I'd heard someone sound like they meant it. But they don't let you decide things for yourself when they think you're a murderer."

"Is that what they think?"

"Yeah. At least most of them do."

"And by them—"

"The doctors. Reporters. Police. People I used to think of as friends."

She touched her ear, reading each stitch like braille. Was it an unconscious habit, or a memory of her time at Whitner Psychiatric Hospital so far?

"Why did you come to the remand center?"

A knock at the door interrupted their conversation. Was it too soon for the truth?

The door opened and Chloe entered, carrying a tray. "Sorry," she mouthed. "I thought you might like some water."

"Thanks, Chloe," said Oscar.

She smiled and turned to Jess. "Dr. de la Nuit is a great doctor, but not the best host." She distributed a glass in front of Jessica and left.

Jess cracked a wan smile. Under different circumstances it might've seemed vibrant and engaging. She sipped some water.

"I saw you on the news. You looked scared and I wanted to talk to you—to listen, if that's what you needed."

Her fingers went back to the stitches along her ear, following the jagged line. She was deciding whether she should trust him.

If Oscar pushed her to talk before she was ready to, he'd lose her. He wasn't sure if he was getting the real Jess yet, or a persona she'd created to get through the days.

He couldn't guess how she would react to a joke, or what she thought about when she was alone. He didn't know what her limits were, or what she was capable of. He had to get to know her better, so he could figure out what she knew. He'd seen people confess under pressure, whether they were guilty or not, but he didn't want a confession. He wanted the truth.

Oscar gestured toward her ear. "I saw what happened. I'm sorry I couldn't get there in time to stop it."

Jess's hand dropped from her ear—she hadn't realized she was fussing at it. She wedged her knuckles under her knees to stop them from creeping back.

"Chrissie said something before she lunged at you. Was it about her chair? It changes every day. Before you arrived, she asked me not to sit there."

"It wasn't about the chair," said Jess. Her arms shifted in closer, as if trying to hold herself together. "She called me a baby killer."

Oscar swallowed hard. He'd heard those words before.

Chapter 6

Then

The first day of kindergarten was always going to be hard. Jess got out of the car, pulled a glittery unicorn backpack from the backseat and adjusted the straps over Zoe's shoulders. She took her hand as they walked to the gate.

"Can I show Aiden my backpack?" asked Zoe, bouncing with excitement.

Jess tucked inky hair behind her ear and looked around. Sure enough, Niki was already there, talking to another parent—probably her motivation for going early. Niki's son, Aiden, would be close by.

Once they were inside the gate, Zoe tried to slip loose, but Jess had a sudden urge to keep her hand safe and warm inside of hers.

"Ma-ah!" Zoe protested, breaking free to find her cousin.

As she moved closer, Jess realized Niki was talking to Meg and relaxed. They had been friends with Meg since school, when Niki befriended her and took her in.

"Jess, get over here," called Niki, spotting her sister. Niki looked immaculate, her dark-blonde hair shining like gossamer. Jess always felt bland next to her glamorous sister. "Lucas and Aiden ditched us already," she laughed.

How were they so blasé? Jess was having a hard time adjusting to Zoe's absence. It felt like her baby—the person she had cared for every day since she came into the world—didn't need her on the most important day of her life. Still, she'd told herself she wouldn't cry, so she forced a smile and joined Niki and Meg.

"Jess, how are you?" asked Meg, hugging her friend.

"Okay. Zoe went to find Lucas and Aiden," she said, smile teetering. If Meg noticed her subtle change of the subject, she didn't show it. She shielded her eyes against the sun to search for her daughter in the glinting morning light.

A stray backpack bouncing on the shoulder of a hurried mother in jeans and a light sweater smacked into Jess's side. The woman offered half an apology and kept walking. Kids ran in every direction, each at a slightly different angle. Jess held her breath as two kids knocked each other over, releasing it when they picked themselves up and ran in different directions, unaffected by the interruption.

Little arms wrapped around Jess's legs. "Aiden!" she said, hugging her nephew back.

"Aunt Jess, this place is the best. They have a sandpit and a swing, and I'm going to play on them all day."

"Awesome," said Jess, matching Aiden's enthusiasm. She waved a hand at Lucas, who stopped behind Aiden, shyly using him as a barrier.

Lucas moved forward and slid his backpack from Meg's hands as a teacher cleared her throat loudly outside of the meerkat room—the room that Zoe would be in this year. "Okay everyone. Thank you for bringing us all to kinder this morning," said the teacher, looking above the children's heads to address the adults. "It's great to see you all. However, we have to ask that you don't come into the classrooms. There's not a lot of room and we find it's harder for the kids to settle with the disruption. Pick up is at 2.30, so we'll see you then."

"Can you believe that?" asked the woman beside Jess.

"Yeah," said Jess, assuming it was Niki. "You'll just have to suck it up."

"I thought we'd at least settle them in first," she said.

Jess looked up, embarrassed to find she was talking to a complete stranger.

"What's your little girl's name? She's beautiful."

"Uh, Zoe," said Jess.

"I wish my daughter was as cooperative as Zoe," said the woman enviously. "But Mia never listens to anything I say. I'm Holly, by the way."

"Jess."

"Nice to meet you."

"Yeah, you too."

"Kids are hard, huh?"

"Yeah, they can be."

"Is Zoe's dad around?"

Jess bit her lip, wondering if anyone else would think that was too personal and a little blunt from a stranger. "He couldn't bring her. He's at work."

"Must be nice. To have someone who loves her as much as you do."

"Yeah, I guess it is."

"Mia's dad doesn't live with us. I had to leave."

Jess shifted uncomfortably and nodded.

The woman took her silence as a cue to continue. "He was violent. I couldn't let Mia stay around that."

"Jess, there you are," said Niki, grabbing her sister's elbow, unwittingly saving her from a silence she didn't know how to fill. "Let's get coffee. It feels like forever since we could talk without getting up for the seventh bathroom break, or a spilled bubbacino."

Niki noticed Holly for the first time, assessed her quickly, and smiled. "Hi," she said, her head whipping towards her sister. "Who's your new friend?"

"Holly," said Holly, stepping forward. "I was just saying that I wish my daughter listened to me like Zoe listens to Jess." She laughed.

"Oh, I know what you mean. I have to fight Aiden to get him to do anything. Luckily, I'm not beyond bribes," laughed Niki.

Holly smiled. "A toy car is cheaper than the dentist, right?"

"Exactly." She turned her attention back to her sister. "Let's grab that coffee."

Niki raised her eyebrows at Jess, then Meg, who nodded. "You're welcome to come if you have time, Holly."

"Oh, that's okay. I should go. I don't want to intrude—"

"Don't be silly. The more the merrier," said Meg. "I've heard Niki's botched eyebrow story so many times, I think we need some new material."

"Hey! They burned it right off—"

"... and it took weeks to grow back," Meg finished with Niki.

"Oh my god! Really?" said Holly, scrutinizing Niki's eyebrow.

Jess stood to the side, a little disappointed that Holly might join them for coffee—she was hoping to talk to her friends about Clay, find out what they thought about his new *nothing bothers me* attitude. He thought it made him seem easygoing, but to Jess, it seemed blasé.

"It's okay. I can laugh about it now that I'm over the emotional scarring. It's nothing I can't cover with make-up." Niki smoothed her brow with her ring finger.

"Oh, come on. There's barely a scratch there," said Meg.

"Yeah, well, that's only thanks to my friend, concealer. Underneath, it's all red and angry."

"So, are you coming, Holly?" asked Niki.

"I have to go, but maybe next time?"

Chapter 7

Now

Oscar sat with his back pressed against his office chair. Hayley was right, he'd put in Jess's transfer without considering the impact on the team, but wouldn't it have been wrong to deny Jess treatment in case it made the hospital look bad?

Oscar took a breather. Right now, all he had were assumptions and deductions. Maybe he was taking Jess's case too personally. He understood what she was going through, but that didn't make them the same.

Oscar used to think that getting emotionally involved in a case was selfish. It put you at risk of personal bias and clouded your judgment. It stopped you from providing the best treatment possible.

The clinical term was *countertransference*, but he wasn't at risk of confusing his experience with Jess's, because he *knew* they were different.

Oscar left his office and walked absently to reception.

"Dr. de la Nuit, can I help you?" asked Chloe.

"Hey Chloe. Busy morning?"

She smiled. "One day you'll ask, and the answer will be no."

Oscar smiled. "But today's not that day?"

Her email pinged on cue.

"Has Jess has been out of her room yet?" Oscar leaned on the front desk.

"Not yet. Other than when the nurses collect her for meals. She doesn't eat much. And she doesn't mingle with the others. She barely lets the nurses check her stitches."

Oscar wasn't sure he would either after her less than warm welcome.

Baby killer.

The words weighed heavy on his stomach. Maybe Jess's reaction showed that she rejected the accusation.

Or she was being defensive because what Chrissie said was true.

"I was on shift yesterday, and I saw her pop out for a bit," said Jason. "I noticed because I'd just checked her stitches and she sat there, acting like she couldn't hear me when I talked to her."

"And you saw her leave her room?"

"Yeah. It was just before lights out. You'd already gone home. She sat in the craft area for about twenty minutes."

"Did she talk to anyone?"

"No. She sat over there," said Jason, pointing to the round table. "She took the rag doll, and then went back to her room."

"Rag doll?"

"Yeah. She took it with her. It's the first time she's shown interest in something, so I let her keep it."

"Good call," said Oscar. "How's her ear healing up?"

"Physically, it's healing well."

Oscar had considered moving Chrissie to another ward. It wasn't the first time she'd started a fight with another patient, but he wasn't in the habit of moving difficult patients when it was convenient. Instead, he'd asked the staff at Whitner to keep an eye on things and work with Chrissie to address what'd happened.

"Where's Jess now?"

"At lunch. She's reluctant to eat with the others, but Chloe convinced her," said Jason, smiling at his colleague.

Chloe shrugged. "I don't think she knows how to be around other people after everything that's happened."

"Bulimic?" asked Jason.

"No, she doesn't eat enough to bring it up," said Chloe.

Oscar remembered something from the remand center about a possible eating disorder. What if Chloe was right? She was a sharp mental health nurse with good instincts about her patients. "Anorexia?"

"Maybe, but when she's alone she seems to eat."

"Thanks," said Oscar. He glanced at the clock. If he left now, he could probably catch her.

In the dining room, twelve patients sat at three round tables, their plates in various states of empty. Except Jess. Her food looked untouched, mashed potato hollowed in the middle like a child's beach project.

Oscar watched from the entrance. Chrissie smiled and waved from the table by the door. He waved back and returned his attention to Jess.

Chrissie followed his gaze, her smile dropping when she noticed who held his attention. "I don't want to eat lunch with a baby killer," she said, her voice peaking. "I want to know what you did to that baby! We all know you did it. Tell us!"

Oscar froze. Chrissie's words echoed in his ears, demanding

a confession.

He turned and saw that the slur was meant for Jess, not him.

Chrissie began chanting. "Tell us, tell us." Lewis joined in.

Jess dropped her fork and hunched over, her hands over her ears, unable to drown their words out.

"Chrissie's going to need something to calm down," Oscar told Karla, the attending nurse. "Offer her Lorazepam, but if she won't take it, Diazepam."

"Okay, got it," said Karla, gesturing for another nurse to help with Chrissie. "I'll get Dr. Manning to write it up."

Oscar went to Jess, ignoring the urge to escape the accusing chant. "Hey Jess, did you want to get out of here? You can bring your food."

She looked up, her eyes shining like a cat in the dark.

"Come on," he said, helping her up. Her fingers curled around the little rag doll, pulling it from the table. Chrissie's chant grew faint behind them, but Oscar still heard them.

That was a long time ago. It wasn't your fault.

He wanted to believe it. He wanted to let go of the guilt. If he could get Jess to talk about Mia, maybe she could let go too.

"Jessica, I was about to come get you," said Jason as they passed reception.

Jessica didn't react.

"You have a visitor. Should I buzz them in?"

Jess kept moving.

"She says she's your sister. Niki?"

Jess stopped. She was listening.

The automatic doors at the front of the ward had circular decals most of the way up the doors to stop people passing by and visitors looking in, but Oscar could see movement through the spots.

The rag doll slipped through Jess's fingers and fell to the floor, soft fabric silent against the carpet. Oscar picked it up and offered it back to her.

"Do you want me to let her in?" asked Jason.

Jess shook her head. The movement was so slight, they might've missed it.

"Are you sure?" asked Oscar gently. "I can sit with you."

"She shouldn't be here. Tell her to go home."

Chapter 8

Now

Jessica shot off to her room and closed the door.

"I can take care of this, Jason," said Oscar. He swiped his key card and exited, making sure the door closed behind him out of habit.

An overdressed woman with salon-lightened hair stood alone in front of the intercom. "Hi, I'm Oscar, Jess's psychiatrist," he said, offering a hand.

"Niki. Jessica's sister. Where's Jess?" She took his hand and held it longer than was necessary.

"Uh, Jess isn't ready for visitors yet. She's still settling in."

Niki missed the apology in his tone. "Well, I want to know where my sister's living. You hear stories about places like this—" said Niki, catching herself. She held up her hands in a stop gesture. "I'm not saying you're like that. I just want to make sure she's okay."

Oscar smiled. "I understand. Perhaps we should step inside for a moment, in case she changes her mind?"

"Yeah, sure."

Oscar swiped again, and gestured for her to go through first.

Maybe she'd feel better if she at least saw the ward.

"This is our common area," said Oscar, aware that Niki was drawing attention from a few of the guests on the ward. New people always did, but Niki seemed used to the attention, and waved hello.

Oscar observed as she looked around at the plain décor, the furniture and walls steeped in light tones and simple lines to look like a home away from home.

"Why won't Jess talk to me?"

Lewis was listening to their conversation with Milo, a patient who was being treated for depression.

Oscar turned back to Niki. "Why don't we have a chat in my office?"

"Okay," agreed Niki, craning her neck to find Jess. "Then can I see Jess?"

"I think we should talk."

Niki's boots clacked against the hallway floor—she made noise even when she wasn't talking. She was a stark contrast to her sister, but Oscar and his own brother were very different.

Oscar waited for Niki to get comfortable. "I have to ask, why do you think Jess doesn't want to see anyone?"

"I don't know."

"Did you visit while she was in preventive detention?"

"I tried. She didn't want to see me. I thought she was embarrassed about being in prison, but I guess a crazy house is just as embarrassing."

Oscar raised an eyebrow, and Niki sighed. "I know that's not the political term. You know what I mean. Jess is a very private person. She doesn't like making a big deal of things. She's a reporter. They stick to the facts. Jessie was always better at writing what she wanted to say than she was at saying it."

Niki crossed one leg over the other, the zip on her boots jingling. "She was secretive even when we were kids. Always writing stories. She wasn't thrilled by parties, no matter how many I dragged her to. She never said much."

"I'd love to read some of her work."

"Before this hell broke loose, she published something for an indie. Google it if you want. It'll be easy to find."

"Okay. What was the title?"

"Um, something about spotting a narcissist. Don't quote me on it. You'd think I'd remember. I joked about it. She didn't appreciate that either, at least not in front of our friends. Like I said, she's very private." Niki lowered her voice and added, "And a bit too serious sometimes."

How would Jess feel about Oscar inviting Niki into her space? He should have checked first, but he couldn't leave Niki out there.

"Was Jess ever violent as a child? Did she hurt you or your parents? Maybe a pet?"

Niki pursed her lips, lipstick staining her lip-line. "If you want me to say that I think my sister killed that little girl, you're wasting your time. There's no way Jess did it." She settled, the fire simmering. "If you want to know if I think she hurt Clay, maybe."

Siblings grew up together, they shared the formative years, and overcame their parent's shortcomings together. Sometimes they made those shortcomings bearable. Niki probably knew things about her sister that no one else knew.

"I just want to help Jessica," he said, "and I think you could help me do that."

"Then I guess we want the same thing."

What would it have been like for Jess, growing up with Niki?

She seemed trusting, maybe a little naïve. If Oscar didn't know better, he'd think Jess was the eldest.

Oscar had grown up with an older brother of his own. When Oscar was eleven and Steve thirteen, their parents divorced. Steve looked after Oscar, especially in the lead up to the divorce, when their parents fought all the time. It brought them closer as kids, but as they grew older, they had drifted apart. Their shared pain couldn't hold them together once they were old enough to escape it.

They'd made feeble attempts to stay in touch, but when their parents had divorced, Steve went with Kiko, and Oscar stayed with Bill.

Oscar went to medical school and Steve landed a job in sales, not wanting to waste time or money on the poor years. But Jess and Niki didn't seem like that. They seemed to remain close through adulthood.

So why didn't Jess want Niki to visit her?

"Can I see my sister now?" asked Niki hopefully.

"I can ask someone to check with Jess," said Oscar.

Niki nodded and he dialed the nurse's station.

"Hello?"

"Hi, Chloe. I have Jessica Green's sister here. She'd really like to see Jess. Could you please check with Jess?"

"Sure. I'll call you back."

"Thanks." He ended the call and turned to Niki. "Chloe's asking now."

"Okay."

"Are you and Jess close?" he asked.

"Yeah. At least I thought we were, but she hasn't let me visit her, so now I'm thinking maybe not. I still love her. I wish she'd talk to me. She shouldn't be going through this alone. I mean, it's bad enough that Holly's going through it. She's a mess, but to be honest, she's doing better than Jess."

"Holly Edwards?" asked Oscar. "Mia's mother?"

'Yeah."

"You still talk?"

"I know that seems disloyal, but I couldn't just abandon Holly. Her daughter's *missing.*"

"Sounds like you're in a tough position. Does Jess know you and Holly still speak?"

Would Jess stop talking to you if she knew you stayed in contact with Holly Edwards?

Niki shook her head, lacquered hair barely moving. "I haven't spoken to her since she came here. She knows nothing about my life now."

"Mia went missing from Jess's house, right?"

"Yeah."

"What does Holly believe happened?"

"Holly thinks my sister took Mia. She's wrong, but she's grieving. She wants to believe anything if it'll give her answers."

Usually, when a child went missing, the parents were reluctant to consider that they might have died. Maybe Holly needed to move on to escape the scenarios her mind thought up.

"Why does Holly think it was Jess?"

Niki filed at a nail with the tip of her thumb. "Mia was at Jess's house. No one saw what happened. Mia just... disappeared. Look, I know my sister. She wouldn't hurt a child, even Holly's child."

Oscar sat back in his chair. "Even Holly's child?"

"I shouldn't have said that. I just meant that Jess is kind, even to people she doesn't like. She wouldn't hurt anyone."

"So, Jess wasn't Holly's biggest fan?"

"No."

The blare of Oscar's desk phone filled the office. He answered before the next ring. "Yes?"

"Dr. de la Nuit, it's Chloe. Jessica's not up for visitors. I'm sorry."

"What did she say?"

Chloe hesitated, then repeated quietly, "She said you can tell her to fuck off."

Oscar put the phone back in its place. What should he tell Niki?

"Sorry, Niki. Jess isn't feeling well."

"What? I have to talk to her."

"Maybe you could try next week, once she's settled in."

"I've been waiting since she left."

"I know it's hard, but give me some time to see what I can do. Check back in a week."

"Why don't you people want me to talk to her? What have you done my sister?"

Chapter 9

Then

Jess watched from the large glass window as Zoe put her bag on her peg and found a seat.

"Aww, look at Aiden and Lucas—they're sitting next to each other," said Niki, waving to get her son's attention. "And there's Zoe. It looks like she's made a friend! She's talking to that little girl with the ribbons."

The little girl Zoe was talking to caught Jess watching and glared.

Zoe tapped the girl's shoulder to regain her attention, pointing out the pages to color on their table. Zoe offered a page and for a moment, Jess felt proud of her daughter for sharing.

The girl pulled away from Zoe and burst out in tears, before running to the teacher.

Ms. Liu shot the women at the window a look.

"I think it's time to go," said Meg. "Before we get a detention."

Niki laughed. "I did my share of detention at school. Let's go."

Jess watched Ms. Liu call Zoe over. "Just a sec," she said.

The crying girl pointed at Zoe, who shook her head, horrified.

Niki pulled Jess's arm toward the carpark. "I need a cup of caffeine, now!" she said impatiently.

"I think Zoe's in trouble," said Jess.

Niki scoffed. "It's the first week of kindergarten—no one gets in any real trouble. The teachers are fresh and bubbly and understanding. Don't worry about it. Can we go now?" said Niki, her wheedling high pitched.

"Okay, I remember why decaff Niki isn't my favorite person," said Jess.

"I'll be fine once I have coffee. It calms me down," said Niki.

"Uh, Nik, you know caffeine is a stimulant, right? It won't make you any calmer."

"Really? Says who?"

"Says science."

"Well, I'm telling you, science is wrong. It definitely calms me down."

Niki pushed forward, already crossing through the car park.

Jess reached to pull Niki back as a car barreled down the parking lot, but it was too late.

Brakes screeched, but the driver couldn't stop in time.

Niki's hands pushed against the hood as if she could avoid the impact.

"Niki! Oh my god! Are you okay?" screeched Meg.

Jess reached out to her sister, steadying her fall. "Just move slowly. Let's make sure nothing's broken," she said calmly.

"I'm fine. I'm okay. Nothing's broken," said Niki, reeling from the shock.

The driver stepped out of their car. It was the stranger Jess had mistaken for Niki. *Holly.*

"Are you okay? I didn't see you. I—"

"I'm fine, really," said Niki.

"Do you want me to drive you to the hospital? You should probably get a check-up or something."

"I don't need a doctor. I need coffee." Niki moved away from the road, clearly rattled. "One day, this'll be a great story, even better than the eyebrow thing."

"You're taking being run over by a crazy driver better than I deserve," said Holly sheepishly.

"Did I damage your car?" asked Niki, assessing the paint on the front of the car. "I think I dented the hood. We should probably swap insurance."

"It was already there. Don't worry about it. I'm more worried about you. Are you sure you're okay?"

"Yeah. A little sore, but I'll be fine." Niki grabbed her elbow and held it.

"Is there something I can do for you? Please, I'd feel much better." Holly placed a hand over her heart.

Niki smiled weakly. "Buy me a coffee and we'll call it even."

"Of course," said Holly.

Chapter 10

Now

Oscar knocked on Jess's door before entering. Inside, the room was clinically neat. There were no clothes strewn over chairs or shoes kicked under the bed. It looked like she wasn't planning to stay long.

The bed was the only thing that looked used, covers crumpled with Jess curled on top. She lay still in the ripples of the cover, as if drowned. Papers littered the bedspread, some scrunched and discarded, others carefully laid flat. Was she working on something?

"Are you okay?" asked Oscar, loitering in the doorway.

There was an incoherent mumble. The answer could go either way.

"I know you don't feel like talking, but sometimes it helps. Can I come in?"

Jess lifted her head, saw Oscar filling the door frame, and shrugged, settling back into a ball.

"I thought you might want this back," said Oscar, setting the little rag doll at the end of her bed. "I heard you borrowed it."

She looked up.

"Why do you like it?"

Jess reached for the doll. "It reminds me of Zoe."

"Your daughter?"

"Yeah. She has one just like it. Suzy. She takes her everywhere." Her eyes came alive when she spoke about her daughter.

Oscar listened quietly, scared to interrupt.

Happy moments were like bubbles here—they burst easily if you disturbed them.

"Zoe gave Suzy to me when I left," said Jess. "She didn't know I'd be gone this long. I wanted to take Suzy with me, but Zoe needed her more."

Oscar hadn't expected an answer.

"Perhaps you can hold on to this one for now?"

"Thanks," said Jess, curling her arm around her shoulder and closing her eyes, signaling she was done talking.

He took the chair across from her, wondering what to say to keep their conversation going.

At Whitner, the staff tried to make patients feel at home by encouraging them to personalize their rooms, and treatment focused on person-centered therapy. Doctors and therapists weren't there to 'fix' things. They provided a patient-centered approach, where they were a sounding board and helped to implement the right tools for patients.

"You know, it seems like your sister really wants to see you."

Jess jumped up in a flurry of papers. "Is she still here?" she demanded. "Tell her to go home."

"She isn't here." Oscar let Jess simmer down. Why was she so agitated by Niki's visit?

"Did anyone come to see you at the remand center besides

Niki?"

Jess sighed. "Clay. My parents. Meg thinks I did it, so she didn't bother."

If he'd claimed he was a friend of Jess's, or a family member, would've they let him talk to her?

"Holly."

Why would Holly visit someone accused of kidnapping her daughter? Maybe she thought that asking her what happened to Mia herself would get a response?

"Did you talk to any of them?"

Jess shook her head. "No, not really. Except Holly."

"Can I ask why you let Holly visit?"

Despite the warm air circulating the room, Jess kept her arms wrapped around herself.

"I wanted to ask her why she was there, visiting me. And I wanted to know if they found Mia."

Her eyes shifted, her fingers fidgeting with the edge of her top, not a nervous brushing of the fabric, but pulling at a thread, as if it was tickling her skin and needed to be removed.

Oscar waited for her to look at him, but the thread kept her attention, even once it was tucked in place. She was lying.

"What did she say?"

Jess eyed the rag doll at the foot of the bed. "She asked where Mia was. I said I didn't know. Then she got angry and said she'll make sure I suffer if I ever get out. She said there are people who think I should get the death penalty."

Her lip twitched, but she'd learned to bottle her emotions and the expression passed.

"How do you feel about public opinion?"

"Honestly, I thought it'd blow over. I'm a reporter. I know how fickle these things can be. One week you're a monster, and the next, you're a hero. Holly wanted everyone to think I did it. She gave an exclusive interview to a magazine and told everyone I hated her. She said I was making her life miserable because Mia tattled on Zoe. She made me seem horrible. I don't blame them for hating me."

Jess pulled at the thread inside her sleeve and it snapped.

"Grief is a desperate emotion. If Mia wasn't missing, I'm sure Holly would take back what she said."

"You don't know Holly," said Jess. "Even if Mia was safe she'd want me to suffer."

"Why?"

"Because none of this is about Mia. Not to Holly."

"What is it about?" asked Oscar.

"It doesn't matter. Just tell Niki not to come back. I don't want to see her."

She stretched out a leg, sending crisp sheets of paper sailing to the floor.

"I'm not here to tell you what to do, Jess. I wanted to make sure you're okay. That chant was hurtful. I know it doesn't help, but Chrissie was angry and looking for someone to take it out on. Her therapist will talk to her about it. I want to focus on your treatment and forget about the other stuff."

Oscar picked the papers off the floor and placed them in a small pile next to Jess, careful not to read the lines of tiny writing.

"You don't get it," said Jess. "They're going to think and say what they want. I don't care. All I care about is Zoe, and what she has to go through because of this. She's too little to understand what happened. She doesn't know why they're calling me a baby killer."

Oscar breathed in and counted to three. He would never

forget what it was like to be called a killer.

"The other parents didn't want their kids to play with Zoe when they thought I hurt Clay. Imagine what it's like for her now."

"Is that why you don't want to talk about Mia? You're worried what it'll mean for Zoe?"

Jess opened her mouth as if to answer, but changed her mind. "You have no idea," she said, ignoring what she really wanted to say.

"Are you looking for someone who understands what you're going through?"

Couldn't she see that he was that person?

"What if I told you that I understand?"

"Does the entire world think you murdered someone?" asked Jess skeptically.

"I know what it's like to be worn down enough that you'd consider hurting someone."

He thought about things he'd said to Prisha, just to get back at her for what she'd said.

Jess moved back, retreating inside of herself. "Okay, so we're talking about my husband now? Or are we still talking about Mia?" She tapped a finger slowly against her elbow. "I'm going to tell you what I told the police and Dr. Redford. I didn't attack Clay."

"Did they believe you?"

"Clay said I hit him with a meat tenderizer and the police believed him. Why wouldn't they? Apparently, people try to kill their partners every day. The police assumed it was an argument that went too far."

Was she telling the truth? Her blue eyes drew him in, clear and bright like the bottom of a swimming pool. She seemed genuine, but Niki said Jess was secretive. Was she just a good liar?

Oscar had kept his own secrets long enough to know the loneliness that came with it. It was a dead weight you carried alone, avoiding people in case they saw the truth. He showed the world one face, but underneath, he locked the truth away.

Maybe Jess felt like an imposter too.

"I'm here if you want to talk," he said. "Whatever you say to me doesn't leave this room."

"If I told you what happened, you'd break that promise." She challenged him with confidence. "It's your job."

"There are some circumstances where that's true, like if you were going to hurt yourself or someone else. But you're already in here."

"It's not that simple. This isn't a movie with good guys and bad guys, Oscar. People are capable of both."

Was she telling him she was guilty or innocent? Or neither? Was she talking about someone else?

She called him Oscar. Not Dr. de la Nuit, or Doctor Oscar, like most patients. She didn't see him as her therapist; she saw him as her equal.

"Do you do good things and bad things?"

"We all tell ourselves a story about who we are. Usually, people want to believe they're good."

"What makes you say that?"

"People want to prove that they're trustworthy. Sometimes, the ones that try the hardest are the worst."

"It sounds like something specific made you believe that?"

"Yeah. I tried to tell the truth, and no one listened. Now a little girl's gone."

Chapter 11

Now

An hour later, Oscar stared at a blank computer screen. A dull version of himself stared back.

Jess was still a mystery. The first image he'd seen of her on the news had captured a sadness etched deep in her eyes.

If Oscar hadn't kept secrets of his own for so long, he might have missed it. She kept a part of herself away from the people in her life. Maybe it was a defense she used to keep the people closest to her, the people she loved, safe.

What is she trying to save them from?

The police had seen it differently—they thought her aloofness was masking her temper and when it exploded, she had tried to kill Clay.

The police were wrong. Jess's fire had no flame. It burned inside. *Tell Niki not to come back.* She was trying to protect her.

From Holly? Jess mentioned that Holly threatened to make her suffer, and Niki would be a good way to do that.

Maybe Jess thought her sister would be safer if she let Holly win.

Oscar lowered the thermostat. He could feel the breakthrough as he worked over their conversation. *'I told them the truth and no one wanted to hear it.'*

Because of that, a little girl was gone.

Did Jess hurt Mia for attention? Infamy over invisibility.

He should have pressed it, but their session had ended because Jess was tired. He was tired too, but he would never admit it.

A gentle rap at the door surprised him. He wasn't expecting anyone.

"Come in," he called, sliding his elbows off the desk and straightening his jacket.

"Hey," said Hayley. She sounded concerned. The lack of sleep must've been showing. "I thought I'd see if you're up for a burger?"

"Hey," said Oscar. Seeing her made him smile despite everything else. He wasn't getting much done sitting here waiting for inspiration. Maybe food would help. "Sure."

"It's freezing in here," said Hayley, looking around for signs of a breeze. "Guess these big old offices are harder to heat, huh?"

Oscar smiled. "I set the thermostat low. I think better when it's cold."

"Maybe you have a fever—it's freezing."

"I like it like this."

"It doesn't slow you down?"

"The opposite." He ignored the twinge in his knee, an old injury that still acted up sometimes.

"You're an easy birthday then—frozen Coke it is." She smiled.

"I look forward to it."

Hayley opened the door. "Meet you out front. Don't make

me wait, I'm starving." She blew him a kiss and left.

Oscar wedged his laptop in his bag and zipped the case. He hadn't finished up by seven in a long time, barely knew what people did at that time of day. He locked the office hastily behind him and pocketed his keys. Seven o'clock looked different when he was married. Dinner. Dishes. Rocking Riley to sleep. Occasionally, a whiskey to wind down.

Things that seemed so ordinary at the time. He missed those moments with Riley.

His appetite faded, but Hayley was waiting, and he couldn't bail at the last minute, even if he knew he should; he wouldn't be good company.

You can't punish yourself forever. You need to move on. He tried to combat the other voice, the one that told him he deserved to suffer for what he'd done. *It was a long time ago.*

The burst of fresh air as he exited the building didn't help him forget.

He saw Hayley standing by the exit and felt a little better.

"Let's go," she said.

Oscar fidgeted with his keys and walked to his car. "I'll see you there."

Her smile faded as she registered the change in his mood.

"Whoa. Where's the fire?" She rushed to keep up. "I thought we could go together. I can get my car later?"

"Sure," said Oscar, hitting the unlock on his key chain. He gestured for Hayley to get in. She climbed into the passenger's seat and buckled in. Oscar threw the car into gear and drove methodically, making a turn onto the main road and accelerating until he was just over the speed limit.

"Are you okay? Is it Jessica Green? You've been so involved in her case, you've neglected everyone else. What makes her so special?"

Oscar flinched. "Is this the new lunchroom conversation?"

He took a breath and tried again. "Someone had to give her a chance."

Hayley's brow creased with concern. "You've been putting in long hours since she arrived. Even for you. Do you ever go home? Do you *have* a home anymore?"

He thought of the house he bought, decorated by a stranger he hired to choose things they thought would fit the space.

"That's a hot lunchroom topic. Jason thinks you live in your office to avoid commuting."

Oscar checked the rearview mirror.

"Oscar, it feels like I reach out, and you shut me out."

"Then why reach?" It came out harsher than he intended, but it was too late.

She watched the road with a driver's attentiveness. "I think you're worth reaching for. But that doesn't matter if you don't want to be reached."

Oscar slowed as the car ahead signaling left, the chance to change lanes gone. "Hayley. We work together. I don't think—"

"You don't think what? You don't think we should ruin our friendship?"

She was annoyed.

The car ahead turned off down a street. Was he pushing Hayley away? He was so good at figuring everyone else out. Why was he so stupid when it came to himself?

Oscar pulled into Carnival's parking lot with a decisive hand brake. "Let's order. We can talk inside," he said.

Hayley's shoes clacked against the concrete. Oscar entered the restaurant, sending the *open* sign dancing. He held the door and Hayley walked through.

An attendant greeted them and invited them to find a free table. "Take a seat," said Oscar. "I'll order if you like?" It wasn't an apology, but it was the least he could do for acting like an ass.

He waited in line, the smell from the grill piquing his appetite. Is this how life would be? Someone tried to get close, and he threw on the brakes?

He couldn't tell her that the Oscar she saw was the Oscar he wanted her to see, not the real Oscar.

Better to seem heartless than to show the real him.

An imposter.

A phony.

A killer.

Chapter 12

Then

Jess parked, savoring a moment to herself, away from the noise of jittery mothers nursing hot mugs of coffee. She breathed in and out, slow and even, just like Dr. Munoz taught her. She felt her shoulders relaxing, her breath filling her diaphragm before she let it out like a deflating balloon before heading inside.

Inside, everyone was already settled at a booth, sipping hot coffee.

"Jessie! You made it," said Niki, shuffling across so Jess could slide in. "I saved you a seat."

"She practically kicked me off," laughed Holly. "I tried sitting with her, in case she fainted from being hit by a car."

"I really am fine," said Niki stubbornly.

Jess smiled. "I'm gonna grab a coffee. Does anyone want anything?"

There was a chorus of 'no'.

"Oh, hang on Jess! Can you get me one of those muffins on the counter? They look amazing. Make it one of the healthy ones, maybe something with fruit in it."

Jess almost argued against the health benefits, but stopped herself. "Sure." She smiled. She wasn't going to begrudge Niki a muffin. She'd just been run down by a car.

Waiting in line, Jess clutched her bag, her bottle of Xanax rattling inside. She glanced at the booth. Holly was admiring Meg's gold ring—an anniversary gift she had been showing off since she got it three weeks ago. Meg pretended she didn't like the attention, but her smile betrayed her.

A bored teenager with colorful hair and an oversized nose ring worked the coffee machine with the finesse of a guitarist working steel strings against a fret board.

"What can I get you?" asked the frazzled-looking barista.

"Just a latte, please. Oh, and an apple cinnamon muffin."

"What size?"

"Uh, regular. Thanks."

The barista pulled a medium-sized cup and began the order, moving two mugs from under the machine onto the counter to pour frothed milk.

Jess tapped her phone and took a table number back to the booth.

The tone of the conversation had turned somber, all eyes on Holly.

"Wow," said Niki. "That's horrible."

"That's why I left," said Holly, almost shyly.

"Well, he doesn't deserve to see Mia, if that's how he treated her. And you, you poor thing. I can't believe how brave you are! Doing it on your own—it must be tough," said Niki sympathetically.

Holly shrugged. "It's better than putting Mia through that."

Holly shifted to Niki's side of the bench. This time, Niki put a hand on her shoulder. "Holly was just telling us what an asshole her ex was. He hit Mia and everything," said Niki, her eyes wide.

Jess eyed the empty seat next to Meg and sat, placing her number in the middle of the table and her bag at her feet. It hit the floor with a *clink* of pills.

"Isn't that *horrible*?" prompted Niki.

Holly watched Jess for a reaction, her dark brown eyes stalking her like prey.

"It's awful," said Jess sincerely.

She stared at Holly, horrified by the clinking under the table as she realized her bag had tipped, spilling her pills across the floor.

Niki investigated under the table and discovered Holly's boot hooked around the bag strap.

"Sorry. My foot must've caught," said Holly.

Jess crawled onto her knees, picking pills from the tiles and dropping them into the bottle.

Niki inched close. "Oh my god, Jess! Xanax? What for?" She looked over her shoulder, as if someone important might see.

"It's nothing, don't worry about it," said Jess, shooting Niki a look to say that now wasn't the time to discuss it.

"I know you've been a little high strung, but who isn't these days with—"

"Really, it's nothing," Jess interrupted tersely. "It's just to help me cope with Zoe going to school."

Niki looked sympathetic. "Not me. I can stop taking Xanax now that Aiden's out of my hair for a few hours a day. Am I right, ladies?"

Holly nodded, and Meg buried her head in her coffee mug.

"It's a big adjustment," said Meg. "Niki only feels like that because she's got two to deal with."

"You're right." Niki paused dramatically. "No, wait. I was fine when Audrey started school too." She grinned mischievously. "I mean, I love them, of course I love them, but sometimes I need a break from being their mother."

With the pills back in their container, Jess snapped the lid closed and rejoined the group.

"I think you forgot one over there," said Holly, squinting across the floor.

"That's okay," said Jess quickly.

"I can get it for you if you like. You might need it," said Holly suggestively.

"It's fine," said Jess, harsher than she intended.

"When I left Ray, I tried anti-depressants for a while," said Holly, her voice low.

Niki nodded. "Of course. It would have been so hard for you."

"The pills didn't do much. You have to ask yourself *why* you need them." She raised an eyebrow at Jess, who downed her coffee, suddenly eager to leave. She'd promised herself she'd take the pills while she got herself together, and then she'd stop. She wouldn't let Holly's words get to her.

Chapter 13

Then

Parents began arriving around the same time, necks craned to catch a glimpse of their children in the classroom, eager to see how their first day went. Did little Timmy remember to close the door when he went to the bathroom? Was Sandy able to make it through the day without interrupting the teacher? Did Amy make any new friends?

Did Zoe get in trouble because of the little girl sitting next to her?

Jess bustled through the gate and waited outside the classroom with the other parents. A swarm of kids sat straight-backed on the mat. Jess could see Zoe, wide-eyed and listening to Ms. Liu at the front of the room. The little girl from earlier in that morning sat towards the back, alone, as if she was in a time out away from the rest of the class. Maybe she needed some quiet time away from her peers?

Two mothers to Jess's right—one with a watermelon belly, the other pushing a baby in a stroller—were talking about pregnancy. Jess looked away when they caught her eye. Pregnancy seemed so long ago, she could barely remember what it was like. She walked on and found Meg sitting under the biggest tree in the yard—she must've arrived early to secure that spot.

They waved to each other and Meg beckoned her over, indicating that she'd saved her a seat.

Jess stepped around the chatting mothers. "Hey," she said when she was closer.

"How are you?" asked Meg with a sympathy that wasn't there before Jess's medication had spilled across the floor.

"Good," said Jess, mustering extra enthusiasm.

"Bell's about to go," said Meg. "I figured I'd let the other parents hustle to pick up their kids. Honestly, it's like they think they'll get their kid a gold star if they show the teacher how good they are."

Jess laughed. A couple of parents closest to the classroom were politely trying to establish that they were at the front of the line, supporting Meg's theory. "What ever gets you a reference for a good primary school, I guess."

"Have you seen Niki? Or Holly?" asked Meg.

"Not yet."

"Holly seems nice," said Meg.

Jess paused. "She uh... Yeah, I guess."

"You don't like her?" whispered Meg.

Jess shifted her weight on the giant log. "I don't really know her."

The bell rang, drowning her words.

Ms. Liu stood in the doorway, clapping her hands to quiet the parents. "Okay, everyone. I'm going to ask that one person collect each child. We'll do this a few at a time. Once you've collected your child, please exit the classroom so that I can call the next group." She clapped her hands together a final time. "Okay, let's go."

The first group was ushered in, followed by a second. "I guess we're up next," said Jess, standing.

When she walked in, Zoe broke into a huge grin. The little girl from earlier sat to the side, one of her carefully tied bows unraveled in her hair. With the classroom emptied, she looked more alone than ever.

Meg told Lucas to collect his bag and waved to Jess on her way out. "Need to get to swimming," she explained.

Jess waved back. "Bye, guys. Have fun."

With five kids left, the teacher went to the girl with the ribbons and crouched beside her.

Two more kids disappeared from the rug and Ms. Liu checked to make sure their parents were with them.

Zoe ran to Jess and hugged her.

"Let's get your bag, Zoo," said Jess, using the nickname Zoe had acquired while learning to say her name.

They walked past Ms. Liu and the little girl, who didn't take her eyes off Zoe. "That's Mia," Zoe whispered loudly. "She told the teacher I hit her, but it was a lie, so I didn't play with her today."

"Okay," said Jess.

"She's mean," said Zoe matter-of-factly.

Mia. Wasn't that the name of Holly's daughter?

"Maybe she was having a bad day. I'm sure she didn't mean it," said Jess.

Mia looked anxiously at the door.

"Is someone coming for you?" Ms. Liu asked.

Mia frowned. "She probably forgot."

"Aw, I'll bet she didn't forget. Maybe she's just late."

"Maybe she knows I got a hole in my shoe by accident. I'm

gonna get in trouble," said Mia, tears welling in her eyes.

"I'm sure you won't get in trouble," said Ms. Liu.

"Daddy wouldn't get mad."

There was a sadness in Mia's voice at the mention of her dad.

"Well, what about your dad? Can he come get you?"

Jess pulled Zoe's backpack over her shoulder, waiting for Zoe to collect her painting.

"I don't have a dad anymore. He died."

Jess's stomach dropped. She hadn't heard Holly mention her ex was dead. Jess assumed he was still a threat.

Jess stopped herself—maybe this wasn't Holly's Mia. Mia was a common name.

Except, looking at Mia, the button nose and turned up mouth, she would believe this was Holly's daughter.

Chapter 14

Now

Oscar knew it was the right thing to do. He'd just about convinced himself that he could do it when he realized that he didn't want to tell Hayley that nothing could happen between them. But this wasn't about him.

"Hayley, the thing is—"

"Stop," she said, her tone still warm. "I told you how I feel because I wanted you to know. I know what you're going to say, but you don't need to."

She pushed her hair behind her ear. "We've worked together for a long time. I've watched you push everything away. I didn't think I'd be any different, but I want you to think about what I said about reaching for you, and then, if you want to discuss it, we can."

The red-haired attendant from last time slid a rectangular plate in front of Oscar, looking at him questioningly, as if the kitchen might've accidentally made the wrong burger, before delivering another to Hayley. "Vegan burgers?" She didn't wait for a response. "Enjoy."

She left before Oscar could thank her.

"Right. We're going to eat these burgers. And you're going to tell me what you really think about them."

Oscar smiled. "Hey, I ate it last time, didn't I?"

"You did."

He took a giant bite and held up the burger in victory.

"Wanna try an onion ring?" Oscar asked.

Hayley pointed to the biggest one. "Are you saving this?"

"No."

"Good." She plucked it from the plate and took a bite. "Not bad."

They avoided work and relationship talk until Hayley broke their silent pact. "I heard Jessica say that she knew you. What did she mean by that? Did you know her before?"

Oscar washed down his burger with a gulp of beer. Hayley's hearing must be exceptional. "I visited the remand center during when she was admitted. They wouldn't let me talk to her."

"Why?"

"They said they didn't want me to disrupt her treatment."

"But she remembered you?"

"Yeah."

"You must've made a big impression."

He turned his burger over and took another bite.

"Oscar, you need a friend who's not afraid to be honest with you, so that's what I'm going to be." She paused, and all he could think was that she'd referred to him as a friend. "Be careful," she said.

"Careful?"

"I think Jessica's developed an attachment to you," said Hayley, sucking in her lip; there was more.

"When you're not there, she asks for you."

"I haven't noticed—"

"That's because you don't see how it is when you're not in."

"It's probably the first time Jess feels like someone's listening to her, not just trying to get answers about Mia. It's not uncommon for patients to develop an attachment to their therapist. It'll pass."

"Oscar, I heard Jessica threaten to hurt Chrissie if Chrissie came near her. When I asked her about it she wouldn't discuss it. She kept asking for you."

"Probably because I'm her doctor," said Oscar.

"She didn't ask for you by name." Hayley looked at him skeptically. "It could be transference, but I'm not sure it's harmless. Oscar, she's been through a lot. It could break the trust you've built, and that little girl will never be found."

"I could use it as a technique?" He knew what Hayley would say. He'd say the same if the conversation was reversed.

"If she starts to see you as part of the problem, it could remind her why she stopped speaking in the first place. She could regress and stop talking again."

It was true. Jess wasn't a good candidate for that technique, which was why he hadn't used it.

"She said she wanted to talk to the 'one that gets it' because you're the same as her. She could be manipulating you to make you think that she's innocent."

"She said we were alike?"

Hayley sighed. "A nurse gave her something for her ear, so I'm not sure she knew what she was saying exactly. She's developed an infection. It's strange that she didn't remember your name, but she remembered your visit."

"And you think she's manipulating me? For what? To get her out of Whitner?"

"I think you should try to get some answers. Find that little girl. If you don't, we might never know what happened to her."

Oscar nodded and set his burger down. "If I push too much, she might stop talking altogether. I don't think she's ready to discuss what happened."

"You don't think she's *ready*? Do you think she knows where Mia is?"

"If she knows, then there's a reason why she's not speaking."

"I know you're trying to be objective, Oscar, but ask yourself why you're so sure. Jessica was there, with access to Mia. They found Mia's hair in her car."

There were too many things that didn't make sense. According to Niki, Jess didn't even like Holly, so why was her daughter at Jess's house?

"I don't know," said Oscar, wondering if he was letting his instinct impede the evidence. If he was wrong about Jess, what would that mean for Mia?

"Push her if you want answers. There's a chance she'll clam up, but she might tell you what happened." Hayley moved her plate to the side, the last third of her burger forgotten.

Hayley didn't offer opinions lightly. She must've really thought about this.

"How can I get her to talk about Mia?"

"Find out why she thinks you're the same. Tell her something personal. Something relatable."

Hayley's eyes were lit with energy. She was making good on her promise to be a good friend. He'd be stupid to ignore her advice, but he still wanted to kiss her.

Before he could change his mind, Oscar leaned across the

table and kissed her, the taste of strawberries on his lips.

Chapter 15

Then

Jess ran through the kindergarten gate, clutching Zoe's hand.

"Hi," called a voice from the logs.

Jess was startled when she saw Holly. The bell had gone a while ago and most parents had already left the yard. Jess gestured towards Zoe apologetically, showing that she was running late.

"I don't want to go," squealed Zoe, pulling back from Jess's grasp.

"Zoe, please. You have to."

"Don't worry, your sister and I were late too. I'm waiting for her now," called Holly, amused by the struggle. "They're impossible when they don't want to do something, aren't they?"

"Yeah," said Jess, losing hold of Zoe's hand.

Zoe continued sliding after her hand was free, falling backwards onto the asphalt. She hit the ground and began to howl.

"Oh, honey! Are you alright? This is why I asked you to hold my hand."

Jess scooped Zoe from the ground and checked her knees

and hands, turning her from Holly's prying eyes.

"No grazes," Jess said, hugging her daughter.

Since Holly had coffee with them that first day, she'd become a regular at their catch-ups. Niki wasn't generally so welcoming to new people. Usuallly, she was the first first to nit-pick.

Jess carried Zoe towards the classroom, aware they were making a scene. "Come on, Zoo. Let's go in. You're already late." It came out harsher than intended, but the day before had been the same, and the one before that.

Niki exited the classroom as Jess went in.

"Jess!" said Niki. Her tone changed when she noticed Zoe's tears. "Oh, no. What's wrong?"

"It's nothing. She fell over and she doesn't want to go in," said Jess, trying to step around Niki to get inside.

Niki pulled gently at Zoe's piggy tail and made a beeping noise. "Wow, I didn't know they did that. Did you?"

Zoe cracked the first signs of a smile and shook her head. "You're funny, Aunt Niki."

"Yeah, well, I tell you what—if you go inside, I might have a surprise waiting for you at pick up this afternoon."

"You will?"

"Yep, but only if you go now."

Zoe slid out of Jess's arms, her tears magically drying, and pulled at the classroom door. "Come on," she said to Jess.

Niki winked. "Talk to you when you get out. Holly's waiting—we'll be over at the logs."

"That's okay," Jess said quickly. She couldn't handle another rolling pill incident after the morning she'd had.

Niki waved a hand dismissively. She'd wait by the tree regardless of what Jess said.

The classroom door creaked, announcing their arrival as Jess went inside.

"Hi, Zoe. Come and join us on the floor." Ms. Liu ushered Zoe over and smiled at Jess.

"Sorry," said Jess, backing out of the classroom quietly.

Niki was waiting at the logs with Holly, as she'd promised. As Jess drew closer, their conversation died.

"Sweetie, we're going for coffee," said Niki, jumping up too quickly and throwing an arm around Jess's shoulders. "And you're coming."

"I—"

"No excuses. You're coming, and that's final." She shot Jess a warning look. "Coffee Bar. I've only heard good things, so we're trying it."

Jess sighed. Niki did this often enough when they were kids that Jess knew she would ramp it up until she got what she wanted.

Jess waved her keys in defeat and went to her car. She'd heard good things about Coffee Bar too.

When she arrived, it was clear how the café got it's name. The front lined with stools occupied by young professionals. Jess caught sight of Niki and Holly and joined them at their table.

"Now that the kids are at school, we should make it a rule to only come to places like this," said Niki, gesturing around at the other adults. "Not a toddler in sight."

"Here, have a menu. There are three whole pages just for coffee," said Holly, sliding a menu toward Jess.

"Thanks," said Jess, opening the laminated menu. "One whole page is just coffee with booze."

"Yeah, we should order that," said Holly.

"It's nine thirty in the morning," said Jess.

Holly's stare was icy. "And? It's not like we do it every day, right? So why not?"

Niki shrugged. "Mocha Toblerone sounds good to me."

They ordered and sat back at their table.

"You know what? I need this," declared Holly. "My ex thinks he wants custody of Mia."

"Oh no," said Niki, eyes wide.

Holly nodded. "The thing is, he doesn't even want to see her. He just wants to piss me off, so he's going straight for Mia."

"Wow," said Niki. "If Bevan ever tried that, I'd—I'm sorry, that's not helping."

"It's fine. Hopefully, he'll realize how much work she is and forget about it."

Niki turned her attention to Jess, widening her eyes. "And how are you Jessie, honey?"

"Are the pills helping?" asked Holly, dark eyes boring into Jess.

Jess nodded, unwavering. "Yeah, they are."

Niki held Jess's hand. "Honey, Holly told me what happened at school."

Jess looked at Holly. She wasn't sure what Holly said, but judging by Niki's tone, it wasn't good.

"It's not your fault. You've got a lot on your plate. We want to help."

Holly raised an eyebrow, an amused child pulling the wings off a butterfly. Most people would have had the dignity to avert their eyes, maybe apologize for causing trouble.

"Don't get upset, Jess. We're worried about you," said Niki.

"Jessica," said Holly in soft tones. "I know I haven't known you for very long, but I already consider you someone I *could* be friends with. It's the only reason I even mentioned it."

Jess glared at Holly until Niki's voice drew her attention back. "You *pushed* Zoe at kinder today? I know they're frustrating sometimes, but Jess, if someone saw you do that, you could get in serious trouble."

"I did *not* push Zoe," said Jess, her voice measured. "I was holding her hand, and she tried to pull away. When she did, she fell backward."

Holly looked at Jess sympathetically before casting Niki a knowing look.

Niki tapped her foot as an attendant delivered their coffee, showing the sense to at least wait until they left before resuming the conversation. "Jessie, please don't get mad. We're on your side. I think you need to vent a little. You bottle everything up. It's only a matter of time before it explodes."

Jess, backed into her chair, cornered by hungry animals. "I'm not bottling anything."

"Jesus, Jess. You're taking pills *because* you bottle stuff up."

Niki had always had a penchant for drama.

"I told you, I was struggling with Zoe going to kindergarten, but I'm doing much better."

"How are things with you and Clay?"

Jess glanced at Holly. She didn't want to discuss her husband or her daughter while Holly was there. The less Holly knew about her, the better.

"Great. And just so you know," said Jess, looking directly at Holly, "I don't push, hit or physically discipline my daughter, regardless of what you *think* you saw."

"No, of course not," said Holly. "Oh god, I'm so sorry. I didn't mean to offend you. I was trying to tell Niki you looked...

flustered."

"Jess, this isn't an attack on you. This is us seeing if you're okay, because we care," said Niki.

"Okay," Jess conceded.

"I know you'd never hurt Zoe on purpose."

Had it really looked like she pushed Zoe? She was annoyed with Zoe's whining, but she was sure she hadn't pushed her—even if a part of her wanted to for just a second.

Chapter 16

Now

Oscar sipped coffee, and found nothing except milk froth stuck to the bottom of his mug like coral. He considered making another, but paced himself when he saw the time. He set down the mug, statistics running through his brain. Fifty percent. One in two. He fell into the 'experienced another episode' category.

A familiar feeling began to surface.

You took a life. You deserve what you get.

A default ringtone echoed through the silence of the room, startling him. He'd been meaning to change it to something more musical, but he'd never found the time.

The mug slid from his hand, ceramic shards exploded in different directions. He imagined taking a piece and pressing it deep into his wrist, ending the torment of living when something inside was long dead.

The ringtone continued—the caller should realize he couldn't talk after a few more bars.

What if it's Hayley?

He dragged himself from the sofa and looked at the screen.

It was work. "Hello? Oscar de la Nuit."

A frantic voice grabbed him. "Oscar, it's Chloe. Sorry to bother you on your day off, but we have a situation here and I thought you'd want to know."

"That's okay, Chloe," Oscar said calmly. "What is it?"

"It's Jessica Green. I think you should come in."

Oscar dodged the shattered ceramic pieces littering the floor.

He changed into fresh clothes and drove to Whitner Psychiatric. He tried calling Chloe on the way, but he couldn't get a connection.

The last time he'd gone in on his day off was because of a wrongly administered dose of anti-psychotic medication. The patient was a nervous girl named Lydia, who had become agitated, and believed the Whitner staff were trying to hurt her.

Once Oscar had calmed her down, he learned she wasn't hallucinating. The medication she took had caused her to relive an experience she had as a child, that she'd kept a secret for a long time.

When he arrived, Oscar knew the situation wouldn't be as straightforward.

Two police cars were parked at the entrance. One of the cars occupied three spaces across. The officer must've been in a hurry to get inside.

Shit.

Sliding from the seat, he raced inside, scanning his id to open the automated doors.

Chloe slid from behind the front desk and greeted him somberly. Jason stood talking to three stern-faced officers in uniform.

"What happened? Is everyone okay?" Oscar asked.

"Jessica left the hospital," said Chloe.

"Is she okay? Where is she?"

"She didn't get far. We called the police to help find her. We were worried what she might do. She was agitated when the police brought her back, saying she needed to find someone. She wouldn't tell us who."

"She flipped out when Jason tried talking to her."

"Where is she now? Is she okay?"

"She's in the treatment room. She has a few scrapes, but we've patched her up. She's refusing to talk to anyone, but I'm hoping she'll speak to you."

Oscar nodded.

"Oscar," said Chloe, placing a hand on his arm. "Charles went in to talk to her when she got back. He might still be with her."

"Okay."

"No one saw her leave, but we think she took a visitor's pass for the door. I was on the phone, and Jason was doing rounds. She must've grabbed it then. I'm so sorry," said Chloe.

"Thanks, Chloe. I'll go see how she is."

The acting manager in Oscar's absence, Charles Aston, walked in, his hands clasped. "Oscar. There's no need for you to be here on your day off. Everything's under control."

"Thank you, Charles," said Oscar carefully. Charles still hadn't accepted that Oscar got the job that he wanted. Now Charles had to content himself with playing director on Oscar's days off, but Charles was an all-or-nothing type, and resented coming in second best.

"I'd still like to talk to Jess. She might like a familiar face."

"Perhaps it would be better if we talked first?"

"Okay, sure," said Oscar, impatient to make sure that she was alright. "Let's talk in the visitor's room."

Charles followed Oscar, pulling out a chair and sitting resolutely.

"What happened?" asked Oscar.

Charles lifted himself up to his full height, his bird-like eyes watching Oscar. "Before we get to what happened today, I want to address a bigger issue that I believe contributed to Jessica Green's escape today."

"Okay," said Oscar, humoring him.

"Ever since Jessica arrived at Whitner, she's had trouble adjusting."

"She's only been here for a short while."

"And in that short while, she's attacked another patient, refused to cooperate with staff, and she doesn't take her medication without significant effort from our nursing staff. Today, she tried to leave the facility—"

Oscar waited as Charles listed each item off on a finger, running out of misdemeanors before he'd ticked off one hand.

"Charles, Jessica Green has experienced significant trauma. We knew there'd be some challenges."

Charles cleared his throat loudly, his neck vibrating. "She has also *caused* significant challenges. Because of her behavior today, I have no choice but to file a report."

"I wouldn't expect anything less," said Oscar.

"I don't know whether you're aware, Oscar, but her treatment is a general topic of discussion at Whitner. Given her resistance, there has been speculation regarding whether she will be responsive to treatment."

Oscar leveled his eyes at Charles. "Well, given the length of her stay, it's too early to say whether treatment—current or revised—is effective."

He'd started cognitive behavioral therapy alongside her medication to maximize its effectiveness. It gave Jess the chance to express things, and gave Oscar a baseline to determine other tools that might assist her. He had also encouraged her to join group therapy—it was easy to get lost in a new environment, and it let her get to know some of the others at Whitner, even if she didn't talk during the sessions.

"Of course. I'm just saying that once I write this report, the clock starts ticking. I'm telling you as a professional courtesy."

The threat was clear.

"Charles, what did you say to Jessica when you spoke to her?"

"It doesn't matter what I said. The point is, she wouldn't answer."

"I'll talk with her," said Oscar.

"That's not necessary," said Charles.

"I'm already here—"

"No one was instructed to call you," said Charles.

"You should get started on that report. I'd like it on my desk tomorrow. Since you're the acting manager today, it would be great if it came from you; don't ask someone to write it for you. It'll give you the opportunity to explain how the situation escalated under your care."

Oscar scraped back his chair to leave. "Oh, and Charles, help Jason first—he looks like he could use a hand with the police report out front."

Chapter 17

Now

Oscar wasn't expecting Jess to look so beaten-up lying in the hospital bed, several pillows holding her up. Her face was drained of color, lips shiny from the ointment the nurse had applied to repair the cracks.

She looked at him with distant eyes, so lost that she probably felt like the only person in the world. It was a lonely place.

"Hey. How are you feeling?" asked Oscar.

She shot him a look.

"That bad, huh? I heard you needed some fresh air. Maybe we can organize some outdoor time?"

"I just need to talk to—" Jess trailed off, as if it wasn't worth the effort it would take to explain.

Oscar caught a pillow as it slid out from behind her, tilting towards the floor. "Who were you going to see?" He readjusted the pillow, propping her up.

She tensed at his closeness. "You wouldn't understand." She'd tried to explain it before, but whoever she'd told didn't get it. Oscar guessed she was expecting the same from him.

"Did you leave to find Mia?"

Jess gripped Oscar's arm and pulled herself up.

"I wanted to tell him to stay strong," said Jess.

Was she talking about Clay? Did she feel guilty about the effect this had on her family?

Was Mia Jess and Clay's secret?

If only he could talk to Clay he might learn something.

"If you want to see your husband, we can arrange a visit."

Jess looked horrified. "No!"

Maybe she was lying about visiting someone? Was she going home to finish what she started by killing Clay? Perhaps the police intervention had saved Clay's life.

"It's okay. I'm not calling anyone unless you want me to."

Panic overtook the vacant look in her eyes. "Don't tell Clay I left. He won't understand."

Jess sounded afraid of her husband. What was she hiding from him?

"What wouldn't he understand?"

Jessica shook her head, strands of hair escaping her loose ponytail. "You'd keep me here longer if I told you."

Oscar tried to conceal his frustration. If Jess wouldn't tell him, how could he help? He had to get her talking before she suffocated on the words she couldn't say. She was already experiencing selective mutism. The past few months had been difficult. What if Jess relapsed?

They were running out of time.

Once Charles wrote up the incident report, Oscar would have to explain why Jess left Whitner, and why he still didn't know where Mia was. At least he could say she was speaking now, if not all the time. If he was going to continue treating Jess, he'd need to show more.

"Jess, you need to talk to me. I mean, really talk. I don't

know how much time we've got before they decide I'm not the right person to be treating you. Since you left Whitner, it'll probably be less time than I thought we had."

She let go of his arm, her hands moving to her sides.

He leaned into her space, occupying it with her. "Tell me what you're afraid of."

"It doesn't matter why any of it happened. They'll keep me here."

Paranoia?

"Who are 'they'? Are you afraid you'll go to prison if you tell me?"

"I'm already *in* prison." She gestured around her. "I have no say in whether I'm here or somewhere else. I can't leave."

"I want to help, but I need to know what happened to Mia so we can figure out what to do next."

She searched his expression, looking for something she could believe in.

"Believe me, Jess—if you know something and you don't speak up now, it'll suffocate you." He paused. "Secrets eat at you, even if they belong to someone else."

"It already does," she whispered. "I can't fix it."

How had life led her to a place where it looked like she'd murdered someone?

"I don't know about that. You tried to get out of here today, because it was important enough to risk getting in trouble for. I believe you wouldn't have done that if you didn't have some hope tucked away."

"I don't even know where he is. It was a stupid idea."

"Who?"

What if he was wrong, and Jess was just visiting a lover one last time? Maybe she'd told Clay she was leaving, and they got into a fight that went too far. Or, she wanted Clay out of the way.

"You're not listening," said Jess. "I don't need help. I'm here because it's the only way to keep me locked up. They don't have evidence, so they can't prove anything, but they don't want to let me go, because as long as I'm locked up, they can pretend they're doing their job."

"As long as they have a reason to believe you committed the crime, they would've kept you at Carlson. I put in a transfer request because I thought you might do better here."

Jess sat up, her back straight, her hands propping her up. "You transferred me here?"

"Yeah."

"Why would you do that?"

"Whitner's nicer than the remand center, and I thought you could use someone to talk to. Someone who understands."

"I'm here because of you?" she asked, as if she couldn't believe it.

"Yes."

"Why did you really visit me at Carlson?"

"I saw what happened to you, and I wanted to help."

"Why me? You could have helped anyone."

Hayley suggested telling Jess something about himself. If he was going to tell her, now was the time, but the words stuck in his throat.

"I know what it's like to be you. I was you."

Chapter 18

Then

Jess picked at her tofu scramble and avocado breakfast. It was much better than the slightly burned toast she'd abandoned as she ran out the door with Zoe, but she was struggling to find her appetite.

She had to finish an article that morning, but Niki promised they wouldn't stay long, so Jess had crumbled and agreed to go. It was nice to catch up without Holly. Jess felt more relaxed, more like herself.

Niki worked a croissant, artfully unrolling the layers of pastry and nibbling on them. "Jessie, are you sure you're alright? You look pale."

"I'm fine." Jess shrugged. "I'm just tired. Clay's always at work. I feel like Zoe's going to forget who he is."

Niki nodded empathetically. "It's difficult."

A phone buzzed. "It's yours," said Niki, automatically checking her own pocket.

Jess rattled around her bag, eventually finding her phone. An unfamiliar number flashed on the screen. "Hello, Jessica speaking?"

"Hi, Jessica? It's Ella Liu, Zoe's teacher. Can you come by the classroom this morning? I'd like to chat about Zoe."

She could feel the digital marketing trends article slipping away into next week, but if Zoe's teacher had asked her to go in it was probably important.

"Um, of course. Is there a problem?"

"It would be better if we discussed it in person. Can you come by around 11:30?"

Jess checked the time. If this was about Zoe doing well in class, she would've mentioned it over the phone, or the kinder communication app. Jess's stomach stirred. "Of course. I'll see you then."

"What was that about?" asked Niki, searching her cup as if it might have a leak. "I should've gotten the large—I'm not done with caffeine this morning. You don't mind staying longer, do you?" she said, gesturing to an attendant to get their attention.

"Hi. Can I have another one of these, please?" Niki asked the gangly man who came to their table.

Jess picked up her fork. "Sure. I've barely started." There was no point trying to work now. She couldn't focus on anything except what Zoe's teacher wanted to talk about.

"Who was the call from?" prompted Niki.

"Ms. Liu."

"Oh?"

"She wants me to come by later this morning."

Niki's eyes widened—she always enjoyed gossip. "Did she say why?"

"No," said Jess, moving the scramble around on her plate.

"I'm sure Zoe's fine."

Jess nodded. "She never wants to go. She's not adjusting

very well. Kindergarten's been huge for her. She's barely even been to daycare."

"It's normal, Jess. Aiden's the same. He complains he doesn't want to go, but once he's there he's fine." Niki smiled reassuringly. "It'll get easier."

"Yeah," said Jess. "Except, she comes home crying, asking me not to send her back. It's not supposed to be this hard."

"Maybe," agreed Niki. "But sometimes it *is*. And we push through until it gets better."

Jess nodded, unconvinced.

"It probably feels worse because Clay's at work. Zoe started kindergarten, and you're taking on more of the home stuff. It's understandable that you're feeling the pressure, honey. Give it a few weeks and you watch; things will settle down and you'll look back on this and roll your eyes."

"Maybe."

"Why do you think Ms. Liu called?" asked Niki.

"I don't know, but I think one of the other kids might be hurting Zoe. Maybe that's what it's about."

"Oh my gosh. Did you ask about it?"

"And say what? I don't want to accuse anyone, just in case it turns out to be a misunderstanding."

"Come on Jess. You wouldn't even *think* that someone hurt Zoe for no reason. You need to stop being so *nice*. Who do you think hurt her?"

Used to Niki's double-barreled questions, Jess waited patiently until she finished. "I found some bruises."

Niki's eyes widened. "Did you ask Zoe if someone hurt her?"

"Of course."

"And?"

"She said she fell over on the playground."

Niki shrugged gingerly. "Maybe she did? Zoe would tell you if someone hurt her. It's a good thing you're going in."

"I don't want to make it worse for her. You know how kids can be. Once you show weakness, they jump on it. One of the bruises went right up her arm. It looked like someone had punched her."

Jess had seen bruises from falls before, but this one was darker, angrier. And it was on the inside of her arm.

"Did you ask her for details? If her story falls apart, you know she's lying."

"Of course. She said she was outside and fell over."

"That must be why Ms. Liu wants you to go in," said Niki. "Do you want me to go with you? I'll get to the bottom of what happened."

"Hey!" called someone at the cafe entrance.

Jess recognized the voice immediately, and forgot Niki's offer. "Oh my god, I just stopped in for coffee, and here you are," said Holly, already at their table. "I keep running into you. I promise I'm not following you."

The way she said it made Jess wonder.

Niki laughed. "Hi Holly," she said warmly. "You caught us at a good time. I'm just about to drink a second coffee, which I never do. Let's just say that I knew I should have ordered the large. Want to join us?"

Holly laughed too, a hollow sound echoing Niki's. "That's okay. I'm just picking up a latte to get me through errands. I'll see you at pick up," she said, starting to move away.

Jess felt relief—she didn't have energy for her today.

"It looks like you two are busy anyway."

"Oh, no. Don't be silly. Join us."

"Really?"

Niki nodded.

Holly scrunched her nose. "I could use a break," she said, sitting beside Niki.

Jess chewed her lip.

"We were just talking about Zoe," said Niki.

Why did she have such a big mouth? Jess tried to catch her eye and discourage her.

Holly set her bag down and adjusted the band of her jeans. "Oh, what's wrong with Zoe?"

"Jess thinks someone might've hurt her at kindergarten."

"Oh no. Who?"

"I don't know," said Jess.

"She came home with bruises," said Niki.

"Kids. They've always got bruises or skinned knees. Well, except mine. I wish she'd play a bit more, get grubby and live it up a little. At least you know Zoe's got an adventurer's spirit," she smiled, flashing pearl-white teeth.

"Yeah. Except it was on her arm, so Jess thought someone might have punched her."

"Actually," said Holly sheepishly. "That might've been Mia."

"What?"

Holly looked apologetic. "I talked to her about it and made her promise never to do it again. I've been meaning to mention it."

"I'm sure Mia didn't do it on purpose," said Jess. What would possess a four-year-old to punch someone so hard they bruised them? Could a child's fist even cause a bruise like that?

"The thing is, Mia said that Zoe was picking on her, and that Zoe hit her first."

Jess's head was reeling. She couldn't imagine Zoe hitting another child.

Was that why Zoe didn't want to go to kindergarten?

Jess shifted the sugar on the table. "I'll ask Zoe about it tonight."

"I'm not excusing what Mia did," said Holly, false red nails covering her heart. "In fact, I suggested she talk to Zoe." Holly looked directly at Jess. "They could be great friends. If she just gave her a chance."

Chapter 19

Now

Oscar waited for Hayley after work. It was his turn to choose where they were going, but he didn't go out enough to know where they should go, so he typed *decent bars New Haven* and let his phone choose.

Looking around, he wasn't sure his faith in a few photos and a quick search was warranted.

He sat on a stool at an elevated table, crunching plum salt dusted onion rings and sipping beer, overly conscious of the people around him. He never knew what to do with himself when he was out. At work he had purpose, but here he had to figure it all out without context or an end goal.

He had seven minutes left to decide what to say to Hayley before she walked through the door.

Trying to keep up with the politics at Whitner was sapping his energy, detracting from work he needed to finish. He'd received notification of the incident report Charles had filed. It focused heavily on Oscar's role in Jess leaving Whitner, but he was trying to let it go, at least for one night.

Charles was lying low. He seemed convinced that they'd

pin the misdemeanor on Oscar. When they crossed paths, he smiled, as if he was winning some imaginary war. Oscar hated himself for wondering if Charles knew something he didn't.

He was ready for a break. This didn't feel like the break he needed, surrounded by people in a noisy bar, but the alternative was to invite Hayley home and he hadn't had time to clean the Brown coffee sludge from the wall.

Oscar forced himself to focus on his beer, tilting the glass to the side. How had he finished half already? He set the bottle down abruptly—he wasn't going down that path again.

Hayley arrived right on time and went straight to the bar to order a martini.

"Rough day?" asked Oscar as brought her drink over and sat.

"Not really. I like a dry martini when I'm thinking."

"What are you thinking about?"

"Nothing." She ran a finger across the tip of her thumb.

"Yes, you are. You trace the edge of your thumbnail when you're lost in thought."

Hayley laughed. "If I didn't know what you do for a living, that could be creepy."

He raised an eyebrow.

"I'm trying to decide if you intentionally made our date this far from work so that no one would see us together. It would've been much easier to grab a drink at any of the bars near work."

Oscar sipped his beer. She didn't need to know that Google chose this place.

"You barely speak to me when we're at work," she said, swirling her glass, watching the alcohol climb the sides, dangerously close to spilling over. "Feel free to cut in," she said playfully, her voice slightly piquing. "I was hoping you'd have an explanation."

"I'm not ignoring you."

"Really? Then what would you call it?"

Oscar sighed. "It's complicated."

"I thought we had fun together, eating burgers, talking. I figured you weren't sure what you wanted, but then you kissed me, and I thought..." She let the words hang, testing his reaction. "Was I wrong?"

"No," said Oscar. "Not wrong. I like you. It's just—maybe now isn't the right time." Oscar stopped. He didn't want to hurt her, but he wasn't sure it was avoidable.

"I'm not asking for anything specific." She shrugged. "Why don't we hang out and see what we think?"

"Things are difficult at work. I have to be careful. Charles filed an incident report questioning Jess's treatment and my methods."

Hayley listened attentively. "Charles is... he's a..."

"An ass?"

Hayley smiled. "Yeah, he is."

"He wants to make it seem like I can't do my job."

Hayley turned. "That's what you're worried about? Look, Charles has always wanted to be the director at Whitner. He's angry and lashing out. If you weren't in his way, I think he believes he'd have your job."

"That's why I have to be careful. Not just that, Charles is trying to get Jessica reassigned."

"That's because it's a high-profile case, and you're making progress."

"Why would he care? Even if we found Mia, it's the police who get the credit, not the therapist."

"Because it seems impossible. Jess wouldn't talk to anyone at the remand center. If you can do this, it shows you were the right hire," said Hayley.

Oscar had never been sure if Charles's dislike of him was as as obvious to others as it was to him. He raised an eyebrow. "Narcissist?"

"Maybe." She smiled mischievously. "Definitely the ass part."

Oscar laughed and offered Hayley an onion ring. He took one for himself. They weren't as good cold.

"He said the same stuff as you in his incident report," said Oscar. "About me taking too much of a personal interest in Jess. He questioned my objectivity said Jess left because I failed as her therapist."

"Really?"

Oscar shrugged. "I don't know if he believes it, but it's easy to blame me. Charles likes easy answers."

"Things are going to happen. Jessica brought her issues with her. If anything, you probably stopped something worse."

"Charles is making fire out of embers, and I don't want to give him more fuel. If he thought it'd get rid of me, he'd say anything."

"Well, it doesn't matter. He can't back up his story."

Oscar turned Hayley's hand over in his, lifting it slightly. "There is one thing he'd try if he knew."

"Me," she said. her voice flat. "You know, it's not illegal to date someone you work with."

"No, but it doesn't need to be illegal to cause a problem. Technically, I'm your boss. Even if it wasn't a problem, Charles would make it one."

She watched longingly as his hand moved up her arm. "I

could get a job somewhere else," she joked, moving closer.

Suddenly aware he was tracing her arm, Oscar took her hand in his. "We need you at Whitner. Your patients need you. You couldn't walk away from them."

Hayley pursed her lips. He was right. "Okay, so what then? We don't see each other anymore?"

"I can't ask you to wait," said Oscar, "but when things settle down, who knows?"

Hayley pushed a loose wave of hair behind her ear. "How about we keep it strictly professional at work, but when we're not at work— "

She trailed off, the question unfinished. Her hair smelled like coconut. She moved her lips across his, stopping his response. He returned the kiss, her lips full and warm against his as he wrapped his arms around her, lost in the moment.

Their bar stools clinked beneath them, teetering off balance, sending Hayley sprawling. Oscar caught her before she fell, wrestling with his stool to stop them both from falling.

They laughed, readjusting themselves so that their arms touched, their faces close together.

"No more ignoring me at work. If you keep acting like that, it'll look suspicious," she warned with mock seriousness. She grazed his arm lightly, sending his skin tingling.

"You're probably right," he agreed.

An attendant carrying a tray laden with food and drinks shot them a look as she passed.

"Was that about the kiss?" asked Oscar.

Hayley laughed. "Oh, come on—I'm sure they've seen worse than that."

"It's lucky I caught you," said Oscar. "There was potential for a broken bone or two."

"Imagine trying to explain why we both had broken legs on the same night."

"Weekend of extreme sport?" suggested Oscar.

Hayley moved closer and kissed him. "Maybe we should make the most of our near miss," she whispered. "Just think, we might've spent tonight waiting on x-rays instead."

"Instead of what?"

"A weekend of extreme sport?"

She kissed him before he could answer.

Chapter 20

Now

Oscar shifted in his chair. He had a session with Jess in an hour, but she had a group session scheduled to start now. It'd been a while since Oscar had taken part in one, and Hayley was running the session today.

Oscar tapped distractedly. Since the incident report had been placed on his desk, every moment felt borrowed.

He stood and stretched, trying to lift the tightness from his shoulders. These days, he was stuck in a chair for longer periods at a time, trying to get on top of everything. He missed doing rounds, and seeing how everyone was. There wasn't time for that anymore. Managing the center had its costs, and he wasn't sure they were worth it.

Oscar threw a jacket over his shirt and walked to the group area. Ten chairs were arranged in a circle so that everyone faced each other. Seven people were already waiting for the session to begin. Chrissie and Lewis sat together, laughing about something Oscar couldn't hear.

Jess was already there, a chair on either side of her. She stared at the wall, slumped in her seat. She was sitting with the group, but wasn't really part of the circle. Oscar was glad she made it to the session, but disappointed she didn't look happier. Part of her treatment included attending group sessions, and she'd promised she'd try.

A chair, slightly further from the others, was left for Hayley. Oscar noticed it was an unspoken rule that staff sat in the red chairs. Oscar took a white chair and crossed one leg over the other.

Hayley joined the circle, smiled sideways at Oscar, and took a gray seat next to Jess. He smiled back, remembering their night. "Oscar, nice of you to join us," she said, nodding slightly.

"Okay, so last time we gathered, we decided to share something we've found useful in our treatment. But first, we have a new participant with us today, so let's all introduce ourselves and say a little about ourselves."

Everyone looked at Jess. Some sized her up, curious about the new patient who never talked to anyone. Others had seen her on the news and knew why she was there, eager to hear her version.

Oscar watched them forming their judgments, deciding if she was responsible for Mia's disappearance. Chrissie glared, making no secret of her opinion.

Jess's hair sat across her shoulders, a dark shroud to disappear under. She avoided their faces, looking at the walls instead.

Was her lack of confidence from her encounter with Chrissie? Oscar could feel the tension, but keeping Jess from the group sessions would ostracize her further, and removing Chrissie could make things worse. Maybe once they got to know each other, they could mend the rift.

"Would anyone like to start?" asked Hayley.

Lydia looked away as Hayley's eyes roamed the group for a volunteer. Suffering from generalized anxiety disorder and a social phobia, Lydia avoided talking. She had been at Whitner for a long time. After a week outside and an attempt on her own life, she was back.

Lydia was being monitored closely after a second attempt. She might never stop trying to end her life. She confused the past and the present. During an episode, she thought Oscar was trying to strangle her. He went home questioning himself when it happened. Did he seem like a predator because of what he did to Riley? Did Lydia pick up on it?

She wouldn't have found him so scary before. What happened to Riley had sharpened his edges.

Chrissie cupped a hand near Lewis's ear and whispered something that made him smile.

"Lewis, did you want to tell us a bit about yourself?" asked Hayley.

"Not really. But I guess I can," he relented. "I'm Lewis. I'm here to learn why I don't get along so well with people. I'm being treated for anti-social personality."

"Thanks Lewis, that was great," said Hayley.

A woman in her early thirties named Emily was up next. "I'm here to manage my post-natal depression," she said. "When my baby was born, I experienced psychosis for the first time, and my husband brought me here. My baby's probably forgotten who I am. I just want to get better and go home."

Oscar smiled empathetically at Emily. Those early days of being a parent were difficult, especially the long, sleepless nights.

"Thanks for sharing, Em. Maybe we can organize a visit

soon. I think Olga remembered you the last time she visited. She didn't want to leave your arms."

Emily smiled at the memory.

"That must be awful," said Jess sympathetically. "Can't your baby stay here with you?" Jess looked from Emily to Hayley. "When Zoe was a baby, I bought a baby sling because she'd only settle when she was strapped to me. I used to worry that my heart was thumping too hard, that it would wake her."

"It's hard, but she's only three months old, and I'm not ready to take care of her yet. I don't want her first months to be spent in a hospital. I want her out with her dad, going for walks in the park until she's sleepy. Then, I want her to curl up at home in her own bed." Emily gave a gritty smile, fighting tears.

"Sorry. I didn't mean to sound rude," said Jess, eyes back to the floor.

"That's okay, really. It's nice to talk about her. I think about her so much."

"I know what you mean," said Jess.

Maybe Jess could make a friend after all—if the group saw that Emily could be civil the others might follow.

"I saw your daughter in a news article. She's cute."

Jess looked shocked. She probably didn't know she'd been a hot news topic for a few weeks.

"My turn," said Chrissie.

"Okay Chrissie. Tell us why you're here," said Hayley.

"I have problems with emotions."

"Would you like to tell us more?"

"I don't feel them," said Chrissie, staring at Jess. "But I know that killing a kid is wrong."

"Okay. Thanks, Chrissie," said Hayley.

"Jessica, would you like to tell us a bit about yourself?"

Jess looked like she might jump out of her seat and run. She searched the group, everyone waiting for her to speak. "They think I killed a little girl, and that I tried to kill my husband. They think I'll do it again."

"Did you do it?" asked Lewis, animated by the drama.

"Maybe."

Chapter 21

Now

Maybe.

Jess disappeared after the group session. Assuming she was taking a bathroom break, Oscar waited in his office, trying to figure out what she meant.

After Jess's turn, the conversation had dried up.

The door opened a crack, and Jess peeked around the corner.

"Come in," said Oscar.

Jess gravitated toward the couches. "Sorry I'm late," she whispered, sitting on the edge of a two-seater.

"How are you?" he asked.

She met his gaze, her face unreadable. He needed to find how to get under her mask, see what she was hiding. There was more to Jessica Green than she wanted to show. How deep did Oscar want to go? How dark would it get down in her core?

Was her maybe an admission, or a cry for help? It felt like she was being vague on purpose, but she hadn't denied kidnapping Mia. Jess always seemed to leave him with more questions than answers.

Maybe. *Maybe not.*

Oscar could bring up the group session, ask Jess what she meant, but that didn't mean he'd get an answer. At least now Jess knew why Chrissie was so blunt. She didn't feel emotions the way most people felt them, didn't understand social convention the same way.

"You went to the group session. I'm impressed."

Jess pursed her lip. "Yeah, well— "

"You didn't find it useful?"

She shrugged. "I don't think Chrissie appreciated me being there."

"Chrissie has a disorder that means she doesn't like anyone being there unless she wants them there."

"Is she a psychopath?" Jess asked.

"That's not what I would call it."

"Is it a specifier for her diagnosis?"

What did Jessica know about psychopaths?

"I can't talk about other patients' diagnoses, Jess. Do you have an interest in psychology?"

Jess shifted, bringing her arms close. "Not particularly."

"How do you know about psychopaths and specifiers?"

She shook her head. "I don't, really. I wrote an article about it."

"Why?"

Jess shrugged. "Because it's interesting."

"Did you choose it?"

"It was a freelance piece." A defensive note had crept into her voice.

"So, why that topic?"

Her eyes flashed. "Are you asking if I was trying to figure out whether I'm a psychopath?"

"Not at all."

She raised an eyebrow, skeptical. He would have to give her more.

"In my professional judgment, you don't seem like you have antisocial tendencies. You're a little reserved, maybe." He shrugged. "That's why I'm curious."

"Like I said, I was writing an article."

"Were you trying to learn about someone close to you?"

"No." She didn't hesitate, guessing who Oscar was referring to. "Clay's caring and kind. He's a great parent. If anything, he cares too much about what other people think. He's always tried to be an involved parent. Sometimes life gets in the way, but mostly, he does an okay job."

She was defending him, but not necessarily because she believed it. Oscar saw people excuse destructive behavior all the time. *He gets angry because he cares so much. She's controlling because she feels like she lacks control in her life.* It was a coping strategy to normalize a situation. Jess sounded like she believed what she was saying, but Oscar had to decide whether he did, which was difficult without meeting Clayton Green.

"If not Clay, then who?"

"No one."

He could hear the lie in her voice, but if he pushed her, she might refuse to say anything more.

The silence stretched. If it became long enough, she might try to fill it. Jess clasped her hands, one in the other, hesitating. She had something to say, but didn't share it.

"What do you want to talk about today?"

She looked tempted by the invitation.

Eventually, she spoke.

"I was thinking about what you said," said Jess, arms

wrapped around her ribs. "What did you mean when you said you know what it's like to be me?"

"I know what it's like to be accused of something horrible. The loneliness that comes with it. The guilt."

"You don't know," she said, her tone prickly. "You can still live your life. You can go where you want, do what you want. I'm stuck here, maybe forever. So, what good would it do me to talk?"

"I want to help, Jess."

"Then tell me, what did you do that was so horrible?"

"I used to have a family." He hesitated. "I thought I would have them forever. Maybe I took them for granted."

Jess pulled her arms around herself, closing the space between herself and everything else.

"We had a son." He pictured Riley, the edges blurred from the years since he saw him. "I loved him. I would've done anything for him." Oscar paused. It was the first time he'd talked about it since therapy, and the words didn't come easily. The shame almost stopped him from continuing.

"What happened to him?" asked Jess.

"Something horrible." Oscar wrestled with the words, struggling to say them out loud. "He was killed. He was just a baby, and he died."

"I'm sorry," said Jess. "Did they find who did it?"

"Yeah. I did it."

Oscar waited for Jess to stand up and tell him they were nothing alike, that he was the worst kind of killer. He hurt his own child.

"How?"

"Excuse me?" he said, thrown by her question.

She spoke gently, asking questions no one else dared ask.

"How did it happen?"

"He was in his crib. Prisha left him with me. She trusted me with our son, and she shouldn't have."

He was skipping parts of the story, unable to find the right words to tell it, unsure which parts he should leave out to protect his family, to protect himself.

I was too tired to go to him.

Jess listened with sad eyes.

"I was meant to check on him, but I didn't. I fell asleep. When I woke up, I realized he hadn't cried for his feed. I was so tired that instead of waking him, I stayed in bed, relieved he was sleeping through."

Jess's arms loosened their hold.

"Prisha came home and went to Riley's room. I thought she was checking on him because she missed him."

Oscar glanced at Jess. She listened with watery eyes. His words had pierced the mask.

"I woke when I heard her screaming. I thought something had happened while she was out. I found her in Riley's room. He was blue in her arms."

Oscar massaged his temple with his thumb. His secret was out there now.

Eventually, Jess spoke. "You're not like me," she said gently. "What happened to you wasn't your fault. It was an accident. You couldn't have known what would happen to your son."

"They called it SIDS," said Oscar. "But my son died because I didn't check on him."

"Is that why you think we're the same?" asked Jess. Her expression changed. "Or did you think that telling me about your son would make me say that I tried to kill Clay or Mia?"

"No, that's not why I told you about Riley," said Oscar. "I

wanted you to know that I understand why you might not want to talk about it. I haven't told anyone else what happened the night Riley died, except my therapist. It's the loneliest kind of secret to keep."

"If you really believe I hurt them, why do you think I did it?"

"I'm not sure that I believe you hurt them. I'm asking so we can figure out how to help Mia. If you didn't do it, I won't waste time getting you to confess."

Jess battened down her defenses. "It wasn't an accident."

Chapter 22

Then

The sound of squealing children greeted Jess before she reached the kindergarten gate. She wiped sweaty palms on her jeans and walked to Zoe's classroom. Ms. Liu sat at her desk, writing something out on her iPad.

Jess knocked and tentatively opened the door. Now that she was this close to knowing why she was there, she wasn't sure she was ready to find out.

"Jessica! Thanks for coming in. Take a seat." Ms. Liu closed her iPad and pushed it to the side.

Jess went to the grown-up sized chair across from Ms. Liu and sat, eyeing the kid-sized chairs. "Is Zoe alright?"

"Yes, Zoe's fine. The children are in an art lesson with our art teacher. I wanted to talk to you about a problem she's having with some of the other children."

Children? Did that mean there was more than one?

Jess took a deep breath to steady her nerves, eyeing the giant alphabet cards lining the wall. An overlap of paintings decorated the corner like wallpaper from an indecisive designer. She saw one with Zoe's name printed neatly in the corner—a picture of a child crying.

Was that Zoe in the picture? Is that how she felt about going to kindergarten? It would explain her wailing every morning. Jess thought it would've passed by now, but what if she couldn't help Zoe, and this was how it would always be? She hadn't mentioned making any friends, and when Jess asked, she changed the subject.

"Another child said Zoe hit her. Apparently, it happened a couple of days ago, but it's just been brought to our attention."

"Zoe *hit* someone? Who did she hit? Did Zoe *say* that she hit them, or did a kid claim that she did?"

"None of our staff saw the incident. Jessica, no one's in trouble. We just wanted to talk to you, to see if Zoe talked about what happened at home?"

"Actually, I was talking to another parent about this earlier. I was saying that I noticed some bruises on Zoe's arms. Maybe she was defending herself?" Jess stopped.

"Has Zoe confirmed that?" Ms. Liu asked again.

"Not directly. But she begs me not to make her go to kindergarten." Jess willed herself to stop talking, but maybe Zoe's best defense was to let Ms. Liu hear Zoe's side of the story. "She cries in the mornings. I thought she needed time to adjust, but I don't know."

Ms. Liu looked surprised. "Zoe's a very caring little girl. She's happy in class—she seems to enjoy it very much when she's here."

Jess stayed silent, unsure what to say.

"We'll monitor the situation and see if anyone's hurting Zoe at playtime."

"Okay," said Jess, forcing a smile. "I've noticed her cousin, Aiden, plays a little rough sometimes. Maybe that's all it is?"

"Maybe. Thanks again for coming in. It might be good to catch up in a week or so, to see how Zoe's going."

Jess stood to leave, but changed her mind and sat back down.

"It was Holly Edwards—Mia's mother—I was talking to," said Jess firmly.

"Oh, okay," said Ms. Liu, clearly surprised. "I wouldn't have expected that. Mia and Zoe have become good friends. I was talking about a conflict with a group of boys."

Jessica's stomach dropped. Was Zoe being bullied by more than one group of kids at kindergarten?

"Who?" asked Jess.

"We can certainly try to find out what's happening," said Ms. Liu carefully.

"Can I go outside for a few minutes, just to see how she's going?" asked Jess.

"Of course."

Jess thanked Ms. Liu and exited through the door at the back of the room. She caught sight of her daughter immediately, recognizing the tawny pigtails and the pink and blue butterfly t-shirt she'd dressed her in that morning.

Zoe walked through the sandpit, her arm linked with another girl. Mia? They grinned as they squished the toes of their shoes in the sand.

Mia caught sight of Jess watching them, staring with the same dark eyes as Holly.

"Mamma!" squealed Zoe, going to Jess for a quick hug. "Come see the sandpit with us."

"Hey, girls," said Jess, giving Mia a quick wave. "Are you having fun?"

"Yep," said Zoe. "We're going to the sandpit," she sang, trying to drag Jess with them.

"Well, I'm not really allowed to play in the sandpit," said Jess.

Mia watched Jess with big doe eyes, as alive as Holly's were empty. Jess couldn't imagine Holly as a child.

"You seem nice," said Mia. "Zoe's nice, too. Can I live with you?"

"Aw, honey, your mother would miss you," said Jess. "And your daddy."

Shit. Jess remembered what Holly said about Mia's dad. She hadn't meant to bring it up.

Mia's attention shifted at the mention of her dad. "Did you know my dad?"

"No. I'm sorry."

"Mommy said he died. That's why he doesn't come to see me anymore."

Holly must have told Mia her dad died to explain why he wasn't in their lives anymore. But why wouldn't she tell her the truth? It could be awkward if Mia ever saw him on the street.

Jess buried her opinion. It wasn't her business—she didn't know everything about their situation. Still, she couldn't help wondering, what if he got help to manage his anger and wanted to see Mia one day?

Would Holly tell Mia he wasn't dead after all, or would she deny Mia the opportunity to see her father?

"Well, I'm sure if he could, he would."

Maybe Holly didn't want to talk about him dying and hadn't mentioned it.

"Daddy was nice," said Mia. "I miss him."

Chapter 23

Now

The phone buzzed on Oscar's desk. He looked at caller ID before picking up. "Hi, Chloe."

"Hi, Oscar. I hope I'm not interrupting anything important, but there's a letter for you at the front. I'll hold it here if you want to pick it up. I signed for it, but I thought you'd want to know when it arrived. Did you want me to bring it in?"

"Thanks. Who's it from?"

There was a rustle as Chloe shuffled the envelope around to read the back. "It's from the board," she breathed.

"I'll be right there."

As Oscar passed the common room, he noticed Chrissie wasn't in her usual place on the sofa. Em sat in a chair, reading a few lines at a time and glancing up from her book as if she knew Chrissie might walk in at any moment. Lewis watched as if he was waiting for something to happen.

With her back to the front desk, Jess sat at the craft table, sewing something on the little rag doll. She looked up when she heard Oscar's voice.

"Hi, Jess." He looked away, more uncomfortable than he

thought he would be after their talk. Now that she knew his secret, did she think of him differently? He hadn't asked her not to tell anyone about Riley, but he hoped she wouldn't. Would she tell them he was a murderer, that he should be receiving treatment instead of pretending he belonged on the other side?

He stopped at the front desk, smiling back at Chloe.

"Here's your letter," she said, leaning across the front desk to hand Oscar the envelope. That explained why Charles had been extra smug lately.

He could be as smug as he wanted. Oscar wouldn't give up his position for someone who didn't care about the hospital. For Charles it was a title for his resume and a dinner party conversation.

"Thanks, Chloe," he said and opened the letter. The board wanted to meet to discuss Jess. It looked like Charles would be there too.

"Shit."

"Oscar, it's not my place to say, but what happened isn't your fault," said Chloe.

Oscar turned. Had Jess told Chloe about Riley? "Excuse me?"

"It's not your fault that Jess left. Charles should've kept things in check. I'm sure the board will see that too."

People were talking. He supposed it was inevitable. A break from routine usually got a few whispers.

"Thanks, Chloe. I appreciate it." Oscar smiled. He had always suspected that Chloe shared his opinion of Charles—the way she reacted to his dismissive attitude with none of her usual warmth.

If this got out, it could be a media frenzy. He could see it now, Charles telling the reporters about Oscar's *attachment* to Jess. He would try to make it sound carnal. In his attempt to ruin Oscar's career, Charles might take Jess down too.

After everything she'd been through, that was the last thing Oscar wanted. He'd have to fight for both of them.

∞

Oscar slammed a fist on his desk, causing pain to blossom through his hand just as the door opened.

"Come in," he said, cradling his fist under the table, trying to relax the muscles.

"Jess," he said. "How are things?"

She pointed roughly at his hidden hands. "I'm sorry I got you in trouble. I didn't mean to. And I'm sorry about your fist. That sounded like it hurt."

"You didn't get me into trouble," said Oscar, regaining his composure. He held up his fist. "And thanks."

"I overheard what Chloe said. I shouldn't have tried to leave like that. I was stupid."

"I won't pretend it was a good idea, but that doesn't make you stupid." He smiled.

Jess rolled her eyes. "Yeah, well, I'm still sorry."

"It's okay."

"If I knew..."

"You probably would've still done it."

"Maybe," she admitted. "But only because I had to."

"Wh— "

"Don't ask."

Oscar changed tact. "If you don't want to talk about it— "

"I don't."

She closed the door behind her and took a seat.

"I was thinking about our conversation about your son. I think you were right."

"I was?" Oscar asked, sounding surprised.

"Yeah, the bit about keeping secrets. It's lonely knowing something that no one else knows, but sometimes you don't have a choice because no one's ready to complicate things with the truth."

He swallowed his questions. If he interrupted now, she might stop talking.

"I want to make this right," said Jess.

"Then work with me."

"Does it mean telling you why I killed Mia? Where I dumped her body?"

He frowned. "That's not what I was going to say," he said. "You can tell me as much as you want, but I'd prefer it was the truth."

She shook her head. "I can't talk about it."

He could see there was more she wanted to say. The side of her mouth twitched slightly. She was so close to saying it, but something held her back.

"Tell me what happened."

"I can't."

"If they're wrong about you, prove it," said Oscar. "Not because you have to," he added, "but because you can."

Jess rested her hands limply on the table. "They have no evidence I did anything," she said, probably tired of defending herself. "I have nothing to prove."

"They can make things look worse than they are, believe me. They can make it look like you hurt Mia, even if you didn't," he said empathetically.

"Who, the police? Why would they want to do that?"

"No. The police largely aren't involved at this point. I'm talking about litigators. Lawyers."

"Holly probably couldn't afford a lawyer," said Jess.

"She doesn't have to."

"What?" said Jess, her voice catching.

If he could show her what she was risking, maybe she'd talk. "There's a crowdsourcing page to raise money for Holly. People have donated thousands. She's getting a lot of publicity."

She looked at him. "And?"

"She has their sympathy, and she's saying you're involved. She implicated you, and your husband—"

"Clay? He wouldn't hurt anyone," said Jess. "Especially a child." She paused until it seemed like Oscar had lost her. "Looking after Zoe must be difficult for Clay. He stepped up when I was taken away. I assumed they'd leave him alone."

"Jess, how sure are you that Clay didn't take Mia?"

She chewed her lip. Oscar had seen people do this a lot, usually when they were about to lie. Sometimes when they were deciding whether they should say what they were really thinking.

"You can tell me," he said.

"No. I can't." The frustration seeped into each word, as if she might want to tell him but had no choice.

"If I told you I hurt Mia, I wouldn't see Zoe again."

Her words gave away her intent. She chose them carefully, testing him. She was trying to figure out what he'd do with the truth before she gave it to him.

"That's not true. I don't have to repeat what you tell me. What we discuss is confidential. I told you about my son in the hopes you would respect that confidentiality, but if you felt you needed to tell someone, I'd understand."

"I have no one to tell," she said. "No one here wants to know me, and I don't see anyone from outside."

He nodded. He knew what that was like.

"Even if I had someone to tell, I wouldn't repeat it."

Oscar believed her.

"I have a question for you, but I need you to tell the truth. No tricks. No pretending. Just the truth," said Jess.

"Okay."

"If I told you I know what happened to Mia, would you have to report it?"

Oscar sighed. It was a complicated question, but he expected nothing less from Jessica.

"That depends. If Mia is at risk, I'd have to tell someone."

"And what if she's not at risk? What if..." she paused, pushing through what she had to say. "What if the police were right, and I killed Mia? Would you have to report it?"

He watched her reaction as he answered, trying to figure out if it was a hypothetical question or something more.

"If Mia's dead, that would mean there's nothing we can do to save her life. So no, if you told me you killed Mia Edwards, I wouldn't have to report it."

He knew it was contentious territory, but there was no point telling her he'd report it if he wasn't sure what he'd do. She'd have to convince him she wasn't lying.

Would he feel the same if Jess told him where Mia was, if she were alive? Who did the rules really protect?

Jess balked at the word 'dead'—not the reaction he'd expect from a killer.

She studied him to see if he was lying. She seemed unsure.

She leaned back in her chair and breathed in, as if storing some spare oxygen in case she needed it later. "Okay then. I need to tell you something."

"Jess, before you say anything, I trust you to tell me the truth. And you need to trust me. Agreed?"

"Yes."

She looked at the letter on his desk. She'd already seen the bold font detailing the meeting time—she knew there was an inquiry, that Oscar might lose his job.

Is that why she was talking now, so that what she said left with him?

"I killed Mia Edwards."

Chapter 24

Then

Jess knocked on Niki's door and stood on the doormat, watching the wind chime dance.

Niki answered in thick house socks, throwing the door open to wave Jess inside. "Hey. I have coffee in the kitchen, but you're gonna have to pour it yourself because you know how you like it, and apparently I don't."

Jess followed Niki in, poured herself some coffee and added sugar. They sat at the table.

"So, how are things?" asked Niki.

Jess rearranged her mug, turning the handle so it fell into her left hand. "Fine," she said, trying the handle with the other hand.

"Fine? Is Clay still working late?"

"Yeah. Things are busy for him at the moment."

"Things are always busy for him."

"Yeah, I know. He said it should calm down soon and we can go away for the weekend, just the two of us."

"That's great. I'm happy to have Zoe if you need someone to watch her." Niki read her sister's face and added, "Except you don't think it'll calm down."

Jess sighed. "It never does. There's always another thing to get done. I don't want a relationship where we have to go away for a weekend every couple of months to make up for not seeing each other for the rest of the week. I want someone who's there with me, watching Zoe grow up. Like you and Bevan."

"Honey, sometimes I wish Bevan worked late, so that I could have some time to myself." Niki rolled her eyes before bringing her focus back to Jess. She slapped a hand down, as if suddenly struck by an idea. "Do you think he's really at work?"

"Where else would he be?"

"Loads of people say they're working late, when they're not." Niki lowered her voice and leaned towards Jess. "I'm not saying he's one of them, but it's code for having an affair." She looked at Jess with pity, still playing the big sister who knew things Jess couldn't hope to know yet.

"No, I don't think he's having an affair," said Jess incredulously. Why did Niki have to turn everything into a drama? "I just wish he was home more."

They sipped their coffee, and Niki opened the cookie jar on the bench, fishing around for one she wanted. "I rarely do sugar in the morning, but I think we can make an exception," she said.

Jess smiled; Niki was always looking for reasons to make an exception.

"It's just, from what you've said... It made me wonder," said Niki.

"Can we drop it?" asked Jess.

They chewed their cookies and let the subject die, neither

of them sure what else to say to keep it from turning into a disagreement.

"So, what happened with the meeting?" said Niki.

"What?" said Jess, distractedly stirring more sugar in her coffee.

"You know, the meeting with Ms. Liu? I wanted to bring it up when I dropped Aiden off, but you didn't mention it, so I figured you didn't want to talk about it at school. And I'm dying to find out, so please tell me already!"

"Yeah, it was fine."

Niki's nose twitched. "Fine? I've been dying over here for '*it was fine*'?"

"What else can I say, Nik? It went well."

Niki contemplated her sister. "I can tell when my baby sister's lying, okay, so just tell me what happened."

"It's a group of boys."

"Well, which ones? I'll ask Aiden to keep an eye out for his cousin."

"I don't know—they don't give out details. She didn't think it was Mia."

"Well, it makes sense that they don't name bullies. I mean, you can imagine some parents getting mad, taking things into their own hands," said Niki pointedly—there was a good chance Niki would be one of the parents she was talking about. "Who else is in their class? There's Aiden and Lucas, but I can't see Lucas hurting Zoe. Meg thinks he has a little crush on her."

"Really? That's adorable," said Jess.

"It has to be someone else. Should I ask Ms. Liu?"

"No, that's okay," said Jess quickly. If she was worried that she might make it worse, Niki had the potential to turn it into a war.

"So, how are Zoe and Mia?"

"Ms. Liu said they're friends. I saw them playing." Jess shrugged. "They seemed fine."

"That's strange. Why would Mia tell Holly they were fighting?"

"I don't know. Maybe they made up. I made a complete idiot of myself."

"Why?"

"Mia asked if she could come and live at my house, and I told her that her mom'd miss her."

"Aww, she would."

"And her dad," Jess added gingerly.

"Jessie, you didn't."

"I felt awful about it."

"The poor thing's probably traumatized by her dad, from what Holly said."

"I don't know," said Jess. "It was strange. It seems like she misses him."

"Well, she's only four. Of course she misses her daddy."

Jess considered mentioning what Mia said, about her dad dying, but she wasn't sure it was true, and she didn't want Niki to think that she was causing trouble.

Jess looked around the kitchen, as if Holly might appear from nowhere.

"What?" asked Niki, noticing Jess's eyes darting across the entrance.

"Nothing. It's just strange not to be interrupted by Holly. I don't know if you've noticed, but she seems to turn up wherever we are. I don't think we've had a coffee together since the kids started kindergarten."

"Oh, come on. You're being paranoid," said Niki lightly.

"You really haven't noticed?"

"Not really. We usually get coffee close to kindergarten. It's not a big jump to think other people might do the same, right?"

"I guess."

Jess nibbled at the edge of her cookie.

"What is it you don't like about her, Jess?"

"Nothing."

"Jessie, I'm going to say this because I'm your sister, and I care. It feels like you're looking for a reason to hate her. She's a nice person, really. You should give her a chance. I think you'd like her."

"Nik, you've only known her for a few weeks."

"We've gone out for lunch a couple of times."

"You did?"

"She was having a rough day, so I offered to keep her company and took her to lunch. It's not a big deal. It turned out it was pretty fun."

Jess sipped her coffee.

"Hey," said Niki, "if you weren't so determined to hate her, I would've invited you."

"That's okay," said Jess. "You like her because she's trying extra hard to be nice to you."

"What's wrong with that?"

"Nothing. I'm not sure how sincere it is, that's all."

"Are you saying she's pretending to be my friend? Come on, Jess. Why would she do that?"

"I don't know. I haven't figured it out yet."

"Well, *don't.* I know you're a reporter, but all that journalist stuff's affecting your brain."

Jess ignored Niki's jibe. As a reporter, she wouldn't write something without confirming the facts, but Niki was her sister, and she had a sudden, overwhelming need to protect her. Something about Holly didn't add up, and Jess needed to figure out what.

"Nik, just don't be your usual friendly self this time, please."

"How am I supposed to be? I'm not as suspicious as you."

Jess swallowed the hurt. There'd be plenty of time to feel bad once she was sure Niki was going to be more careful.

"That's exactly how I want you to be," said Jess, meeting Niki's eyes. "At least for a little while, until we know her better."

A loud rap at the door killed their conversation.

Jess looked at Niki to see if she was expecting someone.

"What?" Niki's eyes were wide and innocent. "I invited her this morning. I thought we could all hang out. Meg couldn't make it."

Jess put her cookie on the side of her plate, brushing her hands together to remove the crumbs.

"Just give her a chance, Jessie. She's had a tough time and she could really use some friends."

Chapter 25

Now

Oscar returned from a walk, wiping his boots on the mat, his thoughts as loud as when he left.

Jess's words played over. *I killed Mia Edwards.*

Their session had ended and the two of them sat in silence as Oscar tried to figure out what he was supposed to say. Was she expecting police officers to storm the room, guns in hand, demanding that she go with them?

Or was she enjoying the silence after almost an hour of discussion? Oscar couldn't tell.

He'd thanked her for sharing, and ended the session by promising they'd talk further at their next appointment, wishing he didn't have back-to-back appointments that day.

She had gone without a word, walking silently through the hallway. She hadn't looked back.

Oscar kicked off his boots and showered. He took his laptop from its bag and booted it up. If he was thinking about Jess, he might as well write up the notes from their session. He typed quickly, fingers struggling to keep pace with his mind as they moved across the keys. He closed his eyes, remembering flashes of the session, until he had it all documented.

His fingers stopped still when he came to the last part. Jess's confession.

What if she'd said it to test him?

He felt the questions on his tongue, like faces in a crowd vying for attention. There was only one question he truly wanted to ask, but he wouldn't allow himself to ask it yet. *Where's Mia?* When he asked, he wanted to be sure he could read Jess well enough to know whether she was telling the truth. Maybe next time.

He snapped the laptop closed, unsure whether to document her confession. It wasn't a *real* confession. It was an emotional verdict she'd placed on herself.

A message flashed on Oscar's phone.

It was Hayley, letting him know she was hoping he'd call. Reminding him that he hadn't.

He dialed her number.

"So, you got my message?" she asked playfully, answering on the third ring.

"Yeah. My phone was sitting right next to me."

"And you didn't message me back?"

"I guess I didn't." He smiled. "It's good hearing your voice."

Hayley laughed. "Well, I'm glad you called."

This must be how people acted when they were flirting.

"Want me to come over? I can't make vegan burgers, but we can order in."

"Sure, why not?" The words were out before he could stop them. He wanted to see her. He'd missed her.

"See you soon then," she said.

He ended the call. He rarely gave in to whims, but Hayley

might be the only thing to stop him from obsessing about Jess and Mia.

He looked around the room, meticulously tidied by a cleaning service. The coffee stain down the wall and leftover shards of mug were gone and he felt bad for leaving them. The cleaner came by while he was at work and finished before he got home. He liked it that way—it meant he didn't have to explain things like coffee on the wall, or dishes in the sink.

Mostly, his house looked unlived in. If Riley was still alive, he imagined there'd be scuffs on the floor from grubby shoes and toys in the living area. It would look like a home.

If Riley hadn't died, maybe Oscar would be sharing take out with Prisha instead of Hayley.

A knock on the door shook his thoughts loose. He shut the door to the room he'd recreated for Riley when he'd moved out. He wasn't ready to tell Hayley about his son yet.

She stood at the door with aromatic containers of food.

He kissed her. "Smells delicious," he said, ushering her inside.

"I stopped off at Masala. I hope you don't mind. I thought we could save their delivery driver the trouble since I was already going by."

"Great. I'm starving," said Oscar, leading her to the kitchen and setting them both a place.

They pulled the dishes from the bag, opening lids, scooping yellow and red sauces onto their plates. "Butter chicken, daal, and Malai kofta," said Hayley, pointing at each dish.

"Butter chicken?" said Oscar, eyebrow raised as she scooped some on his plate. "I thought you didn't eat chicken?"

"Yeah, well, it's the kind of chicken that's not *really* chicken. It's the fake stuff," she confessed. "There's no butter in there either."

He tried a bite, surprised to find the texture was pretty close to chicken. "So, what am I actually eating?"

"Plant protein mostly. Some non-dairy ghee," said Hayley.

He nodded as he chewed, enjoying the flavors.

They talked over dinner and cleared the table when they were done, moving to the living room with two glasses of red wine.

"I hope you don't think I'm rude for not going out," he said. "Long day at work."

Hayley smiled. "I haven't seen your place before. It's really nice."

"Thanks. I can't take any of the credit. It was all done by a decorator."

"You didn't choose any of it?"

"Well, I told the decorator to go ahead and purchase it," he said, gesturing around. "After my divorce—"

Oscar watched her face change for a moment at the mention of his divorce. "Sorry," he said. "You probably don't want to hear about that."

"That's okay. We all have a past, right?"

She smiled encouragingly, and he found himself continuing.

"She kept most of our stuff. She chose it anyway, so I guess it was fair. I didn't have time to buy new furniture. Work was busy and all my time went into my caseload, so I hired someone to decorate."

"You didn't keep *any of it*?"

Oscar glanced towards Riley's room. "Not really. Just a few things that were special."

He sipped his wine, letting the warmth move through him.

"But you're not here to talk about my ex-wife," he said. He

put on some music, aware of every movement Hayley made.

"No, that's okay. I actually came to see how you were going with Jessica Green." She held her glass absently at the stem and watched him back.

"You heard about the meeting?"

"Yeah, I heard. It's doing the rounds in the rumor mill," she said, her nose wrinkling. "Are you okay?"

It was a long time since anyone asked Oscar if he was okay. He wasn't comfortable being on the receiving end of her concern. "Yeah," he said dismissively. "It's just a formality."

"I know," she said. "But it's Charles. He's going to try to make them believe this is your fault somehow."

"Yeah, he is."

"Is there anything I can do to help?" She placed her hand on his arm. "I think I've done a pretty good job staying away from you at work."

"You've done... okay," he said, pretending to think about it.

She pressed her lips together. "It hasn't been easy."

"Really? I've tried to make it easy," he said, smiling to show he was playing. "I've stayed away from your end of the hall. I haven't interrupted you during the day—not even to ask your professional opinion on things."

"That's true," she agreed, moving her hand up his arm.

She looked at him; her face framed with caramel tresses. "Although, I haven't been to your office either. It hasn't been easy. Not when all I wanted to do was this." She set down her wine and leaned in to kiss him, her lips pressing softly against his.

He returned the kiss, setting his glass down on the table. Hayley moved the glasses away from the edge and wrapped her arms around Oscar's neck, resuming the kiss so that it was deeper and more certain than before.

He moved his hands across her back tentatively, down toward her waist, and pulled her in close. She smelled like something floral, her skin drinking in the fragrance. His hands streaked through her hair, and just when he seemed lost in the moment, he broke the kiss, his mind full of questions. *Why did Jess confess to murder?*

Her lips invited him back. He wanted to taste them, but the moment was gone.

"What's wrong?" she asked, lacing her fingers in his.

"Nothing," he lied. "I just—"

What was he supposed to say? That he was thinking about Jess? That he couldn't relax because of what she'd said?

"It's nothing. Just work stuff."

"I have a feeling I know what it's about," said Hayley. "And I want to talk about it, but first, I think we both need a break. There's always something going on at work, or something else to take its place. It's never going to just be a job. For either of us."

She undid the top buttons of his shirt, running a finger along the edge of his collar. "So, work can wait until later."

Chapter 26

Now

Oscar awoke the next morning with one arm wrapped around Hayley. She stirred as he slipped out of bed and into the shower.

By the time he was out and dressed, the smell of fresh coffee was wafting from the kitchen.

"I hope you don't mind, I helped myself to some," she said, holding up a mug and gesturing to another she'd made for him.

"You made me one too, you can help yourself anytime."

She elbowed him playfully. "I borrowed this too," she said, showing a familiar stone-gray shirt he wore around the house.

It looked better on her.

"Also okay. Looks good, by the way."

"Thanks. I'll finish my coffee and get dressed," she said.

"How about you have a shower and I'll make us some breakfast instead?"

"Sounds great, but I can't go to work wearing the same thing I wore yesterday. People might talk."

"How about breakfast anyway?"

In five minutes, he had toast with fresh avocado waiting on the bench. He slid some pan-seared mushroom, tomato and spinach on top, and handed Hayley a plate.

"Thanks," she smiled, strands of hair falling from a loose topknot. "What did you want to talk about?"

"They gave me a date for the meeting. I think they're going to stop me from treating Jess."

Hayley shrugged. "Charles was in charge when Jess left. He's the one they should be questioning." She chewed the nail at the edge of her thumb.

"What if they agree with him?"

"Oscar, I've worked with you for a long time. This wasn't your fault."

"Maybe," he said, trying to convince himself.

What if they knew that Oscar had let his son die? Charles would use it.

You deserve it. You're a fraud.

He considered telling Hayley, but the words stuck in his throat like hot glue.

"Was there something else?" asked Hayley, reading his expression.

If he told her what Jess said, he'd be involving Hayley in something she might not want to be part of.

"Jess said that she killed Mia Edwards."

"Wow, that's huge. Did she say why?"

Oscar shook his head. "I didn't ask. It was kind of a shock. She said it right at the end of the session," he said. "I don't know. Maybe she did it that way on purpose?"

Hayley shook her head. "I don't know."

"I took your advice. I told her something personal to help her to open up a little."

"Have you told anyone else?"

"No. Just you."

"Are you going to take it further?" she asked.

"I don't think so. I don't think it was a real confession. Saying she did it doesn't make it true."

"You think she's testing you, to see if she can trust you?"

"Maybe. I'm hoping she'll tell me what really happened."

"You still don't think she did it?"

"I just want to make sure I can tell when she's lying before I decide."

"Did she say what happened to Mia after she..." Hayley trailed off, her voice somber.

"The session finished, and I had back to back meetings, so I finished up."

"She might need a push— "

"What if she didn't do it?" Oscar cut in.

"Oscar, what if she did? She might know where Mia is."

"Even if she did, she won't tell me if she doesn't trust me."

"If she tells you where Mia is, will you report it?"

Would Hayley think less of him if he said no?

"I'm not sure she murdered her. I think she blames herself for whatever happened. If I report it, we may never know the truth." He looked away. "And if Mia's dead, it's already too late."

"You know you could get in trouble?" said Hayley.

She was right, but if Mia was dead she wasn't in danger. Jess, on the other hand, was. If he couldn't figure it out, she might be stuck in a facility for a long time. Zoe might grow up without a mother.

"So, why are you telling me?" Hayley's eyes searched his.

"Because I trust you." He searched her face to see if it was mutual.

She sighed and picked up her mug. Suddenly she looked vulnerable in his shirt, without her work clothes to armor herself in.

"I just wanted to hear your thoughts," he said.

"I—I uh..." she stumbled, coffee spilling over the rim of her mug.

Was it really that hard? She either trusted him enough to tell him what she was thinking, or she didn't.

"Whatever you said to Jessica must've been pretty personal if she told you she *murdered* Mia. What did you tell her?"

"She mentioned Mia because she knows about the inquiry. She thinks it's her fault," he said evasively.

"Oscar, she confessed to murder. Maybe she did it. How could someone get inside while Jess was in the bathroom and take Mia without her noticing? And if they did, why take Mia and not Zoe?"

Oscar had wondered the same thing, but sometimes things happened and you couldn't stop them. Maybe it was an opportunistic kidnapping and Mia was an easier target?

Unless the kidnapper knew Mia would be there?

"Why would she say she killed Mia if she didn't?" asked Hayley. "Wouldn't you defend yourself? I know I would. Especially if I couldn't see my daughter."

"Unless you knew you were guilty," finished Oscar.

Hayley squeezed his hand. "Unless you were hiding something even worse."

Chapter 27

Then

Jess arrived early to collect Zoe from kindergarten, slowed down by impatient parents who had already arrived, laden with toddlers and strollers.

Niki passed Jess on her way to collect Aiden. "Meg asked if I could watch Lucas this afternoon, so I've got snacks, I've got toy trains, and I've got Netflix. You can come over. Bring Zoe."

"That's okay. I should—"

"Think about it, and message to let me know if you're coming," said Niki, giving Jess a quick hug. Jess knew from experience that it was her sister's way of guilting her into going. Jess had never been good at saying no, which Niki exploited regularly.

"Okay," said Jess reluctantly.

"Oh my god," said Niki, looking over her shoulder at something Jess couldn't see.

Jess spun around and saw Holly walking towards them, her dark hair poorly styled over her eye and a corner of her lip to cover a deep bruise.

"Honey, what happened?" said Niki, going to Holly and resting an arm around her shoulders.

"Oh, I fell over," said Holly dismissively, her eyes flicking past the curious stares from the other parents.

"You fell over and gave yourself a black eye and a fat lip?" said Niki, her voice a shade too loud.

The yard had cleared, but the lingering mothers who usually chattered in circles were trying to get another look at Holly's wounds. They only moved on when they caught Niki staring pointedly in their direction.

"Are you okay?" asked Niki, lowering her voice.

"Do you need something for the swelling?" asked Jess.

Holly shook her head. "Ray came to my apartment. He was upset. He yelled, and then he... it's nothing, really."

"This is *not* nothing. This is something. You should report him," said Niki.

"What good would it do?" asked Holly.

"Well, it would mean that son of a—"

"Niki, I don't think that's helping," interrupted Jess. "Why don't you sit for a minute," she said, pointing to the logs. "I can collect Mia."

"Thanks." Holly peered from under a veil of dark hair. Up close, her eye looked scratched up, as if someone had hit her with a rock.

"What did he hit you with?" asked Jess, concerned by the swelling. "You might need to get something for that, to stop an infection."

"His fist," said Holly, slightly annoyed, adjusting her hair to cover it further.

Niki winced. "He must've hit you pretty hard. You'll have a bruise tomorrow," said Niki sympathetically.

"Yeah, well—Ray's done worse," said Holly, fussing at her fat lip with a long, red fingernail.

"Are you sure you don't want to report it? I can come with you," offered Niki, hand on her hip.

Holly brought her hand to her eye. "No, I just want to forget about it."

"Okay, if you're sure," said Niki doubtfully. "But the offer stands if you change your mind."

Maybe Holly didn't want to report the assault because she didn't want Mia to find out she lied about her dad dying.

"I'll get the girls." Jess thumbed her pockets and walked away. Her instinct told her something was off, but she couldn't talk about it with Niki. Holly had her sister fooled.

Jess turned on her heel and asked, "What's Ray's last name?"

"What?" said Holly incredulously.

"His last name?"

"Why?" asked Holly warily.

Jess worked at making her voice casual. "Just asking in case Ms. Liu asks me which Mia I'm collecting or something."

Was it just Jess's imagination, or did Holly look relieved?

"Oh, no. Mia has my last name. It's Mia Edwards," she said.

Jess smiled. "Of course."

"But just so you know, it's Loxburg."

Jess found Zoe and Mia waiting on the class rug, their giggles snapping like popping candy. Zoe looked disappointed to see Jess.

"Hi," said Ms. Liu.

"Hey. Can we talk?" asked Jess.

Ms. Liu looked at the rug. "Sure. There's no sign of Mia's mom yet, so I'll probably be here for a few minutes and then we can catch up."

"Actually, she's out front. I offered to collect Mia. She's, um... she's had a rough day. Niki's with her now."

Ms. Liu balked. "I'm sorry, I can't release a child without confirming with the parent. I'd need to call her," said Ms. Liu.

"Of course," agreed Jess. "How's Zoe?"

"We're working on her resilience, which is helping when she feels upset about other people's behavior."

Jess nodded. "That's great."

Ms. Liu smiled. "Excuse me for a moment—I'll give Mia's mom a call."

Jess nodded. "She's just outside, if that's easier?"

Ms. Liu looked outside and where Niki sat with Holly under the tree. "Okay," she said. "See you tomorrow, girls."

"Mommy, is Mia coming home with us?" asked Zoe, jumping up and down with excitement.

"No, Zoo. We're just picking her up."

There was a chorus of disappointed 'naws'. "Can Mia play at our house?" asked Zoe.

"Not now, Zoo, but maybe we can organize something for another time."

"Yay!" said Zoe, grabbing hold of Mia's hands and dancing around in a circle.

Mia's face dropped when she saw Holly sitting under the tree, hair pulled back, showing her bruises for Niki to examine.

Jess bent down to Mia, who stared at Holly's swollen face. "She's fine, sweetie. Her eye and her lip are a little sore, but she'll be alright."

"Is she mad?" asked Mia, her lips gathering into a frown. She stepped toward the classroom, like she was considering running back.

"Not at you, Mia. Do you want to give her a hug?"

Mia walked slowly toward Holly as Ms. Liu watched from the classroom.

"Come on," Jess coaxed gently, walking at Mia's pace. "I'll take you over."

"Zoo, you can go play with Aiden and Lucas," Jess said. Zoe shot off, sensing it wasn't the time to argue.

Mia went to Holly, shyly wrapping her arms around her mother, watching Jess the whole time for reassurance. Holly recoiled from the unexpected contact. "Oh, Mia," she said, relief flooding her voice.

"Are you okay?" asked Mia.

"I'm fine," said Holly dismissively, hiding her face from Mia.

"Can I play with Zoe?" asked Mia.

"Sure," said Holly.

"Jess, maybe you could take the kids to your house. I'll take care of things here and then I'll be right over," said Niki, clasping her hands together, silently pleading.

"Sure," agreed Jess.

"That's really not necessary," protested Holly.

"Come on. Jess'll be fine with the kids, won't you, Jessie? We can pick them up later. It'll give you a chance to get your thoughts together."

"Please," said Mia. She lowered her voice. "I won't talk about you or daddy, I promise."

Jess knew first-hand the kind of things kids said. When her niece, Audrey, was little, she told Jess that Niki didn't like Clay. Niki claimed Audrey had misunderstood, that she said she didn't like Clay's new haircut, but it was embarrassing none the less. Jess still wasn't sure who was telling the truth.

Holly looked at her daughter pointedly. “Be good.”
“I will,” said Mia solemnly.

Chapter 28

Now

Oscar rushed to the meeting room, only slowing once his hand was on the door handle. It was the first time he'd been late to a team meeting. Everyone already knew about the inquiry—there would be questions.

"Morning," he said. He checked his watch. "I called a staff meeting to discuss a recent incident involving a patient, Jessica Green, who left the facility."

Charles sat at the end of the table, leaning back comfortably in his chair. Oscar took the empty seat across from Hayley, with Cole and Chloe on either side of him.

David sat off to the side, finger pressed to his lips as if subconsciously silencing everyone.

"There will be a meeting to discuss what happened, to review our processes and make sure it doesn't happen again. This isn't about placing the blame, or finding fault with how anyone does their job—it's about making sure our staff and patients are safe. There's some concern that Jessica Green might have been injured," he said, reluctantly adding, "or injured someone else."

The corner of Hayley's mouth twitched, a brief smile of encouragement playing on her lips.

"I asked everyone in this room to write an account of what happened, and I've compared the responses." Oscar clasped his hands together. "Charles, I haven't received yours yet, so it won't form part of the current assessment."

Charles snorted derisively. "That's okay. I've submitted mine to the board already. If you'd like a copy, you can request it from them—they're free to do with it as they wish."

Oscar smiled. "Thanks, Charles. I'll be sure to do that." He moved on quickly, refusing to give Charles the reaction he craved.

"Don't you think it's inappropriate to request an account from everyone when the board asked you to explain what happened?" said Charles.

Oscar turned to Charles. "The board's trying to figure out what happened, yes. However, I wasn't here, so the best way to answer the question is to figure out how our process failed."

Charles scoffed, opening his mouth to speak.

"I agree with Oscar. We need to take ownership of what happened and provide a solution to mitigate the risk," said David loudly. "Oscar's not on trial here, Charles. It sounds like he's trying to help you out. Weren't you in charge when the patient left the hospital?"

For the next forty minutes, Charles stayed quiet, but the meeting had the effect Oscar wanted. Charles would walk away, doubting which way the inquest would go.

When the meeting ended, Oscar went to the staff room, pulled a mug from the cupboard, and poured coffee. He raided the refrigerator for milk. He shook the carton. Empty. He couldn't tip the coffee back in the pot, and he couldn't drink it without something to soften the flavor.

A carton next to the regular milk had 'Hayley' written across the side in floral script. He read the label. *Almond Milk.* She wouldn't mind if he borrowed some.

"You know, I think that belongs to someone. It looks like it's got a name on it," said Charles, setting his own mug on the bench next to Oscar's with a thud.

"It's fine. I asked to borrow some," said Oscar, pouring the milk. He'd managed to eat a vegan burger—maybe he was ready for this.

"Okay," said Charles skeptically. He rustled around the refrigerator, gave up on milk, and poured black coffee. "I didn't realize you and Hayley were friends."

Oscar shrugged and sipped his coffee. How much did Charles know about his relationship with Hayley?

Oscar found a spoon and scooped sugar into his cup, stirring it quickly to melt the granules.

"Oscar?" said Charles, blocking the exit slightly.

"Yeah?"

"It's nothing personal. It's just, we have people's lives in our hands, and I want what's best for the patients."

"So do I," said Oscar evenly.

"I take what happened very seriously. Maybe more so because of who it was."

Oscar kept his eyes on the door, indicating he wanted to pass.

"What if she'd killed another child?"

"We don't know that she killed anyone."

"But we should know. *You* should know, as her therapist. You put in a request to treat her. Why? It's not like you're getting anywhere—you might as well have left her at Carlson

Remand Center."

Oscar felt the threat in Charles's tone, and suddenly, he knew why Charles chose now to make a scene—he wanted to treat Jessica. He might've even let her leave on purpose.

"Maybe," said Oscar.

"The board will see that you disrupted her treatment for the chance to get your name in a journal."

There was no way to move around Charles without shouldering him. Oscar eyed Charles's collar, contemplating whether it was worth it.

"She won't get you the fame you want. She'd have to tell you where to find the girl she killed."

Oscar waited for Charles to finish. "Thanks for sharing your opinion," he said, emphasizing the word *opinion.*

"It's more like... a gut feeling," said Charles. "Then it's my turn. And I'll get the answers you can't."

Chapter 29

Then

The classroom door was locked. Jess stood in the chill morning air, trying to stay awake after a restless night contemplating life. She was happy, wasn't she? She had the life she wanted—at least the life she used to think she wanted—but anxiety had settled over her, making the good things feel as flimsy as sand on the shore, ready to wash away when the waves hit.

"Your husband made quite an impression on Mia," said Holly from behind, foregoing a greeting.

Jess turned, surprised by how close Holly was. The swelling around Holly's eye had gone down. Make-up hid the greenish tinge but the abrasions jutting across her cheek were still visible.

"Yeah, she's a good kid. It was fun having her over. Zoe hasn't talked about anything since."

"Mia hasn't stopped talking about it either," said Holly. "Anyway, it helped, talking it through with Niki. Mia thought Clay was a lot of fun. She was surprised he played the dance game with them," said Holly.

"It's one of his favorites," said Jess. "I think he had more fun than the kids."

"Zoe's lucky," said Holly wistfully. "Anyway, I just wanted to say thanks."

"No problem," said Jess. "I hope you're feeling better?"

Holly shrugged, hands in her jacket pockets. "Yeah," she said, the words flat. "Ray turned up unexpectedly. I told him to go home and he pushed the door open and came inside. I couldn't stop him. He said that I'm a horrible mother and that Mia deserves more. He wanted me to let him take her. He's going to fight me for her."

"That's awful. Maybe you should report it? Then, if he files for custody you'll have proof he's violent."

"Your sister thinks I have a duty to report it," said Holly.

"Yeah, Niki's always sure about everything," said Jess fondly. She'd always admired Niki's conviction—it must be nice to have that kind of certainty.

Holly swished her hair so that it splayed around her face, hiding her cuts.

"My sister means well. She can be over enthusiastic sometimes, but it's part of her charm."

The yard was filling with parents, ready to unleash their kids onto their teachers.

Holly smiled as Mia ran past, trying to tag Zoe. "Being a parent is great, but sometimes I miss having an adult conversation. Sometimes I even miss Ray." She set her lips together in a pout. "I know that sounds ridiculous after everything he did, but I miss how things might've been."

"It doesn't sound ridiculous," said Jess. She'd written articles about domestic violence. She knew that up to half of the people who left would go back.

What would Jess do if Clay hit her? It was easy to think you'd be rational when it wasn't happening to you. Clay didn't lose his temper easily, so it was hard to imagine.

The bell rang, and kids raced to class. A few boys were reluctant to leave their game. Eventually, they tucked their trucks under their arms and trudged to class.

Mia went right inside while Zoe collected her bag from Jess, raising her arms for a hug and kiss.

"Mia's so independent," said Jess enthusiastically.

"Yeah, she can be," said Holly. "Listen, when I mentioned Mia's dad—" Holly sighed uncomfortably. "Well, he's not a good guy—it's probably better if you forget his name."

"Okay," said Jess cautiously.

"I don't want to sound paranoid, but I'd hate for you to get caught up in this."

Holly looked at Jess, leveling with her. "He's very charming. He seems like such a good guy. I told Mia he died, so she wouldn't try to track him down," said Holly, sounding sorry. "I didn't know how else to keep her safe."

Jess feigned ignorance. "Oh?"

"She kept asking to see him. He's her dad. She doesn't see what he's really like. I thought I could protect her."

Jess nodded, glancing at Holly's face. "What did you tell Mia about your bruise?"

Holly raised a hand to her face self-consciously. "I told her I fell. What am I going to do if he comes back while Mia's there? If she sees him, she'll know I lied."

"Well, if that happens, you can tell her you were just keeping her safe."

"She's four. She wouldn't understand."

"Maybe he said what he needed to and he won't come back,"

said Jess lamely.

"It's not the first time," said Holly, shutting down as quickly as she opened up. "I'm sorry. I don't know why I'm telling you this." She thumbed the strap on her shoulder bag.

"It's okay," said Jess. Years of journalism had made her a great listener. The more you listened, the more people used it as an invitation to talk about things they usually kept to themselves. But Holly was carefully selecting her words.

"Have you got plans for today?" asked Holly, forcing a subject change.

For a moment Jess thought Holly was about to suggest they grab coffee. "Just work," she said. "I have an article to write and a pitch to get in. Then an interview this afternoon."

"Oh, that sounds fun," said Holly with a tight-lipped smile, already bored.

"Yeah, it's fun talking to people."

The people aspect caught Holly's attention. "So, do you get to interview famous people?"

"Not really. I interview regular people."

Holly looked horrified. "And I just told you all that stuff about Ray. Oh god, please don't write about it."

"Of course," said Jess.

"Who are you interviewing?"

"A woman with Narcissistic Personality Disorder." She watched carefully for a reaction.

Holly wrinkled her nose. "Narci-what?"

"It's a psychiatric disorder. People who suffer from it often think they're special, or more important than other people. Sometimes they think others should recognize it too. They like attention, and will do a lot to get it."

Holly's focus drifted.

"Have you ever met someone like that?" asked Holly. "It sounds a bit extreme."

"Niki can seem like that sometimes," said Jess breezily. "But I don't think she has a personality disorder. How about you?"

Holly considered it. "Hmm, I can't think of anyone."

"What about Mia's dad? Do you think he's a narcissist?"

"Who Ray?" Holly roared. "No, Ray's not a narcissist. Ray's just an asshole."

Jess smiled weakly. "How about you... what do you do for work?"

"I used to be an actor. I was pretty good," said Holly. "But Ray didn't like it. I did small theater mostly, until I finally got a role in a movie. Then I found out I was pregnant."

Jess nodded sympathetically. "Did you stop acting?"

"I wish I didn't. I miss it," sighed Holly.

"What do you do now?" asked Jess.

"Odd jobs," said Holly.

Jess couldn't decide whether Holly was being vague intentionally.

"Right now, I'm focusing on getting better," said Holly, looking up to give Jess a clear view of her face. "I hope your interview goes well."

"Yeah, me too," said Jess. She was interviewing someone who was in prison for killing her own child. Jess had left out that Kat had traits associated with psychopathy. If the interview went well, Jess would get a better understanding of what motivated someone with an antisocial personality disorder.

Would it be obvious that Kat didn't feel emotions, or was it something you could fake? Mostly she wanted to know if talking to Kat felt the same as talking to Holly.

Chapter 30

Now

Jess was waiting with her back to the wall by Oscar's door, lost in thought, when he returned from lunch break.

If Oscar were in Jess's position, he'd do anything to see his child. Why wasn't Jess doing the same?

She showed signs of trauma. Her reluctance to trust anyone, the refusal to talk to her sister. Her transfer file said she experienced insomnia and nightmares when she arrived at Carlson Remand Center. Oscar noticed the way she carried herself. She was always tense, her hands up, ready to shield herself.

What was she protecting herself against? He still wondered if it was Clay. She hadn't implicated him. There were no notes, no reports. Was she protecting him?

The thoughts raced, one possibility after another. She couldn't be protecting Clay, she'd left Zoe with him.

"Sorry I'm late," said Oscar, fitting the key in the lock. Cold hit him as he opened the door. He'd forgotten to turn down the cooling.

Jess shivered as she went to the sofa.

"Sorry. The cold helps me think," said Oscar. He went to turn up the heat.

"No," said Jess, her jaw set. "Leave it. It helps me think too." She took the sofa at the far end, away from Oscar.

He joined her on the adjacent sofa.

"It puts you back in your own skin." She tucked her hands under her armpits and glanced at the bumps dotting Oscar's arms. "Does that make sense?"

He followed her gaze, realizing his shirtsleeves were rolled to his elbows.

"It looks like you're punishing yourself," she said.

"How have you been since our last session?" he asked, ignoring the cold creeping up his neck. He didn't want to talk about himself.

"I was waiting for someone to take me to prison after the things I told you."

"But they didn't."

"No," she said, looking at Oscar as if he was a peculiar puzzle; the same way he'd looked at her when he first saw her.

"Why did you keep my secret?" she asked.

"I meant what I said. What you say here stays between us."

"You could give them what they want and be a hero."

"So could you."

Jess wiped at her tired eyes, fatigue clinging to her.

"They wanted easy answers. They didn't care about the truth."

"How can you be sure?"

"I tried. They didn't want to listen," she said, her temper flaring. "They had their minds made up before they even talked to me."

"What didn't they want to hear?"

She shook her head. "It doesn't matter now."

"It matters to me," said Oscar. "And for what it's worth, I'm sorry they didn't listen."

It didn't look like she was going to say any more.

"Jessica, you can trust me to listen."

"If you want to know why I don't want to talk about it, ask Detective Collins. I filed a report, and they wouldn't take it seriously because of Clay."

"The attack?"

"They thought he must've cheated on me or something, and that I snapped and tried to kill him."

"That must've been frustrating."

"It's easier to say nothing. The silence is comforting."

Oscar knew what she meant. For a while, he'd enjoyed being alone, not having to apologize, especially to Prisha.

"The silence feels easier, but it's not. It's like telling the world you've given up. You regress to a place before everything went wrong. But it's not acceptance, not really. It's just admitting defeat."

"The world already won."

"There was a time when you disappeared inside yourself to cope with what was going on around you, wasn't there? You've gone back to that place, Jess. But you need to face whatever happened. It'll come up eventually, no matter how much you ignore it."

"Do you think I attacked Clay?" Jess asked.

"It doesn't matter what I think. I want you to talk to me about what *you* think."

"It matters. You get to decide if I stay here."

That wasn't completely true, but it wasn't the time to point that out.

"Okay. If it matters, the truth is, I don't know enough about it to have an opinion. I was hoping we could work through it."

"Talk to Detective Collins, and then we'll talk."

"That's not usually how it works. I'd prefer to talk to you."

She shrugged. "Talk to him. Until then, don't bother scheduling our sessions."

"What do you want me to ask?"

"I'm sure you can figure out what to say on your own."

She picked herself off the sofa and strode out, closing the door behind her.

So that's why she told him she killed Mia. She *wanted* him to go to the police.

Chapter 31

Then

Jess put Zoe to bed and waited for Clay, their overcooked dinner warm on the stove. Her thoughts bounced between Kat's interview and Clay's absence. She tried focusing on the interview—the deadline was creeping closer, but she couldn't concentrate on writing it up.

The interview hadn't been what she expected. It had been her first time inside a prison, and the inside reminded her of a hospital. After arriving, she had waited in a barren room for Kat, searching the empty walls for something to hold her attention.

Eventually, two wardens sauntered in and sat Kat in a seat.

Jess had always pictured prison inmates as streetwise. She figured it was a survival strategy, but looking at Kat, you could easily believe she was there by mistake. Kat had smiled warmly at Jess.

"Hi, thanks for coming in," she'd said, like they were meeting to discuss a kindergarten bake sale.

Jess had returned the smile, thanking Kat for her time.

"Of course. You'll have to send me a copy of your article

when you publish it. Will it be in a magazine?"

"Yeah, I can send you a link."

Jess had reminded herself she was in a prison, the guards waiting in the corner serving as a reminder.

"What would you like to discuss?"

Jess had a list of questions, but Kat's friendliness made her approach feel too abrupt.

"Mostly life in prison. How did you get here? What it's like day to day."

"Well, I did the wrong thing—that's how I ended up here," said Kat. "But we don't need to talk about that if you want to know about prison life."

Jess remembered the way her skin prickled, so much that she'd shivered. If she didn't know Kat had killed someone, she wouldn't have guessed based on the way she was acting.

"Do you get a lot of visitors? Your partner? Friends? Kids?"

Realizing her faux pas, Jess had bitten down on her lip, punishing the words for escaping.

She'd watched Kat's face drop, her tone hardening. "I don't have a partner. Or children. My friends come when they can." She finished her sentence and smiled, the same as the last smile, as if programmed to respond the same, regardless of the context.

Kat sized Jess up quietly behind the smile, looking for clues to play off of during their conversation. "Did they offer you a drink?"

"No, but that's okay," said Jess.

Kat was surprised. "Not even some water? My apologies. They're not the most socially apt people around here."

Jess smiled nervously—a glass of water didn't seem like that big of a deal. "That's okay. I have a water bottle with me.

Tell me about a day in the life of," said Jess.

"Of what?"

"Of you."

Kat had beamed at that, enjoying the limelight. "Well—"

"First, do you mind if I take notes and record our conversation?"

"It's like being a celebrity," she'd said, clearing her throat. "I start the day early, usually around 5.30am. It's important to make the most of each day."

She'd looked at Jess like she should be taking notes, so Jess humored her, jotting down *enjoy every day.*

"There's always someone around, watching everything you do. They bring you food, like at a restaurant. It's like having a housekeeper, right?"

Was prison a holiday to her—somewhere to be waited on and pampered? Jess couldn't imagine being around people every waking moment—she valued privacy too much. Sleeping in her own bed, setting her own schedule. Most of all, she valued seeing Zoe every day.

"The food isn't exactly gourmet, but we make do," said Kat. "After breakfast I do yoga, before the morning schedule kicks in." Jess had listened as Kat described a very ordinary morning.

When Kat finished, Jess pushed the nice-girl facade. "Why did you do it?"

The sweetness melted away. "Listen to me. You know nothing about my life. Who do you think you are, judging me?"

"I'm sorry, I'm not judging you."

"I did everything for that kid. And for what?"

Kat's raised voice caught the guard's attention. They

hovered closer, ready to step in if Kat became too agitated.

Kat held up a hand, signaling she was calm. "I did everything without help, so don't judge me. I made a mistake. It was tiring and I couldn't do it anymore. You find me someone in the same situation who would've done any different."

Jess nodded. "Sorry."

"Why do you care, anyway?"

"What?"

"It's obvious that's why you really came here—you want to know about my daughter. You want to know why I killed my child. Now I'm asking you why you think it's any of your business, and don't lie, because I'll know."

Jess steadied herself with a deep breath. If Kat knew why she was there, would she answer her questions? Jess believed what Kat said—she'd know if Jess was lying.

"I know someone," said Jess cautiously.

"And?" Kat folded her arms.

"I think she's going to do something similar."

Kat snorted. "And you think you can stop it?"

"I can try to understand it. Maybe I can figure out whether she'll go through with it."

"And you want me to tell you how to stop her from hurting her kid?"

Jess didn't expect an honest answer from someone she'd just met. Kat had nothing to lose, but she had nothing to gain either.

There was a strength in not caring how others perceived you, but at what point did it become a weakness? How did you know where the boundaries were and which ones you couldn't cross?

"Is there anything I can do?"

"Depends." Kat was being intentionally vague.

If Jess wanted answers, Kat would make her ask directly.

"It depends on what?"

"Well, does the person you're talking about know they're a psychopath?"

"I didn't say—"

"You said they were like me," Kat interrupted. "And you're here asking questions about it, so you probably think they're a psychopath, right?" said Kat.

Jess shifted uncomfortably.

"It's fine. I'm not offended." Kat smiled. "So, are they?"

Was Kat being genuine? She couldn't tell. Was that how Kat felt trying to understand social rules? Was it easier around other people like her?

"I don't know." Jess felt suddenly nervous, like she'd unwittingly opened an especially fun playground and given Kat a free ticket. It was controversial to use the word 'psychopath', but Kat sounded proud.

"You should find out."

"Does it change anything if she knows?"

"Oh, it really does. If she knows she's a psychopath, she'll do whatever she wants, even if you try to stop her."

"And if she doesn't?"

Kat grinned, too wide, too sharp. "Then maybe, *maybe,* you can make her doubt what she's doing."

"But how do I stop her?"

"You don't," said Kat, her attentiveness making Jess uneasy. "You should probably just stay out of her way if you don't want to get caught up in whatever she plans to do."

"What would have stopped you?" asked Jess.

"Knowing someone might be watching, that I might get

caught," said Kat, kicking at the leg of her chair. "Knowing I'd end up here."

"Thanks," said Jess with a weak smile, her nerves peaking this close to Kat. The barrier between them felt like cling film holding back a pride of lions at the zoo. How was Kat so calm after talking about losing her child?

"Wait, is this about you? You're not afraid that you might be a psychopath, are you?"

"No," said Jess cautiously. She didn't want to offend Kat.

Kat relaxed into her chair. "It's okay. We're all a little afraid of what we are. Some of us have the courage to face it, and some don't. Who better to ask if you seem crazy than a crazy person, right?" She grinned.

"I should probably go," said Jess. "I've taken up enough of your time."

"One more thing, and you can consider this a bonus," said Kat.

Jessica forced herself to remain expressionless, but it was too late—Kat had seen her squirm.

"One more thing?" Jess was afraid of the answer.

"Find out if she knows what *you* are."

Before Jess could ask what that meant, Kat stood, straightened her chair, and left.

∞

At 8:15 Jess heard the front door open.

"Hello?" called Clay, breaking Jess's reverie. He found her in the kitchen. "Everything alright?"

"Yeah," she said. "I just had a difficult interview today. I waited for you for dinner."

She went to the stove and scooped casserole for each of them into handmade, stoneware bowls while Clay poured two glasses of red wine. "Zoe already ate," she said off-handedly.

"Want to talk about it?"

"Not really." she sat before continuing. "I wanted to discuss something else."

"Sure," he said, keeping his attention on loading up his fork.

Was it her imagination, or was Clay nervous?

"I thought you said you'd be home an hour ago?" Jess was being generous. He was two hours late.

"Did I?"

She scoffed and picked at a carrot on her plate. The conversation already felt like it was going nowhere.

"Well, did you want to talk?"

"I talked to Niki about how you're never home. She thinks you're having an affair."

Clay looked away from his food. "Your sister *would* think that. She's a drama queen."

"Are you?"

"Am I what? Seeing someone else? Shit, Jess, I barely have time to see you."

"That's why I'm asking. You're never here."

"I'm never *here*, because I'm working to support our family. I'm never *here* because there's shit to do. The world doesn't stop so we can spend quality time together."

He was annoyed, but she believed him; after the attack, he'd suddenly gotten busier, as if he was worried the attacker would come back to finish the job.

He shrugged. "I'll cook tomorrow. We can have that paella you like."

"Sounds nice, but Zoe hates paella. She'll refuse to eat it." Jess laughed ironically.

"We'll tell her it's Disney paella—she seems to like anything with a Disney sticker on it."

Niki was wrong. Clay wasn't having an affair. He looked as tired as she felt.

Jess was probably wrong too—he wasn't avoiding her intentionally. Their lives were just busier.

Chapter 32

Now

Detective Collins agreed to talk to Oscar without the usual lecture about poking his nose where it didn't belong.

They met at a busy sports bar, the afternoon sun softened by a blinking window shade.

Calvin Collins was a hefty man. What might've passed for muscle years before had turned to bulky weight. Oscar noticed Detective Collins wasn't in uniform as he entered and walked over. "Oscar?"

"Yeah. How'd you know?"

"You're the only guy in here not wearing a football or hockey jersey."

Oscar looked at his blue striped polo shirt. "I thought one of the teams would be this color," he joked.

Detective Collins gave him a questioning look. "It's my day off," he said. "So, we better make this quick."

"Okay, I'll get right to it then," said Oscar, almost halfway through a coke. "I wanted to ask about Jessica Green? Do you remember her?"

"Jessica? That little girl disappeared from her place. You're her shrink?" Calvin looked at Oscar sideways, like his profession was something he should be ashamed of.

"I'm her psychiatrist."

"You trying to get her out of trouble for what she did? Are you gonna say she's crazy or some shit so she doesn't have to do time?"

Detective Collins didn't think Jess was innocent. *But why?*

"I just want to know what happened. If Jessica knows where Mia is, I want to find out."

"You're a shrink—you're not supposed to be messing around with a police investigation. You're supposed to make your patients feel better about all the shitty things they've done in their lives."

"I'm not messing with the investigation. I want to get your perspective—partly to help Jess, but also to help Mia."

Detective Collins nodded. "And you think you can find her when we couldn't?"

"I'm not trying to find Mia. I'm trying to figure out what Jess knows."

Oscar wished Jess had told him what he should ask. "What was your impression of Jessica?"

Detective Collins wasn't someone who spent time deciding what to say. His mouth sat fixed in a permanent scowl, a skeptic. "Something about her looked unfriendly to me. I always thought she killed that girl, but without a body we couldn't prove much."

"Unfriendly how?"

"Brooding. When we talked to the other mothers at kindergarten, they were happy to help. But not her. She got annoyed."

"Annoyed?"

"I don't know. She said we had some problem with her because we questioned her when she tried to kill her husband."

Talking to Detective Collins, Oscar could see what Jess meant.

"Jessica said she spoke to you about Holly Edwards—"

"Yeah? Did she tell you she accused the poor woman of kidnapping her own daughter?"

"No, she didn't."

"Holly Edwards is going through hell, not knowing where her kid is. Mostly, something like that happens and people show some compassion, help out where they can."

"Did Jessica offer to help?"

"No. Jessica Green told us to question Holly Edwards because Holly knew where Mia was."

Jess said she told the police the truth, but no one wanted to listen. Was that what she meant?

"No disrespect, detective, but is there any chance Jess might have been telling the truth about Holly Edwards?"

The detective sighed. "We searched Holly's house. There was nothing suspicious."

"Why did Jess think Holly knew where Mia was?"

"She thought Holly might be violent, that maybe she hurt Mia and got scared that the kid might tell someone."

"And there was nothing to support that?"

"The kid was fine when she went to Jessica Green's house. She hadn't been to the doctor for anything more than a booster shot, a couple of colds and an ear infection a few years before. There was nothing to suggest she hurt her kid. Only thing that seemed off was the kid missed a couple of days of kindergarten before she went missing. Her mother told the teacher she didn't send her because she was throwing up. Sounded pretty reasonable to me."

"Okay. So, it didn't seem like Holly physically disciplined Mia?"

"No. Seemed like she was a normal parent, struggling to make ends meet. She had pictures of the kid smiling and whatever on her walls. Usually, when there's violence at home, a kid brings signs of it to school—fighting in the yard, mood swings, that kind of thing. The teacher said Mia wasn't scared to go home, and she'd never noticed bruises on her. There were no emotional outbursts."

"Was there anything that might've been a warning sign?"

"Jessica said Mia was complaining about a sore arm when she went to her house. She thought Holly Edwards might've caused it, but the kindergarten teacher didn't remember Mia mentioning it in class."

"And Jess didn't report it, or get any medical help while Mia was at her house?" asked Oscar.

"No. She didn't."

"Did she say why?"

Detective Collins shrugged. "You'd have to ask her. Jessica Green is a strange lady. Not the kind that smiles easily. Suspicious."

Oscar watched Detective Collins as he relayed what happened. His no-nonsense manner made Oscar wonder if he'd ever change his mind about Jess, even if he was wrong.

Oscar would expect a detective to recognize trauma signs. The withdrawal, the anxious energy—things Detective Collins put down to 'an unfriendly woman'.

Oscar hadn't discussed trauma with Jess yet—where it came from and how deep it went. He suspected it was there before she'd had the awful experience of a child disappearing from her house.

"What do you believe happened?" asked Oscar.

"Well, the evidence tells me that Jessica Green was a disturbed lady. It wasn't our first encounter with her."

"Because she had a record?"

"Yeah. She tried to kill her husband. She left him to die in their hallway. Must've reconsidered and called the police."

Oscar could hear it in his voice—Detective Collins didn't believe Jess reconsidered.

"Do violent offenders usually reconsider a murder?"

"We don't get that many women trying to kill their husbands. A man would see the wife was still alive and probably finish the job. Sometimes you get hesitations." He shrugged, apologizing for being honest.

"Jessica Green didn't hesitate?"

"No. Looks like she realized he was alive, but didn't have the stomach to finish him. That's when she called the police, making up something about a break in."

"You don't believe that either?"

"Her prints were on the weapon. She said she'd used it for food prep."

"Is that possible?"

"It's why she wasn't charged. Technicalities like that keep criminals on the street."

Oscar sipped at his soda. He got the feeling Detective Collins would lock Jess up now if he could.

"Detective, would you say Jessica was unfriendly?" asked Oscar, using the detective's language.

"Well, she didn't cooperate with our investigation."

"Was she unfriendly when you spoke to her about the attack on Clayton Green?"

"She was."

"How sure are you that Jessica Green kidnapped Mia Edwards?"

The Detective looked directly at Oscar. "I'm sure Jessica Green killed Mia Edwards and got away with it. Again."

"Again?"

"Her husband isn't dead, but not because she didn't try."

"You think Jessica wanted to kill her husband?" He repeated the detective's statement back to him, encouraging him to elaborate.

"I do."

"Why?"

"Who knows? Marriage is hard."

"You think she hurt Mia?" asked Oscar.

"Yeah, I do."

"Why would she do that? Attacking your husband's pretty different to hurting a kindergartener."

"Rumor is, Holly Edwards was... friendly with Clay Green."

Why would Jess send Oscar to hear this? What was she trying to tell him?

"Who said Holly and Clay were friendly?"

"Holly told me herself. She wasn't proud, but she had the guts to admit it. She thought we should know, that it might've been Jessica's motive."

"Did Clay ever," Oscar searched for the right word, "*reciprocate*?"

The detective poked his tongue through a gap in his teeth. "Depends on who you ask."

Chapter 33

Then

Jess glanced at the time and sighed. Despite an afternoon spent writing an article about narcissism, she was no closer to finishing. She shifted a plant on her desk out of her line of sight. The green leaves usually made her feel connected to life outside her office, but today they reminded her she could be out in the sunshine.

She removed Kat's name and typed *How to spot a Narcissist.* Kat called herself a psychopath, but Jess saw narcissistic traits.

After her conversation with Kat, Jess had considered using '*What makes a Narcissist hate you'* as the title. She filed the idea away and tried to focus on how to spot a narcissist. She needed to get back to the article if she was going to get it finished, but her mind was racing with thoughts.

Why did Holly hate her?

Jess messaged Clay to try to refocus. *Remember to pick Zoe up—she's looking forward to spending some time with you.* He had agreed to an afternoon at the park, giving Jess time to work. It'd been a long time since he had time, but Jess needed to get it in, so she didn't feel too guilty for requesting one afternoon.

Zoe and Clay arrived home just before five, Zoe bouncing through the door.

"Hey, there you are," said Jess, catching Zoe as she ran into her arms for a hug.

"I went to the park with Daddy and we had ice cream and I got to try Daddy's ice cream too," squealed Zoe in a steady stream.

Jess laughed. "Sounds great."

"What's for dinner?" asked Clay, trailing in looking exhausted.

"I don't know. I thought you might make your infamous Teriyaki noodle bowl."

"Infamous?" said Clay indignantly.

Jess scrunched her nose. "Afraid so. Remember last time? I'll need proof it was a onetime thing before I can return it to famous status."

"I'd love to, but I'm exhausted. She's got more energy than I remember."

"Yeah, tell me about it. We could order in?"

"Sure."

"Guess what?" said Zoe, jumping up and down in front of Jess until she had to answer.

"What?"

"Mia came with us! It was the best!"

"Mia?" Jess looked at Clay. If Mia went, Holly must've been there too.

"Yeah, she heard me telling Zoe we were going to the park and begged to come with us." He frowned. "Are you okay? You seem upset."

Jess hadn't told Clay about Holly showing up randomly when

she was with Niki. "I'm fine. Just under the pump."

"You must've stayed late at the park if you're getting back now?"

"We stopped for ice cream," said Clay.

"I had a rainbow one! Mia did too." Zoe bounced on the balls of her feet.

"You took Mia for ice-cream?"

Clay shrugged. "She wanted to go with Zoe. It was nice for the two of them."

"So, you met Mia's mother?"

"Yeah."

Jess waited for Clay to elaborate, but he was scrolling through food options on his phone.

"What did you think?"

Clay glanced up. "She seemed nice enough—lonely, maybe. We should invite them over for dinner sometime."

Jess raised an eyebrow. "Maybe."

"Mia's sweet. Holly said Mia's dad found a new girlfriend and left. Poor kid."

"Really? She didn't mention that to Niki, Meg and me. She told us he was abusive, that he hit Mia."

"Really?"

"Yeah, I'm surprised she didn't tell you," said Jess.

Apparently, Holly's story changed depending on who she was talking to. Clay got the abandoned for another woman version, but Holly's stories didn't add up.

"Maybe she's embarrassed. It's not really something you'd tell a stranger."

"Holly told Mia her dad died. I'm surprised she told you that when Mia might overhear."

"Well, the kids were playing. It sounds like a complicated

situation."

"Yeah." said Jess absently.

Clay put a hand on Jess's shoulder. "You sure you're okay? You're not usually this—gossipy."

"I'm not gossiping, I'm discussing. Jesus, Clay, If I can't vent to you, then who?"

"Well, I feel bad—it sounds like they've had a rough time."

Chapter 34

Now

A knock interrupted Oscar's press-ups. He considered leaving the door unanswered as it grew more insistent.

Oscar caved and answered wearing gray track pants, expecting to find a door-to-door sales rep or an anxious dog owner who'd lost their pet.

"Do you always answer the door half-dressed?" asked Hayley, slipping inside uninvited.

"Not usually. I was hoping to scare off any sales reps. Besides, there wasn't time to dress for the occasion." He smiled as Hayley eyed his bare skin.

Hayley looked away, remembering why she was there. "Sorry to drop by, but we need to talk."

"We do?"

"Yeah."

He ran a hand under his jaw. "Wow, you came all the way here to tell me we need to talk—that's never good."

"I would've called, but it seemed better to talk in person."

"Okay," said Oscar. He offered her a chair and sat, crossing one leg over the other.

"I think Charles is looking for dirt on you," she said.

Oscar almost laughed—he hadn't been expecting Charles to be the thing she couldn't discuss over the phone.

"Why are you laughing?"

"Sorry. It's just... not the worst thing you could've said."

"Charles is trying to get you fired."

Oscar sighed. Charles could've told everyone about Riley if he wanted to make Oscar look bad. When Charles was Oscar's doctor, they'd discussed Riley a lot.

"Charles knows about us."

"Are you sure?"

"He told me not to compromise my career by getting involved with you. He said you're not who I think you are."

Oscar felt her eyes searching his for signs that Charles was lying, but she wouldn't find them. Charles was right—Oscar wasn't who she thought he was.

"Oscar, if there's something I should know, I'd prefer to hear it from you."

He didn't know what to tell Hayley—Charles could've said anything.

What if he told Hayley he killed his son?

Oscar had built a life after Riley's death, but it was fragile. Secrets escaped eventually, no matter how well you kept them. Should he tell Hayley about Riley before Charles did?

"Oscar, talk to me." Hayley's tone was understanding. It made him want to tell her everything, but once she knew what he was, she might never speak to him again.

The silence stretched like a rubber band, ready to bite back on release.

"I want to help, but I can't if you won't let me. There's more to it than you getting the job he wants, isn't there?"

What could he say to that? He wasn't ready to talk about Riley—he shouldn't have to be ready just because Charles was forcing his hand.

"What else did Charles say?"

"If there's something you want to tell me, why don't we start with that, and I'll tell you if it's what Charles told me."

Oscar tried again, faltering over Riley's name.

"Fine. When you're ready to tell me what's going on, let me know." Hayley shook her head and left.

Chapter 35

Now

Jess perched on the edge of the couch, looking out the window. She chose the same spot every time and Oscar thought of it as hers, even though he could explain her behavior using the exposure effect; she'd chosen it the first time, but by her second visit, it was a familiar spot in the room. She seemed calmer when she was looking outside. Maybe it reminded her what was waiting for her out there.

"Did you speak to Detective Collins?" she asked.

"Yeah."

"Did you tell him I killed Mia?"

"No."

Her eyes looked brighter, more energized than he'd seen them. "Why not?"

"Because I don't believe you killed her."

"I told you I did."

"Then tell me where she is. Someone can retrieve her."

Jess flinched. "What would it matter? The only family she has is Holly. She doesn't have grandparents. Her father isn't on her birth certificate."

"How do you know that?"

"Holly told Niki."

"Are you saying you won't tell me where Mia is because no one cares?"

Her cheeks flamed.

"The kids from her kinder class deserve closure. What about Zoe? Doesn't she want to know what happened to her friend?"

Jess looked at her twitching hands, gripping one with the other to steady them.

She was still lying. Jess didn't kill Mia. Why did she want it to seem like she did? Had she done something so bad that confessing to murder was better?

Or was she still testing him?

"Jess, did Mia get hurt by accident?"

"Her arm was already broken."

"You're punishing yourself. Why?"

Jess watched the clouds stroll across the sky, wrapping her arms around her ribs.

He let the conversation settle. If Jess didn't want to talk about it, he wouldn't push.

"I think I understand why you told me to speak to Detective Collins."

Jess turned to Oscar, watching him pour them each a glass of water from a pitcher. "You were right. He has his mind made up about you."

She gave an off-handed shrug.

"He's not the most approachable person, is he?"

The corner of her lip twitched. "I didn't want you to take my word for it."

Her attention turned back to the clouds outside the window. "Did he mention Clay? The detective thought I did it. He told Clay I tried to kill him." She scratched her arm. "He convinced Clay to press charges. When Clay recovered, he realized it wasn't me. He dropped the charges. Clay said all he remembers is having a massive headache, and lots of painkillers."

Oscar listened, afraid to interrupt.

"What did Detective Collins tell you?"

"He said you thought Holly was violent. You thought she hurt Mia?"

Jess chewed her lip. "Yeah."

"Why?"

"A couple of reasons. On the first day of kindergarten, Mia and Zoe had an argument. Another time, Mia bruised Zoe's arm—I thought she might've learned that behavior from home. Then, one day, Mia asked to come home with me. I thought nothing of it, but when Mia came to my house with a broken arm, I wondered if it was more than an innocent request."

Oscar frowned. "Mia asked to live with you?"

"I told the detective, but he thought I was being petty. It sounds petty."

The past was a good indicator of the future. People focused on tragedy once it happened, but sometimes the weeks and months before explained why it happened. If you were lucky, that's where the answers were.

Jess was lost in memories, her expression dark.

Oscar waited.

"Mia seemed scared of Holly," said Jess. "She talked about her dad like he was the Jekyll to Holly's Hyde."

"Was Mia upset with her mother about something?" asked Oscar.

"I didn't know Mia well enough to say." Jess ran her hands across her knees and continued. "Holly told Mia her dad died because he was violent. Maybe Mia knew she was lying."

"Detective Collins said Mia had an injured arm when she arrived at your house. Did you ask Holly about it?"

"Her arm wasn't just injured. It was fractured."

"Did you tell Holly?"

"No," said Jess.

"Why?"

"Because Mia said Holly did it."

"Did you get her arm checked by a doctor?"

"No."

"Why not?"

"I didn't get the chance. I was trying to figure out what to do, and then Mia disappeared. She wouldn't have wandered off with a broken arm."

Jess stopped to gauge Oscar's reaction. "The police thought I was horrible for saying Holly hurt her daughter. I knew Holly would twist the truth to seem like Mia's arm was injured at my house. Detective Collins didn't like me because of what happened to Clay, so I knew they might not take me seriously."

She sounded defensive, explaining herself to avoid more trouble. Her head dropped in her hands, dark hair falling around her like a shield.

"I wouldn't have known what to do either."

She sat up, hopeful. Someone was finally listening. "I couldn't talk about it at the remand center—they were the same as the police. They expected me to lie to protect myself, and they didn't believe the truth."

"Detective Collins said you thought Holly knew what happened to Mia."

"Holly convinced them she had nothing to do with it, so when I suggested she did, I was the monster. One officer said that '*as a mother*' I should know better."

"And what do you think?"

"Mia told me Holly hurt her, and I took it seriously."

"So, you thought she was telling the truth?"

"Yeah, she seemed genuinely scared of Holly's temper. She got her shoes dirty from playing in the sandpit, and she was worried Holly would be mad."

"Detective Collins thinks you might've been getting back at Holly for something."

"By murdering her daughter and lying about it? That's ridiculous." Jess closed her eyes. "I'm sorry, that came out wrong."

"It is ridiculous. You seem rational to me," said Oscar.

"I feel responsible. Mia was at my house when she went missing."

"Detective Collins told me the rumor about Holly and Clay. He thought it could've been a trigger."

"I wouldn't hurt a child because their mother flirted with my husband," said Jess, her tone suggesting how stupid the idea was.

"I know you wouldn't," said Oscar. "Did something else make Detective Collins think you would?"

"Holly and I argued."

"Did it get heated?"

"Not really. Holly tried pushing my buttons."

"I think flirting with someone's husband would annoy anyone."

"Maybe."

"But not you?"

"No."

"Why?"

"I guess I just didn't feel it."

She tried to seem nonchalant, her eyes darting past Oscar.

She was hiding something, and he wasn't sure how to figure out what it was.

Pushing Jess could trigger a trauma response.

Still, she was hiding something, and Oscar could tell that it would change everything.

Chapter 36

Then

"Zoe!" Jess's voice strained over the din of a few dozen kindergarteners riled by the home bell. She waved, but Zoe was busy syncing skips with Mia.

The girls stopped in front of Jess.

"Hey. How was your day? Did you do lots of fun stuff?"

"Yep. I drew a picture for Daddy." Zoe beamed.

"He'll love that. Maybe we can put it on the door of the fridge and surprise him when he gets home?"

"Yay. Can I put it up by myself?"

"Sure." Jess ruffled Zoe's hair, watching Mia scuff her shoe on the ground, looking away as if she were intruding on something private.

"How about you, Mia? What did you draw today?"

Mia shrugged. "I wanted to draw a picture for my daddy too, but Mommy might get mad."

"I'm sure she wouldn't mind, sweetie."

Mia looked at Jess uncertainly, her mouth set in a frown.

Jess put her satchel down and kneeled next to Mia. "You miss your dad, huh?"

Mia's lip wobbled dangerously.

"I never met him. He died before I was born, but sometimes I pretend. All the other kids have one. I wanted one too."

"You never met your dad?" asked Jess.

Didn't Holly say Mia's dad hit them? She had bruises from where he attacked her.

Maybe Ray was Mia's stepdad?

Either way, Jess couldn't ask a four-year-old.

"Mia! What's wrong? Are you okay, honey?" Holly ran toward them, looking accusingly at Jess. "What happened?" she asked, loud enough for everyone to hear.

A couple of parents snuck glances, trying to see what the commotion was about. One woman with a garishly pink mouth stared like a diligent neighbor, ready to name the criminal.

"Nothing," said Jess, abandoning her satchel so that Holly could go to Mia.

As Holly approached, Mia flinched.

Holly cupped Mia's shoulders and pulled her forward in a hug.

Jess watched as Mia's shoe caught on the satchel, spilling notes from her article.

Holly ran after the papers before they blew away. "I'm so sorry." She turned her attention to Mia. "You need to be more careful."

"It's fine. It's nothing important," said Jess.

Holly skimmed the title—*How to spot a narcissist.* Jess had crossed out narcissist and tentatively scribbled *psychopath*?? in its place.

Holly offered the papers back to Jess. "Sounds interesting. So, what're you looking for—narcissists or psychopaths?"

"Thanks," said Jess, taking the papers. "It's just an article

I'm writing."

Holly shot Jess a curious look. "What do you know about psychopaths?"

"More than you think," said Jess, fishing for a reaction. "I did a bunch of research for an article."

Holly turned back to Mia as if remembering she was there.

"Mia, what happened?"

"I didn't get to finish my picture," Mia lied.

Holly looked at Jess for confirmation. Jess forced a smile.

"Well, you can finish your picture tomorrow, can't you?"

Mia nodded.

"Then there's nothing to cry about." Holly wiped at a few stray tears and took hold of Mia's hand. "Come on, let's go. I've got things to do."

"Are you alright, Mia?" Jess asked.

"She's fine. Aren't you honey?"

Holly shot her a look Jess didn't like, daring her to disagree.

Mia looked despondent, her hand resting limply in Holly's. She looked back and smiled weakly at Jess.

"Oh, Jessica—I forgot to thank Clay for the ice-cream the other day," said Holly with a salacious grin. "Thank him for me and tell him I hope to do it again sometime soon."

Jess pretended she didn't notice Holly's implication. "Sure."

"He's a lot of fun," she added.

Jess nodded. There was a time when she would have laughed, secure knowing she didn't need to worry what Clay was doing, but doubt kept her silent.

Chapter 37

Now

Oscar waited for Jess to settle in her usual spot before he began talking.

She ignored the window, fixing her eyes on the gray, patterned rug that stretched between the couches like a river.

"Are you okay? You're quiet today," said Oscar.

She nodded unconvincingly.

"Do you want to talk about it?"

She shook her head.

"It's not easy, but for what it's worth, we're making good progress."

Her eyes flashed. "Progress?" she snapped.

"All I meant was that we've started talking about things that are troubling you."

"I don't care about progress."

He should've chosen his words more carefully. "Before, you wouldn't acknowledge that any of this affected you."

"Until now, there was always someone to twist what I said."

"I won't do that."

"Isn't the medication supposed to do that?"

"Medication helps, but it's more effective when it's paired with something like cognitive behavioral therapy, like we're doing."

"You mean talking?"

"The cognitive part examines your thoughts about what's happened and the behavioral element looks at your response or actions to events."

She retrained her gaze on the perpetual spirals embossed in the floor rug. "Interesting pattern. Does it drive you crazy, looking at it all day?"

"I picked it out," said Oscar. Most people didn't notice the subtle embossing of the spirals.

"Why this rug?"

Interesting that she would ask; it reminded him of his mind spiraling. He seemed to end up in the same pattern, but the rug reminded him the spiral could go up as well as down.

"It goes with the furniture," he said.

Jess looked at him. She knew he was lying.

He needed to give more if he expected the same. *Quid pro quo*. Tit for tat. Except, he wasn't there to barter. Neither was she, he supposed. She attended the sessions because it was expected.

"The rug reminds me that when my mind spirals, I need to bring it back."

"Does it work?"

"Sometimes. Other times it's like a downhill track without brakes."

"What track are you riding?"

He looked at Riley's picture.

"You didn't kill your son. It sounds like SIDS? It's horrible, but it wasn't your fault."

Oscar smiled sadly. It was a nice idea, pretending he wasn't responsible, that he couldn't have stopped Riley's death, but it was a lie. He could've done a lot. Things he couldn't think about when it happened. He still doubted himself, pretending his sleep-deprived mind was playing tricks.

In the following days, with all the time in the world to sleep and think, his mind confused reality with his nightmares. If he hadn't ignored the truth, Riley might be alive.

"Did anyone besides your wife think you hurt your son?"

"No one said it directly, but I think they wondered."

"I know how that feels," said Jess.

"Eventually, they stopped trying to pretend. It's like you become..."

"A monster," finished Jess. "They worry you might do the same to them. It reminds them they're not invincible. Grief scares people, shows them they're not immune."

"Yeah."

"After Clay's attack, even some of my friends thought I tried to kill him."

"That must have been tough."

She shrugged. "*Clay* thought it was me. It made me feel like the years we spent together meant nothing. It made me question myself. How could he know me that well and still think I would do that? I would never hurt him. I wouldn't do that to Zoe."

Oscar had avoided talking about Clay's attack. It was hugely personal, asking Jess why her husband thought she tried to kill him.

"Did Clay say why he thought it was you?"

"He heard someone behind him in the kitchen and assumed." She shook her head numbly, as if she'd gone over the story too many times.

Or rehearsed it.

"Clay saw my hair when he turned around. He asked if something was wrong, and then everything went blank—his words, not mine."

"So, you were in the house when it happened?"

"Yeah. That's why the police thought I did it."

"Where were you?"

"Getting out of the bathtub."

"Did you hear someone in the house?"

"No. I heard the front door open when Clay got home. He said hello and put on some music. The music was loud, but I thought I heard something fall. I assumed Clay dropped something, but when I asked, he didn't answer. I got out of the bath to see what happened and found Clay lying on the floor."

"That must have been awful."

Jess clamped a thumbnail between her teeth.

"Jess? What is it?"

"I wondered for a long time if they attacked Clay by accident."

"What do you mean?"

"Maybe they were trying to kill me."

Oscar nodded, listening.

"I was expecting to find a mess to clean, but Clay was on the floor. He didn't respond when I called his name."

She paused, inhaling a long breath."My husband didn't believe me, so why would anyone else? How could he think I'd do that?"

If Clay thought Jess attacked him, the attacker might've been someone with a small frame and long, dark hair.

"Who'd want to hurt Clay?"

"At first, I thought maybe he was having an affair, like Niki said. I figured maybe she threatened to tell me and he lashed out, so she defended herself."

"Did you tell the police?"

She made a hollow sound, almost a laugh. "Would you go to the police with no evidence? They would've thought I was making it up to cover for myself."

When Riley died, there were things Oscar wished he said, but he didn't, for the same reason Jess didn't. The more time that passed, the less it seemed like a good idea, so he lived with unanswered questions instead.

Jess was watching him, waiting for an answer. "Probably not," he said.

"I haven't told anyone. Until now."

"When did Clay realize it wasn't you?"

"He said he made a mistake, that he knew I wouldn't do something like that—but I'm not sure he believes it."

"Why would he stay with you if he thought you wanted to hurt him?"

"Maybe he was hiding something," said Jess. "Blaming me might've been a cover."

"You mentioned that whoever attacked him might've meant to attack you. Can you think of anyone who would want to do that?"

She ran her hands through her hair, ruffling the strands like feathers. "You'll think it's crazy, like the police did."

Oscar leaned forward and placed a hand on her forearm. "You're not crazy. They should have listened."

Her fingers finished combing and fell from the ends of her hair. "I can't say it," said Jess.

"Why? I won't tell anyone if you don't want me to."

"It's not that. I don't care who you tell. It's Zoe—" She stopped talking abruptly. If felt like she only gave a little before she clammed up again, afraid of what she might unleash.

They were so close to a breakthrough, but distance stretched like a ravine between them. If he missed the mark, he would send them careening until they hit the bottom.

What had she done?

Chapter 38

Then

The morning breeze was fresh and inviting, waiting to be enjoyed. Jess grabbed Zoe's backpack, swinging it over her shoulder.

"Zoe, honey. Come on. We're walking today."

"Walking?" said Zoe, wheedling. "My legs are sore. I don't wanna walk."

"It's not far. The exercise is good for you. Now let's get your shoes on."

Zoe plopped down where she was standing and held out her foot.

"Okay, Cinderella." Jess jammed one shoe on and then the other. "These are getting a little tight. We might need to get new ones. But for now, let's get your bag."

Zoe pointed at the bag hanging on Jess's shoulder.

"Right." They made their way to kindergarten, Zoe reluctantly holding Jess's hand like a puppy on a leash. When they got there, the bell had just sounded, and the yard was quiet without dozens of children playing.

Jess dropped Zoe at her classroom and readied herself for

the walk back, pulling her sunglasses over her eyes.

She walked the long way, past the shops, deciding whether to stop for coffee. She pulled out her phone to text Niki. Maybe she'd want to share a muffin.

How could she ask if Holly was around without seeming rude? There were some things she just couldn't talk about in front of her.

Jess pocketed her phone. She had an article she should probably pen instead. She'd written nothing since *How to spot a psychopath*. Maybe she needed a follow up—*How to survive a psychopath.*

Turning the corner she saw a man and a woman engaged in an argument. Jess walked slower—she needed to pass them to get to the café.

The man gestured, making it look like he was telling the woman to calm down and lower her voice. He looked around, uncomfortably aware that they were making a scene.

Jess was far enough away that she didn't draw their attention, but as she got closer, she realized she knew the woman.

Holly. Who was she arguing with?

It looked like the man swapped money for an envelope. Jess slid behind a tree, waiting for Holly to leave, feeling like she'd seen something she shouldn't.

The man swore as Holly got in a car parked at the curb and drove away.

Jess waited until Holly left before stepping out from her hiding place. She walked past the man, trying not to stare. If this was Ray, he didn't fit the picture Holly painted. This man was clean cut, his dark blonde hair combed and styled.

He moved to the side, watching Jess move past. He muttered an apology, but she walked around him, avoiding his eyes.

"Hey, I saw you watching," he called.

Jess's throat constricted—he knew she'd seen them. What if he told Holly?

"Look," said the man, catching up to Jess as she passed.

Jess flinched.

"Sorry, I uh—I just wanted to say, I looked like a jerk back there. But it's not what it looked like."

"I know," said Jess.

"You know?"

She knew she should stay out of it, knew it wasn't her business, but he'd probably tell Holly he'd seen her, and maybe she could convince him not to. "Are you Ray?"

"Who are you? Why were you spying on us?" he asked, suspicious of her.

It must be Ray.

She shouldn't have said anything. She should have walked on when he called out, but it was too late now. He was blocking her way.

"I didn't. I wasn't. I saw you arguing and didn't want to walk past," said Jess.

"Do I know you?" He pulled off her sunglasses, and she flinched. He smelled like fresh deodorant and shampoo.

He scrutinized her, still trying to figure out where he knew her from.

"I'm sorry," he said, offering the sunglasses back. "That was rude. It's been a rough morning. I *don't* know you, do I?"

"No, you don't."

"Then how do you know me... you *don't* know me either, do you?"

"No."

"Then you must know Holly."

"Yeah. Look, I wasn't spying, I just didn't want to interrupt. It's none of my business." Jess moved around Ray, eager to get to the safety of the coffeehouse. This part of the street was mostly empty, and she didn't want to be alone with him.

"Wait," he said. "If you know Holly, you might know my daughter, Mia. Is she as beautiful as she looks in these pictures?"

He pulled something from the package Holly had handed him and held it up. A photo of Mia with a toothy grin.

Jess shrugged, non-committal. "No, I don't really know her, sorry. I have to go."

"I don't know why I'm saying this, but please, can we talk? I'll buy you a drink or something."

"I'm sorry, I can't help. I have to go."

"Wait. I don't know what she said about me, but just hear me out."

Jess's heart galloped in her chest. Ray definitely wasn't dead like Mia thought. Jess didn't know what to say—just because Ray was calm now didn't mean he didn't have a temper. Holly's face proved it.

Ray stood in the middle of the walkway, clutching the photo's Holly gave him.

"If you know Holly, maybe you know what she's like," he pleaded. "She didn't tell me we had a daughter until she needed money. I paid eight hundred dollars for these photos of my daughter."

The reporter in Jess wanted to ask questions. Why had he agreed to give her money for photographs instead of visiting Mia? How long had he known he had a daughter?

"You obviously aren't friends with Holly, or you wouldn't have hidden from her. You would've come over to see why she was upset," he guessed. "So, I'm thinking that maybe you know."

Jess looked at the ground.

"How do you know her?" he asked.

His words had triggered something in her. *Maybe you know what she's like.* Niki didn't see it, and Meg seemed indifferent. Even Clay felt sorry for her. Only Jess could see Holly was the kind of person who said what she needed to get what she wanted.

What did she say to Clay at the park? What did they do? Did they share more than ice-cream?

Niki had warned her.

Jess chided herself for letting Holly get inside her head. *Tell Clay we should do it again sometime...* she wanted to make Jess wonder. But why?

She remembered Kat's warning. *Find out if she knows what you are.*

What was she?

Someone who knows what Holly is.

"I don't know her well. Our kids go to kinder together."

"You might be the only person I've met who's seen the real Holly, so I'm going to say this. I think she might hurt our daughter."

When Mia asked to live with Jess, it seemed like an innocent request, but what if it wasn't? What if Mia was asking for help?

"You should probably talk to the police about that," said Jess. "I can't help you."

"I've tried. You don't know what it's like being the bad guy when you did nothing wrong. She's a good liar. Better than I could ever be."

Reading people was part of Jess's job. It was how you got

the real story. Ray looked like he'd been broken. Whatever happened between him and Holly, Jess was pretty sure it hadn't happened how Holly said it did.

"She told the police I hit her," he said. "Let me buy you a coffee." He held up his hands. "If you don't believe me, you can walk away and never see me again."

What could one coffee hurt? Like Ray said, she never had to see him again. It was a public place, and she could leave if she needed to.

Ray might know why Holly made her feel like she was walking barefoot across a stage of hidden blades. "Sure," said Jess.

"Thank you."

"I have to make a call. I'll meet you there in a few minutes."

"Okay," he agreed. "Listen, I know you could just leave, and I'd probably understand if you did, but I hope you don't."

Ray walked toward the café. When he was far enough, Jess messaged Clay.

She hesitated, dialing his number instead.

He picked up on the third ring, surprised at her call. "Jess? Are you alright? Is it Zoe?"

"Zoe's fine. Listen, I need to ask you something and I need the truth."

"Okay," said Clay slowly.

"What happened when you went to the park with Holly?"

"Jessica, is this about what Niki said? Because I already told you, there's nothing—"

"Did anything happen that I should know about?"

She waited, the truth filling the silence.

"She's lonely, Jess. She has no one. I don't think she meant anything by it."

"By *what*?"

He cleared his throat. "There was a second where she—I don't know—tried to kiss me or something."

"She *kissed* you?"

"It was nothing. Really."

"Why didn't you mention it?"

"I didn't want to make a big deal out of it, and I knew you would."

His attempt to diffuse the situation made him sound condescending, like she had nothing to be upset about.

"Did you kiss her back?"

"What? No, of course not. She was having a bad day. She probably felt silly afterwards. Let's not embarrass her."

"A bad day?"

"Being a parent is hard. She was struggling with Mia. So, we invited them for ice-cream."

"Was that before or after she tried to kiss you?"

"Really, Jess. I don't know if it was even a kiss. She moved too close, and I moved away. That was it."

"Well, she asked me to tell you she had a good time. She suggested you should do it again sometime."

"Jess—"

"I've got to go. Bye."

Chapter 39

Now

Dark hair fanned around her, edges sharp and dangerous like a knife blade. The new cut canceled the soft edges of her face and her eyes were shining. Maybe she was finally adjusting to life at Whitner. She looked transformed from the person who shuffled in that first day and lashed out when someone hit her, the girl who broke when they whispered *baby killer*. Now she looked unbreakable.

"We need to figure out why someone might hurt Clay, or whether you were the target," said Oscar.

"Why don't you ever say what you think?" asked Jess.

"What do you mean?"

"You ask a lot of questions, or give suggestions, but you don't really say what you think."

"Okay," said Oscar. "Is there something you want my opinion on?"

Jess clasped her hands across her knees. "Do you think I tried to kill my husband?"

"I don't know what I think yet. I'm here to help you navigate what happened."

"I don't need your help."

Oscar paused. "I don't *think* it's likely, but it's not my job to make guesses."

She assessed him quietly, presenting her conclusion. "I think you're afraid of being wrong. You hide behind the facts because you don't want to misjudge someone."

"Was there anything else you wanted to talk about?"

"No," said Jess.

"Are you sure?"

"I'm tired of talking. Unless I walked into the police station and handed them the evidence, they'll believe I tried to kill my husband and that I killed Mia Edwards, even if they can't find proof."

Jess felt frustrated, like Oscar was after Riley died. It was a hard place to come back from. A piece of Oscar would always remain lost. No one could help him find his way back, but Jess had Oscar to look out for her.

"It was as if whoever had attacked Clay just disappeared. They were gone before I was out of the tub. I tried to figure it out, to prove it wasn't me."

She focused on the rug, her eyes following the spirals to the ends, one into the next. "Everything is so fragile," she said. "You can have good intentions and somehow it still goes bad. There's no good and evil. You can be a bad person and still get rewarded, or hide how awful you are and get away with it."

He didn't understand what she was saying. Did she feel like a victim, or the monster?

"Get away with what?"

"Anything you want, if you're not bound by the rules."

"You were writing an article about psychopaths, Jess. Why did you choose that topic?"

She shifted, trying to get comfortable. "People are interested in abnormal behavior."

"Were you researching psychopaths?"

"What?"

"Did you want to know how to tell if someone was a psychopath? Were you figuring out if someone you knew had psychopathic traits? Maybe you were wondering about yourself?"

"I was writing an article. That's all. I thought people might be interested in narcissists, or psychopaths."

"I think whoever you were researching—Holly, maybe Clay or your sister—got inside of your head and made you wonder if you were crazy."

"Niki?" she sounded surprised.

"I met your sister. She likes things to be about her. How does Niki feel about Clay?"

Jess's face dropped. "You're not saying you think Niki hurt Clay?"

"No. I'm asking what you think."

"Niki's not a narcissist, or a psychopath."

"Really? She's friends with someone who accused you of murder. That doesn't sound like a loyal sister."

"Sometimes Niki makes no sense."

"I think you're protecting someone. I'm trying to figure out who. There's a reason you're not telling me everything, and that's my best guess."

"And you think I'm covering for my sister? That's ridiculous."

Jess's expression didn't change, and her voice stayed steady. He believed her. If Niki was involved, Jessica didn't know about it.

Who is she protecting?

"You suggested Holly attacked Clay?"

"She has the same dark hair as you, about the same build."

"So, it would be feasible to think it was Holly."

"I didn't just suggest it. I told the police it was Holly, but they said she had an alibi."

"If the police said she was telling the truth, wasn't that enough?"

Jess glared at Oscar, her body hardened steel. "Maybe," she agreed.

"Why would Holly attack Clay?"

"I've had a lot of time to think about that."

"Do you think they were having an affair?"

"No, I don't."

"Maybe she was angry he wasn't more... receptive to her?" offered Oscar.

Jess hugged her arms closer, shoulders jutting forward. "Maybe." She looked away, avoiding his eyes.

"Do you know why she did it?"

"She was sending me a message. She wanted me to know she could hurt the people closest to me. First, she befriended Niki, but that wasn't enough. She wanted me to know she had the upper hand."

"So even with an alibi, you're sure Holly came into your house and attacked Clay?"

Jess shrugged. "An alibi's easy if someone's willing to lie for you, especially if they're good at it."

He was losing her—he needed to change approach. "I know what you mean."

"Do you?" she asked doubtfully.

"I have an ex-wife who ended up with everything," he said.

"She didn't need an alibi because she was a good liar. She painted a picture of me as a murderer, and she was right. But she made it sound like it was intentional. She's good at manipulating people like that."

"I'm sorry."

Oscar nodded. "Yeah."

"You mentioned Holly might've been responsible for Mia's disappearance?"

"They thought I hated Holly. When I said she attacked Clay and knew where Mia was, they made it sound like I was trying to frame her." Jessica laughed, the sound dry and ironic in her throat.

"Why do you think they didn't believe you?"

"About Mia?"

"Yeah."

"Different rules apply when a child goes missing. I'm a reporter. I know you have to be careful reporting crime against children. People don't hurt children because of anything the child has done, they do it because of who they are. That's why they didn't want to listen when I said Holly hurt Mia."

"I see."

"Sorry, I didn't mean to suggest—" said Jess.

Oscar shook his head. "It's okay. Go on."

"Everyone thought she was a grieving mother."

"If there's a chance Holly hurt her daughter then it's their job to investigate. I think a grieving parent would understand they're just doing what needs to be done to find their child. They might even be grateful that the police are looking into all the possibilities. I know I would've been."

Jess nodded. "For Holly, it got her some sympathy. She had everyone fooled, even Niki."

"What do you mean?"

"Mia's disappearance meant everyone catered to Holly. If she got angry and showed who she really was, it was because she was distraught."

"Niki didn't talk to me for a week after I told the police I thought Holly hurt Mia. Holly made it seem like I'd turned the police against her because they asked a few questions. She convinced them I had an agenda."

"That must've been hard."

"Meg still thinks I killed Mia because of Holly."

"What do you mean?"

"Some people are good liars. Other people are naturals. Holly's a natural."

"Do you think Holly murdered Mia?"

"I don't know," said Jess. "I know she probably hurt Mia's arm. If she needed to hide what happened, who knows what she'd do?"

"But do you think she killed her?"

Jess hooked her thumbs inside her elbows. Oscar didn't blame her for not wanting to answer—it hadn't gotten her anywhere in the past.

Her eyes traced the patterned rug until she reached the end of the spirals.

"I think it's possible."

Chapter 40

Then

Jess threw her phone in her bag, the gel case taking the brunt of her anger at Clay. Omitting the truth was the same as lying if it could change something important.

What else did Clay decide she didn't need to know?

She composed herself, unconsciously pulling her arms in close like she used to when she was a child, afraid of the dark. Ray was probably waiting for her at the café. She knew she had to go in. She needed to hear what Ray knew about Holly.

He sat at a small round table, tapping his fingers on the wood, relaxing a little when Jess walked in. It was true, he'd be a terrible liar. His face was too open, too expressive.

"Thanks for coming," he said. "It would've looked stupid, sitting here by myself with two mugs. I ordered you a cappuccino, because I don't know anyone who'd turn down coffee and chocolate. I hope you don't mind." He allowed himself a smile and gestured for Jess to sit.

"I didn't even ask your name, sorry," he said.

Jess sat across from him self-consciously, shifting her legs to get comfortable.

"Listen, you don't know me and you have no reason to trust me, so you don't have to tell me your name if you don't want to."

"Jess," she said.

"Jess. Nice to meet you. So, what do you do?"

"I'm a journalist."

"Oh," said Ray.

When Jess told people she was a journalist, it usually went one of two ways. They were either careful what they said around her, or they told her their life story.

"Do I need to ask you to sign something or—" Ray let the joke die. "Are you working on anything now?"

Ray's attempts at small talk were awkward, but at least he asked questions, so it was easy to answer. "I just finished an article."

"What's it about?"

"Narcissistic and psychopathic traits," she said, suddenly embarrassed.

Ray thanked an attendant who brought their coffee over. "If you don't want the cappuccino, I'm happy to swap for the latte," he said, watching her inspect the drink.

"Thanks," said Jess. "I'll take the latte, if that's okay?"

She wasn't sure she should drink it—she didn't know Ray, and what she'd heard about him so far made her wary. Still, she'd watched the attendant bring it over from the coffee machine, and she could really go some coffee.

"Sure." He slid a mug with rich, foamy milk toward her, keeping the cappuccino for himself. "Sounds like an interesting article."

"I interviewed someone diagnosed with Narcissistic Personality Disorder."

Jess remembered the feeling Kat gave her with her unstable energy. She'd experienced that feeling before, but without the prison guards to watch her back, it was more unsettling.

"What was it like?"

"It was like being around Holly," said Jess, testing Ray's reaction.

He nodded knowingly.

"What happened between you and Holly?"

Ray leaned his arms heavily on the table, the ceramic clinking. "We fell in love. At least, I thought we did. She was charming and beautiful, and I thought I was the luckiest guy in the world. That lasted almost a year. Then things changed."

"How do you mean?"

"I don't know. It was like there were two Holly's and I never knew which one I'd get. She'd get angry over little things. She would throw things and yell at me. Eventually, she took it too far."

Jess picked up her cup to busy her hands, uncomfortably anticipating where the story was going.

"She threw a knife at me. It landed in the side of my chest." He lifted his shirt and showed her a scar.

"Oh my god," she said, partly at what she was seeing, and partly because they were in the middle of a cafe.

He cleared his throat awkwardly, waiting for the looks to die down. "I haven't told anyone before. She said it was an accident."

"I know what you mean," said Jess.

"There was a lot of blood. I asked her to drive me to hospital."

"Did she?"

"Eventually. She was worried about what they'd say about

her part in it. She made me agree to back up her story at the hospital before she'd take me. I was scared I'd bleed out, so I agreed."

"And what did she tell them?"

"That she found me like that when she got home. She said I hurt myself, and that she didn't think it was on purpose, but she couldn't be sure. I didn't realize it, but she was setting me up. I was stupid for agreeing."

"No you weren't," said Jess.

"I just wanted to stop the bleeding. I won't get custody of my daughter because I seem unstable. She didn't even put my name on her birth certificate. I only found out Mia existed a few months ago."

Ray bounced his leg nervously. "I've been playing by Holly's rules, hoping she'll let me see her. I wasn't sure she was even mine at first, but looking at the photos, I think I can see it. I'm worried Holly'll use Mia to get at me. I can't just walk away until I know Holly's changed—I have Mia to think about."

"Holly told us that you hit her. I mean, her eye was a mess, so we believed her. But you didn't do it, did you?"

"She said I hit her?" he exploded.

Jess pulled back, ready to leave if she needed to.

He lowered his voice. "I'm sorry. Holly hasn't changed at all, has she?"

"She's friends with my sister, and now she's working her way through to my husband. It feels like she's in every part of my life. She hates me, though."

Ray's brow furrowed.

"I know they can speak to whoever they want, but..." she shrugged, disliking how possessive she sounded, but since Holly appeared, it felt like she was on the outside of her own life, trying to get back in. She wrapped her arms tightly around herself. "I don't know why I'm telling you this."

"That sounds exactly like what Holly does when she doesn't like someone. It's like a game to her."

"Why me?"

"You're probably in the way of something she wants."

"I don't think so. We only met because she accidentally ran my sister down."

"With a car?" He raised an eyebrow skeptically. "Accidentally?"

"Do you think she did it on purpose?" asked Jess.

"That was probably her way in. She's good at finding one—or making one."

It sounded a little extreme, even for Holly.

"How did you meet her?" asked Jess.

"She found me at a bar, drinking my loneliness away."

Jess ran a hand through her hair.

Ray's phone beeped. He opened his message and read, turning the phone screen for Jess to read. "It's from Holly," he said.

We need to reassess our agreement.

Ray typed something back. The phone beeped almost immediately in reply. His expression told Jess it wasn't good news.

He spun the phone around for Jess to see. She read his message first.

I'd really like to meet our daughter.

I can make it so you never will, after what you did.

"What did you do?" asked Jess.

"Nothing. She's probably trying to bait something out of me to stop me from seeing Mia."

He wrote his number on a napkin. "Take this, but don't put it in your phone. If Holly sees it, she'll freak out. If Mia's in any trouble, please call me."

"How would Holly know if I put you in my phone contacts?"

He sighed. "If she thinks she should know, she'll find a way."

Jess had a decision to make. Did she believe Ray, or was he a liar, like Holly?

Chapter 41

Now

Oscar waited for Hayley next to her car. He didn't know what to say—he'd never been good at apologizing.

She came through the entrance, clutching the strap of her bag, flustered about something—hopefully not him.

She stopped when she reached her car and fumbled for her keys, waiting for him to speak.

"I should have told you what you wanted to know when you asked. I'm sorry," he said.

"Why pretend we can make things work if you don't trust me?"

It was the first time they'd spoken since she left his apartment. She'd kept her distance at work, unless she couldn't avoid talking to him, but it was painfully formal. Outside of work, she wouldn't answer his calls.

"I didn't know what to say. I froze. I'm sorry," he said, leaning against her car.

She raised an eyebrow. "You're lucky my car's not locked," she said. "I have a killer alarm system."

"I noticed, or I wouldn't have risked standing this close."

"It's not too late." She held up the keys, her thumb over the lock.

Oscar stepped away from the silver paint, hands up in surrender. "Okay, but I'd really like to talk. Maybe I can explain—"

She slid into the driver's seat. "Hop in."

Oscar jumped in beside her. The smell of her perfume filled the car. She stuck a travel mug in the cup holder—she must have refilled before she left. She was probably taking work home if she was drinking coffee at this hour.

"Do you want to get a drink?" He pointed at her coffee. "Have too much of that stuff and you won't sleep."

"I have a lot to catch up on," she said, gripping the steering wheel.

"I hate how things are with us, Hayley. I wanted to say something, but I couldn't think of the right thing. I'm sorry, I messed up."

Hayley loosened her grip on the wheel. "You're right, we should talk. There's something I need to tell you, but not here." She searched the shadows through the windscreen, as if someone might be watching them.

"Where do you want to go?"

"I think I know somewhere. Buckle up."

Hayley parked in the parking lot at Fluid, a bar known for its cocktails. No one from work was likely to show up here.

"Happy to give up my coffee for something a little stronger," she said, using the handbrake.

"I'm game if you are." He took her hand.

Her fingers tensed. "I didn't invite you here to kiss and make up," she said, strands of hair flying on the breeze.

"I know."

She looked at their hands, almost together, and laced her fingers with his, dragging him toward the bar.

They ordered drinks and sat at a glass-topped table, with bar stools covered in black, gray and pink pvc. It was Oscar's first time at Fluid, and he felt out of place among the women out for drinks with the girls, laughing too loud and letting loose after a stifling day at work.

"What are we drinking?"

"I don't know. I just looked at the pictures and picked one with no dairy that looked good." Hayley laughed and held up her glass, the colors of the drink glistening like a traffic light over the ice. Oscar lifted his glass and sipped. "Fruity. Not bad."

Hayley tasted the cocktail and raised an eyebrow. "Not bad at all."

"I didn't think this would be the kind of place you hang out at."

"I don't, but I figured no one we know would either."

"What? I can't hear you."

"I said, I figured—"

Oscar sidled around and put his ear close to Hayley's mouth to catch the rest. He scouted the bar, looking for familiar faces. "Good call. I can't see anyone."

"Well, you're getting noticed anyway. There are a few girls by the bar who'll remember you." She tilted her head towards a table where three women were stealing glances their way, trying to look subtle while they figured out if Hayley was a friend or something more.

"I know how to fix that," said Oscar, brushing back Hayley's hair to kiss her cheek, his nose lingering in her hair. He put an arm around her shoulder.

"Okay I get it, if you act really into me—"

"I've never been a good actor," he said.

The three women shot Hayley looks before searching the bar for someone else.

"You said you want us to trust each other, so I'm just going to ask—did you tell Charles what Jess said about killing Mia?"

Hayley pulled away, throwing Oscar's arm from her shoulders. "No. He already knew. I don't know how, but I didn't tell him anything." She looked hurt. "I can't believe you have to ask."

"I don't. I just needed to hear you say it."

He meant it, but she didn't seem sure. "There's something else you want to say," she said. She could read him well.

The noise from the bar swam inside his head. He couldn't stall any longer. "I saw a psychiatrist a few years back. I thought it'd help me make sense of some things that happened."

"Did it?"

Oscar sighed. "In some ways, maybe, but I never forgot. I don't think Charles forgot either. He'll use it."

"Seeing a psychiatrist won't get you fired. Everyone says stuff during debriefing, it means nothing."

"Charles was my psychiatrist."

Chapter 42

Then

The key rattled in the door, releasing the lock.

"I'm home," called Clay. It was after eight on Friday and everyone had already started their weekends.

"Jess?" He threw his briefcase on the bed. "Did you save me a plate?"

Friday night, and the house was silent, Clay's Oxfords tapping against the tiles, echoing back at him like a faraway voice. Usually Jess was home by now, but there was no sign of her.

"Jess?" he called again, listening for her voice. She must've gone out. He swung by Zoe's room. Empty. Did Jess mention a sleep over at Niki's? She was probably dropping Zoe off.

Then he remembered. They had dinner reservations for an hour ago. That's why Zoe was going to Niki's. Shit.

Maybe Jess went alone?

Clay kicked off his shoes and searched the cupboard for something to eat. He grabbed lettuce, cheese and tomato from the fridge and fixed a sandwich, biting in without cutting it into triangles, like Jess did.

He played music to break the silence. Without Zoe running around, the sound was amplified. He turned the volume down.

His phone rang. It was probably Jess, but he didn't want a fight. If it was important, she'd leave a message. He picked up his sandwich and took a bite.

Clay heard someone behind him. "Jess?" He looked over his shoulder.

A flash of dark hair caught his eye—why wasn't she answering?

He turned, as something smashed against his head. Pain exploded as his vision wavered like a bad AV cable. Before he could call out for help, everything went dark.

∞

Clay woke up in hospital feeling like he had a hangover, his head wrapped in a bandage.

A doctor in his late fifties came into the room wearing a white coat, glasses, and a name badge that said *G. Hernandez.*

Clay made it through a round of checks, blinking against the light as it flashed across his eyes.

"You might have some light sensitivity, but that's normal with a hit to the head. You were very lucky. A blow like that can be fatal. When you're up to it, there are a couple of police officers here. They would like to talk to you."

"Okay," said Clay, feeling around his head to assess the damage. A lump above his left ear hurt when he put pressure on it.

"Do you want me to send them in?"

"I want to talk to Jess."

"Are you sure you're up to it?"

"I need to talk to my wife," he said firmly.

"Okay."

Doctor Hernandez left the room.

Moments later, Jess came in with her hair down around her shoulders. She wore make-up that highlighted her eyes. The blue jeans and blouse she wore looked made for her—a glimpse of the woman he had married.

"What happened?" she asked, hugging Clay carefully so that she didn't bump his head.

The smell of her perfume made him pause. He hadn't smelled perfume when she snuck up on him—maybe she'd showered before visiting.

"Come on, Jess," he said coldly. "What'd you hit me with?" He tried to sit up, dizziness making him sink back into the pillows.

"I was taking a bath. I heard a crash and got out to see what happened. When I found you, you were on the floor. Your head was bleeding."

"You were in the *bathtub*?"

"Yeah."

"I called out, but you didn't answer."

She looked away. "I was mad at you. You missed dinner and didn't even call to say you couldn't make it—again. Where were you?"

"You were upset, so you attacked me? Jesus Jess. You could've killed me." His expression changed. "Is that what you were trying to do?"

"I didn't attack you."

A tear started at the corner of her eye, gathering eye liner as it fell.

"I saw you, Jess. When I turned around, you attacked me."

Chapter 43

Now

"Charles was your doctor?"

"Yeah."

"Wow."

Oscar sipped his drink, crushing cold ice between his teeth to slow himself. He needed to be sober for this.

"When I said Charles knew about us, you clammed up. I thought you were giving up, but I wanted to find a way through, but this is what you were worried he'd use against you." She thought about it for a moment, and added, "He'll try to pin Jess leaving on you."

"Hayley, I—"

"He told me to ask you who you really are."

Oscar ran a hand across his chin, sending pins and needles across his fingers.

"Oscar, what does Charles know?"

"Before I was at Whitner, I had a son. His name was Riley."

"You have a son?"

"He died." Oscar's stomach turned, anticipating her response. "And I fell apart."

"I'm so sorry. I didn't know," she said, squeezing his hand.

"I wanted to tell you, but I couldn't get the words out."

Her hand rested on his, scaring him from telling her the worst of it.

"I got help to deal with Riley's death. My ex-wife, Prisha, blamed me because Riley died while she was out with her friends."

Hayley moved her other hand across his. He held onto the feeling. Once he'd told her it was his fault, she mightn't talk to him again.

"I was supposed to check on him, but I fell asleep. I woke up to Prisha screaming."

Hayley listened quietly, her hands still around his.

"I couldn't move past it, so I saw a psychiatrist."

"And *Charles* was the psychiatrist?"

"Yeah."

"Did he help?" she asked, as if she couldn't imagine Charles helping anyone.

"No. I mean, at first he tried. His methods were unconventional. He wanted me to take responsibility for what happened, and I assumed it was to get to a place where I could let go of the guilt, but it wasn't. I think I was waiting for someone to tell me it wasn't my fault."

"Oscar, your son dying is *not* your fault."

"But it was. When Prisha came home that night, I heard the door open, but I didn't get up. She went into Riley's room. She was in there for hours before I heard her scream."

"Do you think she needed time to process what happened?" asked Hayley, breaking the image.

"Maybe. Prisha and I were already drifting apart, but after Riley died, she blamed me and left."

"Her son died, Oscar. She was probably projecting her feelings onto you. Maybe she was sad she wasn't there."

"Want another drink?" asked Oscar, pushing back the bar stool.

"Sure."

He waited at the bar, under the fairy lights until a barman in a tight-fitting black t-shirt took his order. Oscar chose something similar to their last drink and watched as the bartender mixed different colored liqueurs together.

Oscar carried their drinks back to the table, getting ready to continue the story.

"I was at Whitner when Charles arrived three years ago. I was trying to rebuild my life. No one knew about Riley. It was easier that way. Everyone kept asking how I was, and I never knew how to answer."

"Do you think he'll tell them about Riley? Is that what you're worried about?"

"Maybe. There was some... speculation about how he died."

"Well, it's just speculation," said Hayley. "I don't think you'll lose your job because of a rumor."

"I don't care about that. I went for the promotion because I thought Charles might leave. I'm not proud of it, but I thought if I didn't have to see him every day, no one would find out about Riley. Instead, I made Charles angrier, and he held it over me."

"I know what you're thinking, Oscar, but resigning won't fix this. You're not giving up your job for some asshole. If he wanted to bribe you, he would've done it when you got the job."

"He couldn't. He didn't have enough to back it up."

"He still doesn't," said Hayley.

"I don't want them to use Riley to get to me. He doesn't deserve that."

"Oscar, don't let him get to you. Keep letting him do what he's doing—he'll only show them what he's really like."

"I can't fight this. He said he's spoken to Prisha—she's willing to give a character statement saying Riley died before she came home."

"What?"

"Prisha always said I killed Riley that night. She didn't report it because she couldn't prove it, but she reminded me every chance she got. I think Prisha and Charles are going to use it."

"Oscar, they can't *say* anything. Your son died tragically. It's awful, but it happens. It's no one's fault."

Oscar frowned. "Someone told me that some people are good liars, but others are naturals. Prisha's a natural."

"Well, maybe you could talk to her about it?"

"And say what? *Please don't say I murdered our son?* If she's going to do this, there's nothing I can say to stop her."

"Do you have someone who can tell them what really happened? Maybe your family?"

Oscar sighed. "I have a brother, but we don't talk."

Hayley looked sympathetic, but Oscar didn't want her sympathy. He needed a solution to stop Prisha and Charles. If he resigned, maybe he could avoid the whole inquiry, but resigning didn't mean that Charles and Prisha would let it go.

"Maybe your brother could write a statement?"

Steve and Oscar hadn't really spoken since they were kids. When their mother left, she took Steve with her, and for a long time, Oscar wondered if he was the reason she left, and why she didn't take Oscar too. He'd stayed with his dad, making sure he didn't die in an alcohol-soaked stupor.

"Steve didn't know Riley."

"Oscar, listen to me. I get that you don't want to ask, but Mia needs you. If there's a chance you can find her, then try."

Did Hayley think this was about finding Mia? He didn't get Jess transferred just for Mia; he'd always suspected that Jess didn't know what happened to her. It had been too long—the chances of finding Mia weren't good, but there was still hope to save Jess. He put in the request because he knew what it was like to be in her shoes, to have no one care what happened to you.

"As much as I want the police to find Mia, it isn't my job to help her, Hayley. My job is to help Jess, but I'm not getting anywhere. Maybe it's someone else's turn to try. Maybe I've done as much as I can."

"You fought to bring her here. Why give up now?" Hayley rested her arms on the table. "Finding Mia *is* the way to help Jess. She's trapped in the aftermath. She can't move on until it's resolved."

"Do you still think she killed Mia?"

"I never said I thought that. I just asked you to consider it."

"But do you think she did?"

"I don't know, Oscar." She shrugged. "Maybe she's protecting someone."

"I've been wondering the same thing. I tried asking her about it, but it doesn't fit. Who is she protecting?"

"If she's willing to let people think she's a murderer, it must be someone close to her. Maybe her husband? Maybe it was an accident?"

Someone close to her. From what she'd said, Oscar wasn't sure Jess would lie for Clay. "I don't know—he accused her of trying to kill him. Why would she protect him?"

"Maybe that's exactly why," said Hayley. "Maybe he's using the attack to keep her quiet."

Oscar didn't believe it. "She's already locked in here. What more does she have to lose?"

"Think about it. What if Jess attacked Clay, and he agreed to drop the charges if she met the conditions he set for her?"

"Why would she cover for him? If she told the police that's what she was doing, it'd only look better for her, and show why she'd been angry enough to attack him," said Oscar.

"Yeah."

"That's why you think she attacked him, because he kidnapped Mia?"

"It fits. Maybe Mia wasn't the first." Hayley shifted uncomfortably. "Oscar, there was no evidence of a break and enter. Jess and Clay were home alone at the time. Do you really believe she didn't do it?"

He stared her down, unwavering. "No. I believe her."

"Have you met Clayton Green?"

"No, but I'd like to," he said. "I considered calling him in to see how he reacts to some gentle questioning."

"Yeah, it could provide some perspective, but it might cause Jess more problems."

"That's why I didn't call. It's strange how he hasn't even tried to see if she's changed her mind about seeing him."

"Maybe she thought he was going to hurt Mia, and she tried to stop it before it happened?" said Hayley.

Oscar flinched. That'd be a normal response, wouldn't it, to stop him from hurting Mia? Except, it wasn't that simple. Knowing someone was capable of horrible things didn't mean you could stop it.

"If not Clay, then who is she protecting?"

Oscar sighed. "I thought it might've been her sister. Jess was researching narcissists and psychopaths. She wrote an article about it. After meeting her sister Niki, I wondered if Jess was trying to understand her better."

"Is her sister a narcissist? Could she have hurt Mia?"

"Maybe."

"But why would Niki kidnap Mia?" said Hayley.

"Maybe Jess is researching narcissists and psychopaths because she's trying to understand herself?"

"I considered that too. I don't think Jess is a narcissist, and I doubt she has an antisocial personality disorder. She's compassionate."

"What does Jess think she is? Maybe she wrote the article to understand what's happening to her. If she's not ready to admit it to herself, how is she supposed to communicate it to anyone else?"

It was true. Jess might be trying to understand darker aspects of herself, but he doubted it.

"Maybe she suspects someone close to her has a personality disorder. It's not uncommon for a narcissist to turn on someone who might expose them. Maybe they got to Jess, convinced her she's the problem," said Oscar.

"Do you believe that?"

Oscar sipped his drink thoughtfully. "It would explain why she doesn't want to talk about it."

"I wouldn't want to either, especially if it gave them something to use against me," agreed Hayley.

"Exactly." He said it too sharply, as if Hayley's words were accusing him.

"Oscar, I didn't mean your—"

"It's fine. You're right. If your opponent's willing to play dirty and you're not, then guess who wins?"

"Sometimes, maybe. But not this time."

He looked at Hayley quizzically.

"This time, someone believes her—someone who's willing to fight for her, because he knows what she's going through."

"This isn't the same as Charles or Prisha. Jess still has a little girl out there waiting for her to come home, and if she didn't kidnap Mia, that little girl's growing up without a mother for no reason. I didn't have anyone relying on me when I fell apart, so it didn't matter. But if Riley was still here—"

He paused. "It's why I know she didn't kidnap Mia. If she could be with Zoe, she would."

Hayley moved a hand across Oscar's cheek and kissed him. "I don't know what I believe, but you trust her, and I trust you."

He returned the kiss.

"Fight dirty if you have to," she said.

Chapter 44

Then

Jess burst outside the hospital doors, into the fresh air. She needed to get away from Clay's accusation.

I saw you, Jessica. When I turned around, you hit me.

He had a head injury; he didn't know what he was saying.

Fighting down the pain, Jess felt around her pocket and pulled out Ray's number. She'd been carrying it with her—it made her feel less alone somehow, knowing there was someone to call if she needed to, someone that understood. She thought Clay would always be that person, but he wasn't.

They should've been there for each other, but they stopped talking. Jess told herself they needed a reason to talk again.

I know you attacked me.

Clay's words severed her hopes of reconnecting. Had they drifted so far apart that he believed she'd hurt him? Did he really think she was capable of killing him?

Jess sat near a planter box, drawing deep breaths, turning her phone over in her hands, too upset to call Ray now. She breathed deep to calm herself down. People stared and walked around her. They probably thought she was grieving a sick relative.

She took a steadying breath and stood, wiping at her eyes as she left the hospital. She dialed Ray's number and waited for a ringtone.

"Hey."

"Ray? It's Jess. I uh—Can we talk?"

"Sure. Is everything okay? You sound upset?"

"It might be better if we talk in person."

"Okay. Where are you?"

"I'm at the hospital. I can meet you in twenty minutes. Same place as last time."

"I'll be there."

∞

Jess arrived before Ray and ordered coffee. She watched the door, waiting for him to walk through. She probably shouldn't have called, but it was too late for regrets.

Ray found her as soon as he walked in. He took the chair adjacent, brow etched with concern. "What is it? Is it Mia?"

"No, Mia's fine. Someone attacked my husband last night. They broke into the house and tried to kill him."

She watched for a reaction, something to suggest he already knew about the attack, but Ray looked horrified.

"Shit. Is he okay?"

Jess looked deeper. "He will be. I thought you might've done it at first."

"Me?"

"Given what Holly said... and we met not long before the attack..."

"Why would I attack your husband?"

"I thought you might've been looking for me and found Clay

by accident."

"Okay. Remind me why I'd want to hurt you?"

She shrugged. "I don't know. Maybe something to do with Holly."

"Right. What changed? You wouldn't be here if you still thought I wanted to kill you."

"My husband, Clay, thinks I attacked him."

"What?"

"He saw dark hair and assumed it was me."

Ray nodded. "Except it wasn't, was it?"

"No."

He looked at her dark hair. "You think Holly did?"

Jess raised an eyebrow wryly.

"Why would Holly attack your husband?"

"I don't know. Maybe she was looking for me and he interrupted her. Maybe she was mad because he didn't kiss her back when she made a move."

"That sounds like Holly," said Ray knowingly. "She doesn't like hearing the word no."

"The thing is, I'm not convinced that Clay didn't kiss her back."

"Maybe he tried to end whatever she thought they had, and it made her angry?"

Jess steeled herself. She'd wondered the same, but hearing it out loud made it seem more likely. "Angry enough to try to kill him?"

"Holly has a temper, but she also has a way of making you feel like you're the problem. It's how she gets away with it."

"Surely people notice?"

"She's charming when she wants to be. The people who notice the real Holly have to decide—they can stay quiet and make sure they aren't her next target, or fight it and risk her noticing. Most people are chicken shit. I was. But you're not Jess, that's why she noticed you."

Kat's words rushed back. *Find out whether she knows what you are.*

Is that what Jess was to Holly—someone who might bring her lie undone?

"What if we're wrong and this isn't about Clay?"

"What do you mean?"

"What if she saw us talking, Ray? It could be a warning."

Jess looked around. Holly seemed to turn up everywhere else. Why not here? She hadn't told Clay she was meeting with Ray. If Holly saw them together and told Clay, it would look bad. *Bored wife tries to kill her husband so she can move on with her boyfriend.* She wouldn't put it past Holly, who had already made her look unstable to her friends. Jess still felt the embarrassment when she remembered her pills tapping against the floor as she scrambled to catch them. She wouldn't forget Holly's smirk as she scooped pills back into the bottle.

"How would she know we talked? I gave her the money, she gave me a couple of pictures of Mia, and she drove off."

"Maybe she saw us and decided to hang around to see what happened. What would Holly do if something spooked her?"

"Shit. Mia."

"Ray, I think you're right to worry about Mia."

"You think I don't know that? If Holly snaps, she could hurt her. If Holly put your husband in hospital, I don't want to know what she could do to a four-year-old."

"It's okay. Mia's her daughter. Hitting a grown man with a meat tenderizer is different to hurting your own child."

"You don't understand," said Ray. "Holly's not like you or

me. She doesn't feel things the same way. To her, Mia's no more important just because she's her daughter."

"What do you mean?" said Jess.

"I think Holly's a psychopath. She looks at the world in terms of how everything affects her. It's like she's the axis and everything spins around her but she's not affected by any of it."

"She's affected. She doesn't always show it. Holly thinks she controls everything. She's afraid of finding out that's not true," said Jess.

"Maybe." Ray would need more convincing.

"Maybe we should show her what happens when it stops."

"How?"

"By stopping her from hurting anyone else."

"I don't know if we can. Things could get pretty bad if it backfired."

"I interviewed someone similar to Holly recently. It was for an article. I chose her because she was the most like Holly. I thought it might help me figure out why Holly hates me, so I can stop her from hijacking my life."

"How can we stop her?"

"Ray, the woman I spoke to—she killed her own child. I asked her what would've stopped her."

"Did you find out?"

"She said the risk of getting caught. Knowing that someone could stop her might've changed it."

"What Jess? Why are you looking at me like that?"

"The way she said it. I don't believe her. She might've been more careful if someone knew. I don't think she was trying to help me. I think she wanted to help Holly."

Ray took his time contemplating how things might unfold.

"If Holly thinks we're watching, or that we might interfere, she'll escalate it. You said your husband believes you attacked him—what would he think about this?" Ray pointed a finger in the air, drawing a circle around them.

Jess's phone vibrated. She answered automatically.

A stern, unfamiliar voice spoke. "Mrs. Green, it's Detective Calvin Collins speaking. We need you to come to the station."

"Is everything alright?"

"We'd like to ask a few more questions about your husband's attack." His tone turned accusing. "We were hoping to finish up at the hospital, but you disappeared."

She had to go, or it would seem like she was avoiding their questions. "What time works for you?"

"You can come down now. Someone will be there to speak with you."

"Now?"

"Is that a problem?"

"No. I'll be there."

Jess ended the call. "The police want to talk to me. I think Clay told them I attacked him."

"What did they say? Are they arresting you?"

"I don't know."

"We need to find out if Holly saw us talking."

Chapter 45

Now

Oscar knew it was Clay as soon as he walked into Whitner.

In summer, his light brown hair could pass for blonde. Like his clothes, his hair was neat and styled stiffly. Oscar could tell he wasn't the type of person who dressed for comfort. Clay Green looked showy and preoccupied with achievement.

Oscar observed at a distance, trying to find out the sort of person Clay was underneath the veneer. A little girl with the same brown hair held his hand obediently, a rag doll tucked under her arm as she looked around, eyeing the walls as if Whitner was too big to take in. Oscar couldn't imagine Clayton Green at the park with his daughter, or sitting on the floor having a tea party. Zoe must be missing her mom.

"Mr. Green, I'll have to ask before I can let you through," said Chloe, smiling politely.

"I have her daughter here to see her. Please, make sure she knows Zoe's here."

"Of course," said Chloe, excusing herself.

Oscar watched Clay wriggle his hand from Zoe's. He leaned across the desk, flicking through the visitor's sign-in log.

What was he looking for? Was he checking who'd visited Jess? As far as Oscar knew, Clay didn't know anyone besides Jess at Whitner.

Who would visit her? Niki?

It was a skill of Oscar's, blending into his surroundings, observing people before they noticed they were being watched. You could learn a lot.

Oscar wanted to learn how Clay acted when no one was watching, but Clay's guest had already spotted him.

He waved at Zoe, who watched curiously with inky blue eyes. She waved back, the movement catching Clay's attention. He leaned down and whispered something to his daughter, who nodded apologetically at Oscar—whatever warning he'd issued, she didn't agree.

Oscar approached Clay, who straightened to his full height. It looked, like he'd dressed up to visit his wife, but Oscar guessed the gelled hair, the jacket and the pants were part of Clay's everyday uniform.

The smell of cologne wafted, something from this year's collection—a smell Oscar remembered from the lifts in his financial advisor's building. It was over applied, the stronger tones overpowering the subtleties of the fragrance.

Clay eyed Oscar derisively.

"Hi. I'm Oscar de la Nuit, Jessica's psychiatrist."

"Clayton Green. I'm Jessica's husband."

"Hello," said a little voice.

"And this is my daughter, Zoe."

"Nice to meet you," said Oscar, smiling at Zoe.

"Do you know my Mommy?"

"I do," said Oscar.

"I came here to see her," said Zoe. "I miss her. Does she

have her own room? At home she has to share with daddy. I made her a picture. Can I give it to her?"

Oscar smiled. If Riley was alive, he would be a little older than Zoe. Would've he visited Whitner, maybe to surprise Oscar with a drawing like the one Zoe was holding?

"She'll love it," said Oscar.

Zoe tucked the paper under her rag doll. She'd folded it twice, the edges not quite meeting.

"What did you draw?" asked Oscar.

"It's a drawing of me and Mommy. Daddy's not there because I'm staying here, and Daddy can't stay."

"When can we see Jessica?" asked Clay, moving Zoe slightly behind him, as if shielding her from Oscar.

"I don't know if that's a good idea," said Oscar softly, so Zoe wouldn't hear.

"The woman at the front said she'd find out. Who does she need to ask before I can see my wife?"

"She's probably asking Jessica, but please, don't get your hopes up—she might not be ready for visitors."

Oscar stood unflinching as Clay's words ripped through his tense jaw. "We're not visitors. Zoe's her *daughter.* It's been so long since Zoe saw her that she asked if Jess was dead. She didn't believe me when I told her Jess was alive, so I brought her here to show her."

"I understand. That must be difficult, but I don't want to get your hopes up."

Oscar looked at Zoe's expectant face. How would she feel if her mother couldn't see her—would she take the rejection personally? Of course she would—it would confirm her worst fears, that her mother must've done something bad.

"I can talk to her, see whether I can coax her out," Oscar

offered for Zoe's sake. Clay Green seemed angry more than concerned for his wife's well-being.

Zoe traced the pattern on the facade of the front desk.

"Zoe, don't go too far."

Is that how it was at their home, with Clay calling the shots and everyone going along with his decisions?

"First, I need to ask something."

"What?"

Oscar lowered his voice, watched Zoe's little hand move across the raised silver panels on the desk, intentionally avoiding eye contact as he spoke to Clay. "Do you still believe your wife attacked you?"

He caught Clay's expression, the flash of annoyance. "If the coward didn't attack me from behind, I wouldn't have been the one on the floor," said Clay.

"Do you think someone else might've attacked you?"

"You're her doctor, what did she tell you?"

"Jessica thinks someone was in your home. Can you think who it might've been and why they'd do that?"

Clay watched Oscar, his expression guarded, deciding how much to say. He didn't realize he was already telling Oscar a lot, even in his silence.

He turned to look at Zoe, who was happily engrossed, exploring a new environment. "My wife was the only other person there. Zoe was at a sleepover, and when I turned, I saw a brunette. That's why I thought it was her."

Clay hadn't answered the question.

"Do you still think it was Jessica?"

Clay's shoulders moved upward, the shrug involuntary. "I don't think this is the place to discuss it," said Clay stiffly, missing the irony.

Zoe hummed a tune, letting her rag doll take a turn tracing the patterns. She guided its arm across the edges, avoiding the smooth parts. Had she talked to someone about the changes in her life? It must have been hard losing her mother so suddenly.

"Of course," said Oscar.

Clay sighed. "When I asked her why she did it, she acted... hurt."

"And that's why you thought it mightn't have been Jessica?"

"Maybe—"

He stopped short, something ahead grabbing his attention.

Oscar's eyes followed.

"Zoe, come back here!" called Clay, but Zoe was already in motion, her legs gaining speed as she ran, the rag doll discarded at the foot of the desk.

She stopped in front of Jessica and threw her arms around her. "Mommy. I miss you. Can I stay with you?"

Jess caught Zoe before she crashed into her. "Zoo, what are you doing here?" she asked, her voice breaking. She held Zoe, leaving a gap between herself and Clay.

"Jessica—I had to bring her. She's five. She doesn't understand. Hell, I don't understand. Zoe won't stop asking for you. She thought you were *gone*." He said it with finality. The kind of gone that only happens when you die.

"I told you I didn't want her to come here," said Jess robotically, looking over Zoe's head at her husband.

Clay pulled at the bottom edge of his jacket, aligning the sides as he stepped forward, ignoring Jess's tone.

She tensed as he moved forward, but if he noticed, it didn't stop him. Gently, he took Zoe from Jess's arms and set her down. "Pick up your doll, Zoe. I need to talk to your mom."

Jess nodded. "Go on sweetie."

Clay wrapped his arms slowly around Jess and whispered in her ear. "Why didn't you want to see us? I know you didn't attack me," he said, trying to smooth their visit for Zoe's sake. "I know you didn't kill that little girl. I want to be here for you."

Jess looked at Oscar, her chin resting over Clay's shoulder, her arms at her sides. Oscar felt like he was intruding on a private moment, but he couldn't look away, searching for hints of what'd happened.

Did they share a secret? Were they hiding Mia somewhere together?

Zoe sat with her back against the front desk, drawing her knees close. She picked up her rag doll and hugged it, watching her parents with big, bright eyes.

"Jess, you can't do this alone. You need us to get through it."

Jessica withdrew from Clay's hug. "You told me you wouldn't bring her here. You told me you understood, that you'd look after her."

"I know what I said, but you don't know what it's been like for us, for Zoe. I've stopped reporters from talking to her when they think no one's around to stop them. We don't watch television in case they say something about you. We don't listen to the radio. I can't take Zoe out for ice cream or a movie, in case someone recognizes us."

"I know," said Jess. "That's why I told you to leave, and start again where nobody knows who you are."

"And what then, Jessica? Once we do that, it's like admitting you're guilty. It'll show them we've given up on you too."

Jessica's face changed, warning bells going off in Oscar's head. The rage and frustration burst, releasing everything she'd been holding in. She had the same expression Oscar saw when Chrissie called her a baby killer.

"Clay, move," said Oscar, pressing the alert button behind the desk.

Clay turned towards Oscar.

"Jess, don't!" called Oscar, hoping he could change her mind before she acted.

She drew a knife, looking wistfully at her daughter. It looked like Jess was about to make a decision that would keep her here for a long time.

"Sorry," she whispered, and plunged the knife into Clay's leg.

Chapter 46

Now

Oscar pulled Jess to the floor, but the knife had already hit. Clay howled in pain, Zoe matching his howls when she saw the blood.

Hayley emerged from her office, calling directions for everyone to follow.

Oscar kept a hold of Jess as she sobbed, the fight gone now that she'd done what she needed to. "I told you not to bring her here. Go home and don't come back," she said, her tone cold.

Zoe looked at her father as he cradled his leg, rocking back and forth. She ran toward Jess, lost in the chaos, as Charles tried to pull Jess away.

She resisted, pulling free from his grip.

"Someone call an ambulance," said Charles, trying to take charge of the situation while Hayley soothed Clay.

"It's fine. I don't need an ambulance," said Clay.

"You're the only one with a free set of hands, Charles," said Oscar. He caught sight of Zoe, lost and unsure of what to do. Oscar smiled. "It's okay," he said, as she ran to him.

"I've got it," said Chloe from behind her desk.

Charles took Jess by the arm and led her away from the commotion, her feet dragging behind her. "Don't just stand there," he called to a young orderly. "Help me out."

Zoe called after Jess with a terse voice.

"It's okay," soothed Oscar. "She'll be alright." Why didn't Zoe run to her dad? Maybe the blood dripping from his leg scared her?

"Hey, it's okay, Zoe. I'll look after her, I promise."

Zoe gathered herself the best a five-year-old can, talking in bursts between her sobs. "I don't want to go back," she cried. "I want to stay here."

"Zoe," called Clay in a booming voice.

She turned away from Clay, dark pigtails swinging, reminding Oscar of Lila's plaits. "Are you really going to look after my mommy?"

"Of course," said Oscar, charmed by Zoe's bravery.

"Promise?"

"Yeah. I promise."

"Mommy's going to get in trouble for hurting Daddy, isn't she?"

"Yeah, I think she might be in trouble."

Zoe hesitated before stepping forward. "Can I tell you a secret?" Zoe steadied her breath and avoided looking directly at Oscar.

He rested an arm gently on her shoulder, shocked at how tiny they were. Riley would have probably been a little bigger than Zoe at the same age—he was a big baby, outgrowing his newborn clothes in the first few weeks. Would've Oscar remembered details like that if they had more time together, more memories, or would've his first words and first steps replaced them?

"Mommy isn't bad."

"Of course she isn't."

"Mommy didn't hurt Mia," she whispered.

Oscar's heartbeat quickened. This could be nothing more than a little girl protecting her mother. Zoe would've seen the papers, and he could imagine what the kids at school said—he still remembered what they said to him about Lila.

But what if Zoe saw what happened to Mia?

Even a week was a long time for a child, but what if Zoe remembered? Zoe was there when Mia went missing.

"Why do you say that, Zoe? Did you see what happened?"

Zoe nodded.

"We were playing hide and seek, and Mia found a really good spot. I couldn't find her. Mommy couldn't find her either."

Chapter 47

Now

"Hey, did you want this?" asked Hayley, thrusting a coffee at Oscar. "I was wondering where you got to. I didn't expect to find you out here, hiding in the courtyard."

Oscar brushed her hand as he took the coffee. "Thanks. I needed some air."

"You look like you need some caffeine too," said Hayley.

Oscar pretended to be offended. "I just finished writing up an incident report." He tested the heat of the coffee with a sip.

She rested an arm around his shoulders. "You couldn't have known she'd snap."

"I should've seen it coming."

"Come on, don't do that to yourself," said Hayley, balancing her over-full mug in her free hand.

"Are you worried this'll affect the inquest?"

"I don't care about that," said Oscar.

Hayley retreated, her arm hovering across his shoulder.

"Sorry," he said. "It doesn't matter."

"Of course it matters. You can't give up."

"Everyone saw Jess stab Clay."

"It's not for you to ask *what* happened—that's for the police. You need to keep asking *why*."

"What if we don't find Mia? What if it really is too late?" asked Oscar.

Hayley sipped her coffee, lips lingering at the edge of the mug.

"Why did she stab him?" Oscar sat up a little straighter. "It was so cold—almost as if she wanted to keep him away."

"Oscar, maybe Jess knows what happened to Mia."

"You're wondering if she killed Mia?"

"It's looking more likely," said Hayley regretfully. "You saw what she did to her husband. It's not the first outburst she's had. He'll need stitches."

"That's not the same as kidnapping," said Oscar, abandoning his coffee in a potted plant. He'd never been much of a gardener.

"Oscar, please. I'm not saying she did."

"Really? Because it feels like you think you can do my job better than I can."

"I thought we were having a discussion, like we used to, before..." she trailed off.

"Before what?"

"Before we became—I don't know, Oscar. You tell me. What are we?"

Did Hayley really want to discuss their relationship now? "I can't do this now. I'm sorry. I need to take care of this mess with Jessica," said Oscar. He left, wishing he could make things better, but knew he'd probably made them a whole heap worse.

Chapter 48

Now

Oscar found Jess's bed made up, white sheets wrapped around the mattress like a Christmas present, rag doll leaning against the pillows.

He inspected the rag doll closer and found stuffing oozing from its back like an open wound. He took the rag doll with him to the lobby.

The front desk was quiet. Chloe had gone home for the day, a bored-looking woman named Eloise taking her place. "Was there something you needed?" she asked, adjusting her oversized cardigan to stay on her shoulder.

"Yeah. Jessica Green isn't in her room. Do you know where she went?"

"Just a sec." She typed something and hit the mouse.

Oscar drummed his fingers across the front desk, the impatient gesture earning him a look he ignored.

"She's in recovery. Go through and ask at the triage desk. They should be able to help."

Oscar thanked Eloise and went to triage, where he was directed to Jessica's temporary bed.

Four beds occupied the room, plastic curtains separating patients just enough to provide some privacy.

Oscar found Jess in bed three, staring at the ceiling. Her eyes were flat and disinterested, despite Oscar ruffling the curtain.

"You can go in, doctor," said a passing nurse.

"Thanks." Oscar stepped inside. "Jess?"

She turned, looking him in the eye. "Where were you?"

"I asked to visit earlier, but they were still fixing you up," said Oscar, looking her over for injuries. "I thought they would've released you by now. How do you feel?"

"Fine," said Jess, glassy eyes belying her tears.

"You said you didn't want trouble," said Oscar. "But we're gonna have a world of it now."

She turned, rolling across the pillow, away from him.

"What happened?" he asked, holding the rag doll up to show the damage.

"I found it like that in my room. I was going to fix it."

"It reminds me of a scarecrow, full of stuffing instead of straw," he said, poking the stuffing. He ran a thumb across the smooth fabric on the front of the doll.

"A straw man," said Jess.

"Yeah." Her words made Oscar think. "Have you heard of the *straw man fallacy*?" he asked.

"No."

"It's used to discredit someone's argument by drawing conclusions that aren't based on that argument. Like someone asking someone if they prefer chocolate or broccoli, and then arguing the person is against healthy food when they say they prefer chocolate."

Jess considered the concept.

"Or someone choosing not to speak to the police, and being

labeled guilty because only a guilty person wouldn't talk."

"Yeah," said Oscar. "Like that."

Jess sighed. "Or keeping someone locked up when you have no evidence, but releasing them might seem negligent."

"I think you use the same logic to punish yourself."

"How?"

"You took responsibility for Mia because she went missing from your house. You tell yourself you weren't paying enough attention to stop it."

"Is that what *you* do?" She turned back to Oscar.

"It's partly why I transferred you here. When Riley died, I thought the same things about myself. I told myself that I didn't check on him because I cared more about some extra sleep than I did about my son."

"That's not true," said Jess, taking the rag doll from his hands.

"I might lose my job," said Oscar. "Charles is saying we haven't made progress. He'll recommend someone else take over your treatment."

"They're firing you?"

"I don't care if they do," he said. "I never liked the politics anyway, but I want to help you before I leave."

"You're leaving?"

He looked away, unable to meet her eyes. "I thought I could help you, but maybe I'm not the right person."

"Charles?" said Jess. "I know him. He came in earlier, asking me questions about Clay. He said he should've been my doctor."

"Charles was here?"

"Yeah."

"Did you talk to him?" asked Oscar.

"Would you?" she scoffed.

Oscar shrugged and sat in a chair next to Jess. "I did once. He was my doctor."

Jess snorted. "You saw a psych?"

"Yeah. It's part of debriefing as a psychiatrist. After my son died, I had a lot to work through."

"I overheard him talking about you with another doctor. He doesn't seem to think you're cut out for psychiatry."

"He knows a lot about my past," said Oscar.

"Like what?"

"My childhood, for one. It was tough. My dad was violent to my brother and I. He gave my mom a rough time, too. The only redeemable thing about him was that he never hit my little sister. I didn't think I'd survive it, but I did. Then I had a son, and I wanted to give him everything I didn't have."

"I understand," said Jess, her words loaded with layers Oscar might never peel away.

"Sometimes, you can't give them the important things. It was like that with Riley. I couldn't protect him."

"You tried. The way you talk about him—I can tell."

"Don't make the same mistake. If you wrote that article about psychopaths because you know one, you need to be there to protect Zoe. You can't protect her in here."

Jessica's eyes welled. "I can't protect her out there."

Oscar moved closer.

"I worry every day about how the world could hurt her."

"Protect her from what you can, and be there through the things you can't. Don't let her grow up wondering if she can trust you."

"You don't understand."

"Don't I?" He pulled up a chair.

Working at Whitner, around Charles every day, was a constant reminder of another time. Oscar thought if he helped Jess and Mia, it'd make up for the things he couldn't do for Riley.

He couldn't keep living as if he'd died with Riley.

Watching how Mia's disappearance had affected Jess showed Oscar how guilt kept you trapped, but he owed it to Riley to live.

"We protect the people we love because we don't think they're capable of terrible things." He paused, deciding how to continue. "When we find out they are, it seems surreal. When Riley died, it seemed like Prisha found him in his crib."

"That's not what really happened, is it?" she asked.

"I heard the nursery door open. Riley stirred, but he settled, and I went back to sleep. Prisha's screams woke me; she must've realized what she'd done."

"Did you tell anyone?"

"Yeah. I told Charles during therapy. He convinced me it was grief playing tricks on me, that I was trying to find something to blame to make sense of what happened."

"Is that true?"

Oscar shook his head. "I didn't have evidence. I couldn't put Prisha through that before I knew what'd happened. If I'd checked on Riley, he'd probably be alive. If Prisha killed him, I could have stopped her."

"Is that why you think you and I are the same? You think Clay hurt Mia and I'm scared to say it in case I'm wrong?"

"Did he?"

"You're the doctor, you tell me?"

Oscar steadied his thoughts in silence. The rest of the hospital was hotter than his office. The heat made it hard to think, just like the night Riley died, coated in a warm haze that lulled him to sleep.

"At first, I wondered if you stabbed Clay because he hurt Mia and left you to take the blame. I thought maybe Clay triggered a response in you," said Oscar. "I saw you look at Zoe before it happened. You were sorry that she was there to see it."

Jess hugged her knees, folding herself until she occupied as little space as possible.

"I've been thinking about it since," said Oscar. "When you saw Clay, you told him to go home, like your house was somewhere he belonged."

Tears fell across Jess's cheeks, streaking her neck like old scars.

Oscar placed his hand over hers. "If Clay hurt Mia, you wouldn't have told him to go home."

Jess nodded.

"You wanted to make sure he didn't bring Zoe back. You were trying to keep her safe, weren't you?"

"Always," said Jess, her throat constricting.

"Zoe knows what happened, Jess. You can't protect her from it. She was there when Mia went missing. I think she saw what happened."

"What do you mean?"

Jess eyed Oscar cautiously. "She told me they were playing, and that Mia hid somewhere," he said.

"They were," said Jess wistfully. "I hoped her memories would fade. I wanted her to move on and have a normal life, but she can't do that with me there, and everyone thinking I murdered her friend."

"Jessica, Zoe isn't likely to forget her mother disappearing from her life, or why it happened. She'll probably remember this forever."

"Zoe and Mia had a rocky start. When I found out Mia was Holly's daughter, I was worried about the girls being friends, but then I met Mia. There was something about her that seemed... lonely. I don't think Mia had a friend in the world until she met Zoe."

"Why was Mia at your house? I mean, it sounds like you and Holly weren't really friends."

"Holly was going somewhere with Niki, so when Niki dropped Aiden off, Holly dropped Mia too. It was her way of letting me know they were having fun without me."

"Why would she do that?"

"I know how it sounds," said Jess. "But that's why she did it. It was always just enough to notice but not enough to make a fuss about without me seeming petty."

"Holly wanted me to know she was calling the shots, going to lunch with Niki while I watched the kids. She sent Mia to my house with a broken arm. I knew she'd say it happened at my home. If I'd known she was setting me up for this..." She gestured around the room.

Why would Holly stage Mia's kidnapping just to make Jess suffer?

"I believe you saw something in Holly no one else wanted to see. You saw she was hurting Mia, and you tried to stop her, but things got out of control."

"I tried, but Holly won."

Oscar squeezed her limp hand, as if trying to bring it back to life. She curled her fingers and squeezed back.

Chapter 49

Then

Word spread that Jess had tried to kill her husband. She walked Zoe to class as parents stepped out of the way, not hiding their surprise at her presence. Complaints would follow. It didn't matter whether she was innocent. What mattered was the reputation of the kindergarten.

When Jess made eye contact, they looked away. Their conviction made her question whether they were right—was she the sort of person who'd hurt someone? She always believed that if it came down to it, she wouldn't be able to save herself, but now that someone had entered her house and threatened her family, she wasn't so sure.

What if someone had hurt Zoe instead of Clay? The most infuriating part was that the police refused to listen when she asked them to find the intruder. They were still out there. They could come back.

"Jessie, honey—I didn't expect to see you here. Are you alright?" asked Niki, curling an arm protectively around Jess's shoulders. "How's Clay?"

Niki grabbed Aiden's bag as he threw it and ran off to play, hauling the strap over her shoulder, catching other parents' watching Jess as if she might explode into a fit of rage.

Jess had seen them too. She almost felt sorry they couldn't see the real threat in their lives. They'd prefer to blame her and maintain their sense of security. If it was Jess who attacked Clay, there was no stranger out there, ready to do the same to them.

"I'm sorry you're caught up in this," said Jess, worried the mishap with Clay would affect Niki too.

A woman with a son in another class whispered to her friend and pointed at Jess. The friend gasped, probably hearing the news for the first time, and stared at Jess. "Her?" she whispered, loud enough for them to hear. "She doesn't seem like the type."

Niki moved Jess to the other side, shielding her from the looks that followed them.

"What the fuck are you staring at?" demanded Niki. "You've seen the news, huh? Well, newsflash—she *isn't* the type, but I damned near wish *I* was, to wipe that stupid look off your face."

"Nik, don't. It's fine," said Jess uncomfortably.

When she was satisfied the women had moved on, Niki grabbed Jess's arm, leading her away. "Let's get the kids to class and get out of here. It's like they think you don't have ears to hear their stupidity." She looked behind, making sure they heard.

"Let it go," said Jess. "Things are bad enough."

The bell signaled the start of class, and Jess and Niki rounded up the kids, avoiding another confrontation. Jess kept her eyes on the ground, embarrassed by the looks Niki was giving unsuspecting parents.

Once the kids were in class, Jess left, breathing easier.

The sound of boots clapped against the sidewalk, grabbing Jess's attention.

Niki's arm slid away as the boots stopped in front of them.

"Holly!" said Niki, leaning in for a quick hug.

"Hi," said Holly, almost including Jess. She looked from Jess to Niki. "Is everything okay?"

Jess saw a hint of amusement in Holly's eyes. Holly knew. Word travelled fast. She was just being cruel, trying to make Jess say it.

"It's nothing. Don't worry about it." Niki rolled her eyes, ignoring the exiting kindergarten moms sneaking glances at them.

"Well, we're late again," said Holly, despite no one asking. "Mia wouldn't get ready this morning." She nodded toward Mia, who was balancing her backpack, trying not to topple with the weight.

"The bell just went, so we won't keep you," said Niki.

"Ah, five minutes more won't hurt," said Holly, turning to Jess. "I heard what happened to Clay. How is he?"

"He's fine. Thanks for asking," said Jess tersely.

"Yeah, he's fine, but the rumor mill is going full speed. I overheard some of it. They think Jess attacked Clay," said Niki.

Holly's eyes widened. "Really? That's awful."

Niki missed the amusement in Holly's voice. "Yeah. I'm taking her for coffee now," said Niki.

"Well, I can come. I'll drop Mia off and be back in a sec."

Niki's brow creased apologetically. "Sorry. It's just sister stuff today, but maybe next time?"

Holly narrowed her eyes, almost imperceptibly, watching

Jess. "Oh, that's okay. Have fun then."

They reached Niki's car. "Oh no," said Niki.

"What's wrong?" asked Jess.

"I think I left the keys in Aiden's bag. Wait here, I'll get them."

"Okay," Jess called to Niki's back, but Niki was already racing toward the classroom.

Jess waited, head down. If people were still staring, she didn't want to know. The sound of buckled boots made her flinch, the noise reverberating through her head.

"Well, Mia's in," said Holly. "Better late than never, right?"

"Yeah," agreed Jess. "Zoe's the same some mornings—it's like you can't get moving, but then when they need to stay still, they go into over-drive."

Holly laughed. "Yep, that about sums it up. Listen, how is Clay, really?"

"He's recovering," said Jess.

"Maybe it was an intruder looking for things to sell?"

"Maybe."

"Either way, I hope he feels better soon. Tell him for me?"

"Yeah, sure." Jess wrapped her arms around herself, silently hoping Niki would hurry back so she could leave without seeming rude.

"You're lucky, Jess. Clay's a nice guy. We're not all that lucky. Maybe he has a friend he can introduce me to? I haven't dated much since Ray."

Jess avoided eye contact with Holly. What if she knew Jess had spoken to Ray? "Maybe," said Jess non-committal.

"You know, sometimes people seem nicer than they really are. It's only when you're in the pits with them that you see what they're made of. Ray was always charming to everyone else. He was a great liar. People bought it. If you met him, you'd see what I mean.". Her knowing tone made Jess uncomfortable. She stepped back, creating distance between them as Holly closed in like a piranha, all sharp teeth and no substance.

"Relationships can be tough. We've all thought about it."

Did Holly think Jess would talk to her about Clay?

"I didn't attack my husband."

"Fine. I'm just saying, you're the only one who knows the truth. And Clay, of course. But the truth won't stop people talking." Holly raised an eyebrow. "See you around, Jess."

Jess watched Holly leave, her footsteps heavy, like she was trying to crack the concrete, dark hair swishing against her back.

Holly's words felt threatening. Maybe she was driving the rumor that Jess tried to kill Clay.

Clay was probably sitting in his hospital bed, a food tray off to the side, the pain in his head numbed by morphine.

He said he remembered dark hair, but lots of people had shoulder length black hair, including Holly.

Except Clay wouldn't expect Holly in their kitchen. He barely knew her, so why would she attack him?

Maybe he'd realize the head injury was clouding his memory and figure out that Jess wouldn't hurt him.

Perhaps Holly had set Jess up? Clay could've told Holly anything about their relationship on their ice cream date—he might've given her enough information for her to formulate a plan. He had a habit of saying what he thought, even to complete strangers. All Holly needed was an inkling that Clay would doubt Jess in order to exploit it.

"Got em," said Niki, returning with keys looped around her

finger. “What’s wrong? You look like you’ve seen a ghost.”

Jess couldn’t make small talk over coffee now.

“Niki, I really appreciate you trying to distract me, but I have to go. Sorry.”

Chapter 50

Now

Jess entered Oscar's office, closing the door gently behind her. She sat uninvited, testing Oscar's mood with a tentative smile.

He recognized it as an apology, silent but sincere.

"You look better than last time I saw you," said Oscar.

"Yeah well, last time I was out of my mind on meds and in shock from what I... Well..."

From stabbing Clay. She didn't have to say it. It was a last resort, and Oscar wouldn't make her relive it. If people doubted if she was responsible for the first attack, they were probably more certain now.

"I still don't understand what happened. You surprised me, and that's rare."

"Did I get you in more trouble? You're still here, so that's got to be a good sign."

Oscar smiled. "Yeah. For now."

"If you're still here, they'll probably keep you, right?"

"Well, I haven't had that meeting to discuss how you left Whitner, and now they'll probably want to talk about what happened to Clay."

"Sorry about that. About all of it. Actually, I wanted to thank you."

"What for?"

"You didn't give up on me. I seem to make things difficult for everyone, but it hasn't stopped you from trying with me. At least not yet." She looked pointedly at Oscar. "You said a few things that made sense—so thanks for that too."

"Jess, I probably won't be allowed to treat you anymore. They'll find someone else, and I'd like to say it'll be great, but there's a chance it'll be Charles."

"Shit," said Jess. "I thought he was just trying to scare me when he said that." She looked out of the window. Oscar tried to guess what she was thinking. "The plant's new," she said.

"Yeah, I put it on the sill to brighten the window."

"It's so... green," said Jess.

"It's also easy to grow. I'm not good with plants. That plant is my entire garden, and I still don't like its chances."

"Clay's the same—not that he has ever *tried* to grow a plant."

Whenever she started talking about anything personal, she stopped herself, afraid to say too much.

Oscar waited for her to continue, filling the silence when she didn't. "Why do you do that?" he asked.

"What?"

"You open up a little, then clam up even more."

She shrugged.

"I think you're afraid that if you open up, you'll keep going. There's something you're avoiding, but part of you wants to talk about it."

"And you think I should tell you?"

"Maybe. That's up to you. But if I'm not the person to

talk to, tell me now and I won't fight for it tomorrow when they're deciding whether I should continue your treatment. I'll suggest someone who I think could help instead."

"Maybe you're the right person," she said. "I just, I don't know what to say—it's my fault Mia went missing."

"You're still blaming yourself. Maybe the guilt's stopping you from moving on. It might be stopping you from remembering what happened that day."

Jess claimed she was in the bathroom when Mia went missing. Did whoever took her wait until Jess left before they took Mia?

"I don't know," she wiped at her forehead with the back of her hand. "Maybe we could talk about something else."

"Sure."

Oscar turned down the heating and poured cold water for them both.

"You want to know why I attacked Clay when he was visiting, don't you?"

He could mull it over forever with Hayley, but he needed to hear Jess say why she did it. "Yeah."

"You want everything to have some kind of reason, but sometimes it just is what it is."

"I think there's more to it than that. Maybe you need some help to figure it out."

"I don't need help. I'm not some basket case." She sounded defensive—the help she'd received before wasn't really helpful, so it wasn't surprising.

"I know. I want to work through this with you."

"There's nothing to work through. Leave me the hell alone."

"Is that really what you want? Or what you're telling yourself?"

She chewed the edge of her thumb, working the nail until it started bleeding. "At first, I thought you attacked Clay because you wanted to hurt him for leaving you in here. I thought that maybe he kidnapped Mia and let you take the rap."

Jess frowned.

She didn't believe Clay had anything to do with Mia's disappearance. "I already told you," said Jess, looking at Oscar. "I know. But you also told me that Holly kidnapped Mia, and we both know that's a lie."

Jess looked away.

She acted disinterested, fixating on her fingernail. Oscar could feel the question burning, but she couldn't ask how he knew that without raising more questions. "I'm not saying that Holly's a good person, or that she didn't hurt Mia, but she didn't stage a kidnapping."

Jess bit down harder on her thumb, using her teeth like a clamp.

Oscar couldn't watch her hurt herself. "Does Zoe know what happened to Mia? Is that why you've kept her away?"

She released her thumb. "I kept Zoe away because it's a *psychiatric* hospital, and she's just a little girl. Would you want your son to visit you here?"

Oscar closed his eyes, shielding himself against the pain Riley's memory evoked. He opened them and looked at Jess. "Honestly? If I could have my son back, I wouldn't care where I saw him. I'd take every moment I could."

"Sorry," said Jess. "I shouldn't have said that."

"No, I'm sorry. I know you want what's best for your daughter. Maybe keeping her away is the only way you can help her right now, but your absence will leave a gap worse than anything else in her life."

"I couldn't stand if Zoe thought I did it." Jess slipped her hands into her sleeves until just the ends of her fingers poked out. "She's five. Her biggest worry should be how much glitter her backpack has on it, and if her plaits are the same length, not whether her mother killed her friend."

"Then help me prove you didn't, so she doesn't have to wonder."

Oscar read her reactions to his words, despite her best efforts to seem aloof. "I already told you I killed her. If my daughter looks at me like she doesn't trust me, it's because I deserve it."

"You don't deserve that."

"Yeah, I do." She held his gaze. "But Zoe doesn't."

Chapter 51

Now

Oscar stood on Prisha's doorstep and rang the bell. This was his last chance to find out what Charles had on him before the inquiry. He almost backed out, afraid of making things worse. If Prisha wanted to help Charles, then showing up at her house might encourage her, especially if she was still mad at him. Even if he was fired, leaving Whitner might not be so bad.

Seeing Prisha at the door, highlights in her hair, looking like a stranger, reminded him how much he hated change.

"Oz," she said, her voice conveying her feelings. It was one of the things he used to love about her—she never left you wondering what she was thinking.

"What are you doing here?" She sounded weary, like she didn't have the energy required to deal with him.

He smiled. No one had called him Oz in a long time. "I need to talk. Is now a good time?"

"Not really." Her hand clutched the door frame, cutting her personal space off. "You didn't think to call first?"

"Yeah. I thought about it. But I figured you wouldn't

answer."

She shrugged, conceding. "What do you want?"

"I think you know. Which is why you wouldn't have answered."

She cleared the back of her throat, something she did when she was uncomfortable. She knew she was doing the wrong thing. Was she still angry enough to go through with it?

Was he still that angry with her? They'd channeled the pain from losing Riley at each other. Then Oscar realized it didn't matter whose fault it was—nothing would bring Riley back. If Prisha had hurt their son, hurting her back wouldn't make up for it. Nothing could fill the empty space he'd left.

"Okay," she said. "I'm going to need more information."

"Prisha, what did Charles say to you?"

She looked away. "He mentioned there was a situation at work. Apparently, all the women you're around want to run away. A patient of yours?"

Her attempt to pick a fight was indelicate, an attempt to deter him. If she was successful, he'd leave and she could pretend she was doing the right thing.

Oscar wouldn't make it so easy. If he left now, he wouldn't be able to bring himself to come back. He let out a slow breath, counting as the air left his lungs. It was a technique he ran through with patients who had anxiety.

"Can I come in for a few minutes?" He moved forward as he asked. Most people naturally moved out of the way. If she stood there, that would be openly confrontational, and most people wanted to avoid seeming unfriendly.

It worked. She stepped to the side and Oscar walked through. "I heard you're making a statement?"

She raised an eyebrow, and Oscar stopped. She was enjoying

this too much. Oscar needed something, and she'd make him work for it.

"Prisha, I could get fired."

"What do you want, Oscar?" she asked, already bored.

"I want to know what you said to Charles. Why are you helping him?"

"I didn't need to say much. Charles knew about a lot of things." She folded her arms and waited, daring him to answer.

"Charles was my therapist. When Riley died, I needed to work through some things." Oscar sat on the sofa that used to be theirs.

"It sounds like you had a lot to say about me," she said. "Which is probably why you never told me about it."

Oscar sat on the edge of the sofa, his feet on a thin cotton rug that looked new. Somehow, she'd managed to make all the things they'd shared look different. Their sofa faced the opposite wall, new pillows peppering the back. He felt a pang of nostalgia.

"We both had things to work through."

Her anger was like a strong wind, a warning the hurricane was still to come.

"He was my son too. Don't you think I needed someone to talk to too?"

"By the time I saw a therapist, we weren't trying to work things out together. That's why I didn't talk to you about it."

"Charles told me what you said. How could you blame me for what happened?"

"I didn't say that—"

"You didn't have to. You never do, Oscar. It's just that you don't know how to keep your thoughts inside. You feel things.

And you're bad at hiding them."

"Charles shouldn't have discussed my therapy—that was confidential."

"You think I'm stupid enough to tell them what he told me? You'll finally get what you deserve for what happened to Riley. I'll do everything I can to make sure you do."

"I came here to try to reason with you, Prisha. I wanted to talk. How are you?" he asked too late.

Prisha folded her arms. "I have nothing to discuss with you."

Oscar stood to leave, stopping next to Prisha. "Just so you know, Charles will use you for what he wants and spit you out."

She shuffled her feet, the tips of her toes flashing red with polish in her navy-blue platform sandals. "What are you worried about, Oscar? You don't hide as well as you think you do."

During Oscar's sessions with Charles, he'd said that Prisha had come home and stayed in Riley's room for hours, until he'd heard her screaming and took Riley from her arms, but it was already too late.

It took a long time sitting there for her to cry out, after she realized he was gone, and what she might have done.

"Whatever Charles said, whatever you think he has on you—don't do this. He'll use it as soon as you stop giving him what he wants."

She folded her arms. "I haven't given him anything I didn't want to give him. And once this is over, everyone will know you killed our son."

"Prisha, please don't do this."

"It's already done."

Chapter 52

Now

Oscar slammed his car door and drove without looking back or waving goodbye.

Prisha was a last ditch; he knew she probably wouldn't help him. She still blamed Oscar for Riley's death, but this was more than just taking her anger out on Oscar.

The thought of going home to an empty house made Oscar sick. He did a U-turn, speeding away from home, rows of street lights illuminating the way like beacons in the haze.

It wouldn't be difficult to move towards the light until he collided with the utility pole, free from Prisha and Charles, oblivious to what Hayley would think of him after the meeting. It wouldn't matter.

Hands off the wheel, Oscar let the car steer itself. The wheels edged to the right.

Oscar thought about Jess, trapped in the broken car, the metal bending and breaking around her. Once he let himself crash, what if he never broke free? He could stay like Jess, stuck in his own kind of hell.

Is that what it'd take for Oscar to realize he'd taken his

freedom for granted?

A car honked its horn and Oscar jerked the steering wheel, directing the tires back inside the lines. Until he knew Jess was okay, he couldn't give up. If he really wanted to end it, it didn't matter if he did it now or later.

He drove until he found a bar. He could only have a couple and still drive, but it was enough to clear his head and figure out what he should say to keep treating Jess. Charles had probably rehearsed his speech a dozen times, but Oscar wouldn't waste his time; if he had to fight that hard to prove he deserved his job, he probably didn't want it.

The phone rang, and he pulled into an empty parking space to answer it. As he cut the engine, Hayley's name lit the screen.

Oscar pocketed the phone. Talking to Hayley was too much effort—he needed to think without distractions.

The phone continued buzzing.

Hayley again.

Why is she being so insistent?

He sighed and tapped the screen. "Hey."

"Oscar! Where are you? I went to your house, but you weren't home."

"I went to Crafters for a drink."

"Okay. I'll be there soon."

"It's okay, I'm just gonna—"

Hayley ended the call before Oscar could finish his sentence. He tried calling back but she wouldn't answer, so he watched the door until she entered three drinks later.

She smiled when she saw him and strode over purposefully.

They stared at each other until Hayley broke the silence. "I'm sorry about our argument. Jessica's your patient, but when you ask what I think, it's my job to tell you the truth, like I always have."

"That's fair."

"I was trying to ask if you should consider why the police thought Jess hurt Mia. Don't ignore the evidence."

It didn't matter that she was right, what mattered was that she could be wrong.

"The evidence is only as good as its interpretation," he said.

Shadows fell across Hayley's face in the bar light, giving her a dark edge. "If you're not careful, you're going to go down with her."

"Is that what you came to say?"

She looked at his empty glass, and the one before, which wasn't cleared yet. "No. I came to keep you company. You shouldn't be alone tonight."

Oscar heard her words as if they were swimming through his head. He was feeling the effects of the alcohol—too much, too quickly.

He ordered two glasses of scotch, handing her one.

She took the glass and set it down with a thud. She was formidable when she was on a mission. "Work problems shouldn't get in the way of our personal lives, but they do anyway. You're distracted and I don't know if I should try to talk to you or stay out of your way until it's over."

"Hayley, I have to prepare for tomorrow. I might lose my job."

She sat, folding her arms. "If you don't discuss this now, the meeting won't go well anyway."

He swirled his glass, creating a whirlpool. "You know how the meeting will go? The same way you know Jessica killed Mia?"

Her eyes flashed, giving just a hint that he'd hurt her, but she hid it well. "You'll take the blame. You won't mean to, but you will, because you won't be able to hear that what she did was wrong."

The scotch stopped spinning and Oscar took a sip, pacing himself so that he could carry on their conversation.

"You think she was outside before anyone noticed because of the security measures at Whitner, but I doubt that's what happened."

"Why?"

"Jessica's an opportunist who knows how to pick the right moment." Hayley searched the bar. Oscar followed her gaze, attempting to pinpoint what she was looking for. The recycled bench tops and tables at Crafters made it feel like nothing was squandered except the customers whittling away their time with a glass in hand, making small talk and trying to forget things they didn't want to remember.

"You're saying I shouldn't take responsibility for what happened, that I should blame a *patient*?"

"No. I'm saying that you're going to take the blame for what happened, but Charles won't. I'd much rather have you as my boss than Charles." She smiled, her teeth showing.

What would she think if he told her he was considering leaving?

"Why is Jessica so important? She's your patient and I get wanting to help her, but it's like you have more invested."

"She's been through a lot. When no one believes you, it reminds you how alone you are. It's like speaking a language no one else can learn."

Hayley put a hand on his arm. "Helping her won't change what happened to you. I was wrong when I said to open up to Jessica. She's using it to manipulate you."

"Maybe, but I'm gonna try anyway," said Oscar.

"I know." She smiled. "But I had to still had to say it."

"I don't know how to reach her. We've been moving forward, but it's like walking into a hurricane."

Oscar felt Hayley's hand wrap around his. She squeezed gently.

"Oscar, Jessica *is* the hurricane."

Chapter 53

Now

Oscar went into the meeting expecting an inquisition. The room was already as full as it was going to get, with everyone who needed to be there seated.

Oscar's mentor, Caroline Taylor, waited patiently, thin arms folded atop the desk, champagne gray hair tied in a soft knot. He didn't see her much now that she was busy with board meetings, but he took her slight smile as a vote of confidence.

To her left sat the chair, Franklin, stuffed into his clothing like a sardine, uncomfortably stewing in his own skin. Each time Oscar saw him, his health seemed to have deteriorated further.

Lastly, a man Oscar's age—probably the impartial third party—sat in a navy business suit, his hair fluffed as if he had just gotten out of the shower and left it to dry.

They usually met in the boardroom as colleagues, making the meeting even more awkward. Oscar established eye contact with each of them. "Hello," he said, taking the seat Franklin offered. It already felt like they were sizing him up.

He'd been expecting Charles, but there was no sign of him.

Three was a democratic number. If it came down to a vote, it'd all be over quickly. Maybe they'd already met, and they were just there to relay the outcome.

"Thanks for coming, Oscar," said Franklin. "I know everyone's busy, so let's keep this short." He clasped his hands, making a fleshy clap, the sound peaking in Oscar's head.

He stayed out too late the night before. If Hayley hadn't been there, he might've stayed until the bar closed. Instead, she coaxed him home and stayed to make sure he was okay. It'd been a long time since anyone looked out for him. He didn't want to get used to it, in case he lost it again.

"I believe you already know Caroline?" Franklin said.

"Yes. Hello again, Caroline," said Oscar, shaking Caroline's hand, then Franklin's.

"And this is Matt Landon—Matt forms part of our legal team."

Legal team. That couldn't be good.

"Hi," said Oscar, shaking Matt's hand.

"Don't worry, I'm only here to make it official," said Matt in a tone that gave Oscar hope.

"We've reviewed an incident report that detailed the events of a patient at Whitner Psychiatric Hospital leaving the facility. I believe she is being held here voluntarily; however, she isn't allowed to leave. She may be a threat to herself or others?"

"Yes," said Oscar. He'd decided to answer only the questions they asked. Franklin enjoyed talking, so it was better to leave him to it.

"Okay, good." Franklin flicked through notes on a laptop, rejoining the conversation when he found what he was looking for. "And I believe the patient in question is in your care here at Whitner?"

"Yes."

"For the record, can you confirm that the patient in question is Ms. Jessica Green?"

"Yes."

"How is Jessica's treatment going?"

The question felt unorthodox. Was that Franklin's attempt at being social?

Oscar kept his expression unreadable—there was no point in giving them something to make out of nothing.

"Good. We've made more progress than Jess did at the remand center," said Oscar.

"Okay, such as?"

"We've discussed the events that led to her detainment," said Oscar.

"Did she say what happened to the little girl who went missing from her home?" asked Franklin, his voice even.

"We've discussed Mia Edwards, but it's not clear if Jessica knows what happened to her."

"So, you can't tell us where she is?"

Oscar cleared his throat and sipped a glass of water set out for him. "With respect, it's my job to treat Jessica Green, not to find Mia Edwards."

Caroline looked down at her hands for a moment, folded neatly in front of her, considering Oscar's words.

"Is that why you requested Ms. Green's transfer to Whitner?" asked Franklin. "You thought you'd be the best person to treat her?"

"I thought being here might help her."

"And why is that?"

Oscar straightened up. "I thought that receiving care from trained mental health professionals might help. How can someone talk about what happened to them when they're locked up, waiting to be found guilty of a crime?"

Franklin grunted. "You don't think she's a criminal?"

"It's not a judgment I'd be willing to make at the moment, no."

Matt typed notes, keys clicking under his fingers.

"We have highly trained staff at Whitner, and so far, the environment has proved a better fit for Jessica."

"Is that why she attempted an escape?" asked Franklin.

Caroline shifted in her seat, the movement making Oscar feel fidgety. He focused on Matt instead, who stared fixedly at his computer screen. Oscar suspected Matt didn't want to be here.

"Her treatment's progressing. She didn't talk while she was in preventive detention, but now she is. She left the facility because she wanted to visit someone. As much as it was the wrong way to go about it, it suggests that she's considering life after the incident."

Franklin cleared his throat. "While that might be true, from the outside it looks bad, which brings Whitner Psychiatric Hospital into question."

Oscar gave the conversation room to breathe, refusing to fill the gap Franklin left for him to defend.

"How can I prove we take this seriously, and that it won't happen again?"

Oscar considered the question. "With respect, it was my day off when that incident occurred. The team have reviewed the policy, and it seems like it was a human error."

"The report we received from Charles Aston suggests that the policies we have in place aren't being enforced under your care."

"Charles Aston was the acting director."

Franklin turned to his tablet and scrolled through his notes. "Jessica Green also attacked a visitor."

"Yeah. Jessica attacked her husband. If there was any sign she was about to hurt him, their visit would've been monitored."

Franklin sighed. "Things happen quickly. I remember what it was like working on the ward—you can't always stop the inevitable. Nevertheless, Jessica Green has a history."

"The charges were dropped," said Oscar.

"It might be in your best interest to stop treating Jessica. Charles mentioned that your relationship has crossed professional boundaries."

"That's his opinion."

"Yes. You've done a good job as director, Oscar. However, we take all claims seriously, so I'm asking for your version of what happened. We'll assign Jessica another doctor, for your protection and hers."

The bastard was waiting for something like this. He'd only been able to catch him on a couple of dirty dishes left in the staff room sink before.

"Dr. de la Nuit, that's an invitation if you'd like to take it. Why does Charles want you removed from your position? It's not the first report he's filed against you."

Franklin leaned back, readjusting his chair. "Dr. de la Nuit?"

"Not that I'm aware of. Charles went for the director's position. Maybe it has something to do with that?"

"Are you suggesting Charles Aston wants your job?"

Oscar shrugged, letting the words hang.

Caroline seemed visibly uncomfortable now, one hand working over the other soothingly.

"I don't like to bring personal matters into these things, but in this case, it's required," she interjected, ignoring the look Oscar shot her.

Damn. She remembered. And she was about to tell everyone, right in the middle of an inquiry.

Chapter 54

Now

"Go ahead," said Franklin.

"I've known Oscar for a long time," said Caroline, her voice gaining momentum.

"I don't think—" started Oscar. This wasn't the direction he wanted the meeting to go in, but Caroline had the wheel.

She looked at Oscar kindly—maybe she was trying to help, but he didn't want it.

He wanted this to play out quickly and quietly.

"That's how I know Charles Aston was once Oscar's psychiatrist."

"I see," said Franklin.

"That was a long time ago," said Oscar.

"Still, it gives Charles knowledge that could stop him from remaining impartial," said Caroline. "Oscar was going through something deeply troubling."

Franklin considered Caroline's words before turning to Oscar. "And Charles helped you through that time?"

Oscar shrugged. "He was my psychiatrist, yes."

How would Franklin react if he were the one sitting in front of his peers? Would it horrify him if his personal life was dragged out in the open?

"Oscar was working through the death of his son," said Caroline. "Which I only bring up to show that Charles isn't impartial."

They hadn't brought up Prisha's character statement yet—had she decided not to give one?

Franklin cleared his throat again. "I want to hear more about Jessica Green. When she arrived, there was an altercation with another resident. Is that correct?"

"Yes. She responded defensively to an attack."

"The day she arrived?"

"Yes. One of our long-term residents called her a baby killer—"

"And she responded with violence?"

It was easy to twist what happened, to make it seem as if Jess was violent.

"And after Jessica attacked another patient, were measures set up to prevent it from happening again?"

"We revised her medication. There's a list of what she was taking written in her notes. She also agreed to group therapy sessions to help her settle in."

Franklin flicked through the notes.

"She also attacked her husband during a visit, this time in front of their daughter."

Oscar nodded. It didn't matter what Oscar said in response; Franklin was making a point. Jessica had shown violent tendencies during her stay at Whitner Psychiatric Hospital, which showed what she was capable of.

"Oscar, you will remain in your position at Whitner Psychiatric Hospital—there was no negligence and, as you said, the day Jessica Green left the facility, you weren't there. However, someone else will oversee her treatment."

Caroline shot Oscar an apologetic look. Surely she didn't agree with their decision?

"Would you like to add anything?" asked Franklin.

Oscar sat there, processing what'd just happened. Jess wasn't his patient to help anymore. He wasn't going to find Mia, and now, he couldn't find Jessica. It was over.

He'd failed.

"Oscar, would you like to add anything?"

"No."

"The new arrangement is effective immediately. Thanks for your time, everyone," said Franklin.

Matt gathered his things and left with a quick goodbye. He clearly felt bad about removing Jessica from Oscar's care, but Oscar wasn't mad. He felt bad for the guy. He'd made a career from pissing someone off every time he did his job. How much self-loathing would you need to think that'd be a fulfilling career?

Franklin rested a hand on his shoulder. "You've handled this well. I hope you understand."

"Yeah. Of course," said Oscar, still sitting after Franklin left the room.

Caroline was the last to leave. She moved to Oscar and shook her head as if disappointed in him. "What happened? It's not like you not to fight for someone you believe in, especially a patient."

"It doesn't matter," he said.

"I remember a time when it mattered a lot, when you were studying psychiatry, and you came to me, determined to make a difference, asking if you could do an internship. What changed?"

"I was just a kid then."

Caroline softened. "I know you, Oscar. I don't see you as much as I'd like, but I know you well. After Riley died..."

"Caroline, I didn't stay in touch with anyone after Riley died. I couldn't."

"I know. But I wish if you'd reached out when you were ready."

"Sorry."

She waved a hand. "You don't need to apologize. I was worried. I just wanted to know how you were."

"I'm fine."

She saw through the veneer. "I know what you're doing. You think if you can find this girl, if you can get the truth from Jessica, it'll help make up for what happened to Riley."

"Am I that transparent?"

She moved closer, lowering her voice. "I read the report Charles filed. I'm telling you because you're my friend, and right now you could use a real one."

He worked at his brow with his thumb and forefinger, massaging the tension out.

Caroline waited until he finished. "I read Prisha's statement too."

Caroline knew Prisha. There was a time when she seemed to like her. "I want you to know that we didn't use it. It was low of Charles to ask for it."

"She's angry with me, Caroline. She still blames me for what happened. I tried to talk her out of it, but she was still so... angry."

"I remember a time when you thought she might've hurt Riley."

His face snapped up. “I never said that.”

“Not directly, no. But I remember how you punished yourself for thinking it. You were trying to find a reason for Riley’s death, but eventually you took the blame, even though you knew it wasn’t your fault. You protected Prisha.”

Oscar sank down into his chair.

“You’re doing the same thing again. Ask yourself why you’re protecting Jessica Green.”

He nodded. Caroline was one of the most perceptive people he knew. Nothing got by her. He didn’t know how she realized he was questioning what Prisha did to Riley, but if Caroline was saying he should ask himself why he was protecting Jess, there was probably a good reason.

“When you’re feeling up to it, come have coffee with Jane and I. She’d love to see you.”

Chapter 55

Then

Jess needed to warn Ray that Holly might've seen them talking, but how? A public place wasn't ideal, and she couldn't invite Ray to her house.

She sat in her car, deciding what to do. She could forget about it and get groceries to make Zoe something special for dinner—she'd be upset when she heard that Clay was in hospital.

She dialed Ray's number to warn him—if Holly paid him a visit, too, who knew how it'd end.

"Hello?"

"Hi. We uh, met the other day... it's—"

He cut her off. "Yeah, I remember."

"I'm calling because there's something you should know."

"Sure," he said easily. "You can buy me a drink at The Hull and Anchor."

"I don't think that's a good—"

"See you there in forty minutes." Ray ended the call.

Shit.

It didn't mean she had to go. What good would it really

do, telling Ray that Holly knew they'd spoken? There was no guarantee Holly would do anything, even if she knew.

Jess saw herself in the rear-view mirror and looked away. She was lying to herself about why she wanted to see Ray. He knew the real Holly too. He would understand. Usually, she'd go to Niki with something like this, or Clay, but if she tried to talk to Niki about her suspicions, she'd probably brush it off.

The engine turned, kicking over at the last second. When she arrived, she parked and went inside. The worn pillars replicating the remnants of a shipwreck, with wooden booths set up with sails separating each section.

Pictures of old ships amidst tumultuous waves lined the walls, and although it should feel suffocating, it made Jess feel energized and alive.

Ray waved her over from a table at the back.

"I wasn't expecting you yet." She slid across from him. "You said thirty minutes."

He shrugged and sipped his half-empty beer. "Yeah, I wanted some time to finish my beer."

"Jesus, why are you drinking at this time of day? Shouldn't you be at work or something?"

He shot her a look. "Shouldn't you?"

"Sorry," she said. "I'm a little irritable."

"I noticed."

It took some effort, but she ignored his comment. "She knows."

"What?"

"Holly knows we were talking. She said that even I'd fall for your charm, despite being a journalist. It might've been a random comment, but I don't think so. I don't trust her. I'm scared of what she'll do next."

"What do you mean?"

Jess shook her head. "Everyone at kindergarten knew Clay had an accident. They think I caused it. Holly made an off-handed comment about relationships being hard and wanting to leave. If she believed I hurt Clay, I don't think she would've been so understanding."

Ray shook his head, confused. "I'm not sure where this is going."

Jess glared at him, exasperated. "She knows I didn't attack Clay, because she *did.* She was playing with me."

"Okay," said Ray, processing her words.

"She started a rumor that I attacked Clay. No one'll believe that it was her. She made them believe it was me."

"I see," said Ray.

"Anyway, I thought you should know. She hates you as much as she hates me, so who knows what she's planning for you."

"She'll never let me see Mia," said Ray. "She can't do anything worse than she already has." He upended his glass.

"Yeah."

"Why would she care if we talk, anyway?" asked Jess.

"It's what she does. Her lies only work if she can isolate you. You could show everyone who she really is." Ray leaned over the table to grab Jess's hands before she moved. "Figure out what she wants, because this is nothing."

"Nothing? She tried to make it look like I wanted to kill my husband."

"That was just a warning shot. There are things you care about more than him. It's the only warning you'll get. Next time, she'll hit where it really hurts."

Jessica pulled her hands back, pressing them against her

stomach as if she could stop it from dropping. "I love my husband," she said, wondering what else Holly would do to teach her a lesson.

"Oh my god. Niki. She's been spending time with my sister lately, but they're friends. She wouldn't hurt her, would she?"

"I don't know. It might be too obvious, and she wouldn't risk blowing her cover. She needs to keep your sister on her side."

"You don't think it's Niki?"

"No. I think your sister is just another way to piss you off. And it's working. If I can see it, she can too."

"Maybe I should talk to Niki."

"And tell her she shouldn't be friends with Holly? I wouldn't. Not yet."

Jess swallowed down her frustration. Ray was right. She'd sound paranoid and vindictive if she said anything to Niki now.

Zoe.

If Clay was a warning, then Holly would use Zoe to punish Jess. She had to figure out what Holly wanted and stop her.

"Why is she doing this? What have I done to make her so angry?"

"Nothing. Or everything. It doesn't matter. Trying to understand Holly is like trying to understand how many raindrops are in a storm."

"Why me?"

"I don't know much about you, but knowing Holly, you probably got in her way. You didn't fall for the charm. You didn't jump in line to be her friend. You didn't admire her and love her. She wants you out of her way."

"Why would she need to do that?"

"So that she's free to do whatever she wants."

Chapter 56

Now

Oscar had an appointment with Jess's remand center psychiatrist, Sarah Redford.

He parked his car and walked through the lot, hands in his pockets.

Carlson Remand Center didn't look like somewhere you'd go to improve your mental health. It made Oscar think he'd made the right decision, transferring Jess.

The entrance looked cold, in cheap, clinical gray brick. The kind that was strong but gave the impression it was being used for something that wasn't worth spending money on. Even the waiting room felt forgotten, the off-white paint dull and faded straight out of the can.

"Hi, I'm looking for Sarah Redford?"

The administration officer looked from her screen to greet Oscar, a permanent smile plastered on her face. "Do you have an appointment?" she asked.

It'd always amused Oscar how some people could train themselves to look perpetually happy. He'd gotten better at it, but he'd never be good.

"My name's Oscar de la Nuit. I called earlier and Sarah said to drop by around two."

"I'll let her know you're here. If you'd like to take a seat, she'll be right with you."

Oscar sat and folded one leg over the other. Unable to get comfortable, he shifted position. He was risking more trouble by posing as Jess's doctor after she was assigned a new one, but he needed some perspective. He couldn't walk away without knowing he'd tried everything, without digging a bit deeper to find out what happened.

Oscar waited while the receptionist, whose name tag he couldn't see, called Sarah Redford. He pretended not to listen to their conversation.

"Yes," she said, glancing in his direction and lowering her voice. "He says he's Jessica Green's psychiatrist. He wants to talk to you."

She paused and nodded. "Yes. Okay, thanks."

She looked at Oscar. "She'll be with you shortly."

"Thank you."

He didn't have to wait long. Sarah looked the same as her online profile picture. She smiled, lips pursed, red curls tickling the tops of her shoulders. She sized him up with brown, unreadable eyes. By the time she reached him, she had her opinion under wraps, but he was good at reading people.

She didn't want to talk about Jess. After the media circus, he didn't blame her.

"Dr. de la Nuit, is it?"

"Yes," said Oscar, taking her hand and shaking it lightly.

"Follow me."

Oscar kept pace behind her as she walked to her office, afraid he'd bump into her if she stopped. She ushered him inside and closed the door behind them. "You're treating Jessica Green?"

"Yes."

"Please, have a seat."

He sat, looking around her office. The sofa was a muted, light gray, overshadowed by shiny vases draped in greenery. Oscar imagined Sarah had similar vases at home.

"Well?" she blurted. "What was it you wanted to talk about?"

"I was hoping to hear your professional opinion regarding Jessica Green."

"My professional opinion?"

"Yes, as her previous psychiatrist."

"She's not talking to you about what happened, is she?"

"We've made some progress."

Sarah watched him knowingly. "But not enough?"

She was right—it wasn't nearly enough, and they were out of time.

"I couldn't reach Jessica," said Sarah. "She didn't want help. She wouldn't talk to me about Mia Edwards, so I asked a colleague to speak with her. They had the same result. She was very... secretive. If you're looking for an assessment, the consensus was possible Borderline Personality Disorder."

"I'm not here for the consensus. I'm here for your assessment."

"You want me to tell you if I think she orchestrated Mia's disappearance?"

"I want to help Jess," said Oscar, "and I'm thinking that finding Mia might be the only way to do that."

"Did you ask Jessica where she is?"

He looked away.

"Okay, so you did. What did she say?"

"She wouldn't tell me."

"She told you something, or you wouldn't be here looking for more information."

Oscar shrugged.

"There's no doubt in my mind that Jessica knows where Mia Edwards is," said Sarah.

"Why do you think she won't tell anyone? She's not getting out until they find out where Mia is—there's a chance they'll try her for murder anyway—so why not tell someone?"

"I always assumed she was avoiding legal consequences," said Sarah.

"If she hurt Mia and lied about it all this time, the consequences will only be worse," said Oscar.

"Fear makes people do strange things."

"Should I keep trying?" asked Oscar.

"I can't help you with that, Dr. de la Nuit. That's up to you. She didn't tell me what happened, or where Mia was, the entire time I treated her. Not one word. So, if she's in a place where she's talking, maybe that matters."

"Do you think she killed Mia?" asked Oscar.

"I don't treat Jessica Green anymore, so it doesn't matter what I think. You should ask yourself what you think."

Chapter 57

Now

Oscar threw his wrapper in the trash. After forcing down a tortilla wrap for lunch, he still wasn't ready to tell Jess he wasn't treating her anymore.

He knocked on Jess's door. There was no answer. "Jess?" he called, knocking a second time.

The door swung open and Jess peeked around, hair swept into a ponytail. Her eyes were bright, too bright, as if she'd been crying.

She wiped her eyes with a sleeve. "So, how did it go?"

"What?"

"The meeting. It's not good news, is it?"

"No."

Jess looked like she might start crying again.

"Are you alright?" asked Oscar, sliding inside the room. The rag doll lay propped up on the bed, the stuffing sewn back in.

"I'm fine," said Jess.

"No, you're not," said Oscar, his tone matter-of-fact.

"What if she hurts Zoe anyway?" said Jess.

"What do you mean? Who's going to hurt Zoe?"

"Holly. She said if I ever got out, if I didn't pay for what I did to Mia, I'd never see Zoe again, but what if she does it anyway, while I'm locked in here?"

"Did you tell the police that she threatened you?"

"They thought it was an empty threat. She'd lost her daughter, she was grieving. Holly did a great job painting herself as something she's not. They acted like it was insensitive of me to take what she said the way I did when I still had my daughter. Holly's dangerous. And I'm in here." She held up her hands, defeated.

So that was it. Jess was afraid of what Holly would do to Zoe if they released her from Whitner.

"Is that why you won't talk to me? You don't want to put Zoe at risk?"

Jess didn't answer, leaving Oscar to fill in the blanks.

Oscar leaned closer to her ear and whispered, "You told me you killed her. If there's something else you want to tell me, now's the time."

Jess moved away. "It's complicated."

"I'm not your doctor anymore—this might be your last chance. Trust me. Tell me what really happened."

"Why do you want to know?"

"Like I told you, I've been where you are," said Oscar. "It took me a long time to come back from it. When I saw you on TV, with the headlines saying you killed Mia, I wanted to talk to you. I wanted to hear what you had to say. I have a feeling that whatever happened wasn't your fault. You didn't mean for Mia to go missing."

Jess sucked in a breath, fingers unfurling at her sides. "Mia deserved a home with parents who loved her. She didn't deserve Holly as a mother, but that saying about not getting to choose who your family is—it's true. But what about the kids in dangerous homes, the forgotten kids with no one to help them? I wanted Mia to have somewhere she could belong without being scared."

"Like Zoe had—like she could still have?"

Jess piqued at her daughter's name. "Zoe has a home. With her father."

It was becoming clear why Jessica wouldn't discuss what happened to Mia. Each time they talked, he learned a little more. His instinct had been correct. She *was* protecting someone.

Mia.

She deserved a home.

"Did Mia find a home that she deserved? Who took her?"

Jess fretted over her ponytail, pulling at the end to tighten it.

Oscar watched her fussing, visibly uncomfortable with his question. "Jess, I have to ask. Did you take Mia somewhere?"

"Why would I do that?" said Jess defensively.

"Listen to me, Jess. I won't be here to talk to anymore. I shouldn't be talking to you now. But if you honestly believe Holly'll hurt Zoe, let me help."

She looked at him hopelessly.

"I came to say goodbye, so that you didn't think I'd abandoned you. I would never do that."

"They can't just reassign me. I'll tell them I don't want another doctor."

"Jess, it doesn't matter. It's already done."

"Well, can't you talk to them?"

"I don't get a say in this either."

He hesitated. He didn't want Jess to think he was just trying to get answers from her, not when it might be the last time they spoke.

"There must be something," said Jess, challenging him to find a way.

Oscar put a hand on her shoulder. "Not anymore," he said. "It really is too late."

"When you said you were like me, I thought it was to make me feel safe at first, so that I'd talk. But you meant it, didn't you?"

"Yeah," said Oscar. "I really did. I have to go. I shouldn't be here." He laughed at the stupidity of it, at how paranoid he probably sounded.

Jess smiled—a hint of what she was like before her life took a turn.

"What happened between you and Charles? He seems really pissed."

"I don't know. Maybe he doesn't like me."

Jess looked through him. "Come on. I might only talk to couple of people a day, but I can still tell when someone's lying."

"Charles went for the director position at Whitner at the same time as me."

"And you got it."

"Yeah."

"Well, that'd be it. There's got to be a way to smooth things over."

"Short of handing over my job, not really. I'm definitely considering it."

"No, you're not."

"Yeah, I am."

"And they really won't let you be my doctor anymore?"

"I'm sorry. I tried, but I don't think it's possible."

"Because I left the hospital?"

Oscar sighed. "Charles would've found another way."

"How? If I didn't leave, he wouldn't have anything else to use against you."

Oscar shifted uncomfortably. "Charles made it seem like we were getting close. He made it sound inappropriate."

"What? That's ridiculous!"

"I know."

"There's more. Tell me."

Oscar hesitated.

"Just tell me."

"When Clay visited, with Zoe..."

"Ah. They think I'm unstable because I attacked Clay."

Jess moved to the bed and perched on the side, covering her face in her palms. "That wasn't your fault. I stabbed Clay on purpose, not because I lost it."

Oscar sat with her. "Do you want to talk about it?"

"I wanted to stop him from coming here. I needed something that he'd talk about, so it'd get back to Holly and keep her away from Zoe."

"It seemed like an extreme response," said Oscar gently.

"I don't want to give Holly a reason to hurt Zoe. I'm trying to keep them safe."

"Jess," said Oscar gently, "What do you think Holly would do?"

Jess's eyes were flat. "Whatever she wants."

"I have a theory about what happened," said Oscar.

"Okay."

"I think Mia's dad lied about his alibi. At least the timing."

"You think *Ray* took his daughter? They'd be all over him.

There's no way."

"I know he lied."

"How do you know that?" asked Jess, clearly surprised.

"Because you just told me," said Oscar.

"I didn't. I don't know if he lied."

"I want to help you keep Zoe safe, but I can't if you lie to me. You can't keep her safe while you're in here. I'm going to walk out those doors in a moment, so it's up to you. What do you want to do?"

"Maybe I should tell you what happened," said Jess, lowering her arms to sides.

Oscar swallowed. "Only if you want to."

She nodded, her blue eyes looking directly at him. This was it. She was finally going to tell him what happened to Mia.

The door opened, killing their conversation.

Chapter 58

Then

The phone on the bench buzzed, impatient and consistent, an unwelcome interruption to the weekend.

Jess considered letting it go to voicemail—whatever it was, she could deal with it later.

A name on the screen caught her eye. *Niki.* Grudgingly, she scooped it up and answered. "Hey."

"Jessie, do you want to get coffee? And before you say no, I want to remind you that you bailed on me last time."

"I can't. I've got Zoe with me."

"Well, can't Clay watch her? Actually, I was going to ask if he could watch Aiden too—Audrey's at her friend's house. It'd just be for an hour or two," she said.

"Clay went out. I'm not sure when he'll be back."

"Oh, okay."

"You go, Nik. Bring Aiden over to spend some time with Zoe."

"That's okay."

"Really. I don't mind."

"Are you sure? I feel bad dumping the kids on you."

"Yes! They can paint masterpieces to cover our refrigerators."

"Well, if you're absolutely sure."

"Yes."

"Okay. See you in a few minutes. And thanks."

Jess found Zoe riding her tricycle on the deck. "Zoo," she called. "Aiden's coming over. I thought we could do some painting. What do you think?"

"Yah! Can we use the paintbrushes?"

Jess laughed. "I hope so. I'll see if I can find them."

Jess found the paint and some brushes and placed them on the bench. Next, she searched for snacks to feed the kids. Aiden loved cheese puffs, so Jess looked for a bag.

The dull hum of an engine in the driveway diverted Jess's attention.

Jess went outside to meet Niki, waving as her sister beeped the horn of her blue Toyota. There was someone in the passenger seat, but Jess couldn't quite see who it was under the glare of the windscreen.

Doors opened and closed, and Aiden stepped out as Zoe raced past, brushing Jess's leg as she squealed and hugged her squirming cousin. A second door opened, and Mia stepped quietly out of the backseat.

"Mia, get back in this car right now," said Holly from the passenger's seat.

"Aww, ma—can't Mia stay and paint with us? Please."

"I don't think—" started Jess.

"Mia'd love that. She'd probably get bored with us anyway," said Niki, cutting off any protests.

Zoe ran to her friend and took her hand. "Yes! Come on, I'll show you my room." Zoe dragged her friend away as Mia looked at Holly for permission.

Holly stepped out of the car, one foot still inside, and leaned on the roof. "Wow, your house is beautiful," she said, emphasizing that she was seeing it for the first time. "Mia—did I say you could go?"

The tone in Holly's voice made Jess soften. She didn't want Mia to get in trouble. Maybe coffee would calm Holly enough that she'd forget about it. "It's fine," said Jess. "Go ahead. We're just painting, and there are plenty of brushes to go around."

"Are you sure?"

"Of course. I think the girls have already made up their minds. We'll see you soon."

"Thanks," said Holly.

Niki beeped the horn again. "See, I told you—Jess is amazing," she said, hands sliding onto the wheel. "We'll bring you back a capp. Want sugar?"

"Yeah, thanks," called Jess, waving them off as they reversed down the driveway.

Jess went back into the house, closing the door behind her. Zoe was waiting, wide-eyed, looking concerned.

"Zoe, what is it? Why don't you go play with Mia and Aiden?"

"Mia's crying. She said her arm's sore."

"Okay. Well, where is she?"

"She's in my room. Aiden didn't want to play with us, so he took my basketball outside."

"Well, let's go and see how Mia is," said Jess, leading her daughter to her room.

Mia sat cross-legged at the end of Zoe's bed, cradling her arm. Tears pooled under her chin.

As Jess approached, Mia shuffled her knees away from her.

Zoe rushed to Mia's side, catching Mia's shoulder.

Mia flinched, her face grimacing in pain.

"Let me see that, honey," said Jess, kneeling gently beside Mia.

Mia shuffled, bringing her arms up to her sides as if she could avoid Jessica's attention if she made herself small enough.

"Okay," said Jess. "How about this? You don't have to say anything, but your arm can tell me how it's feeling. Would that be okay?"

Mia shrugged.

"The thing is," whispered Jess, "I don't really speak arm, so you might need to help me out by answering for your arm. You can just nod or shake your head if that's easier."

Mia nodded bravely.

"Okay. Arm, can you hear me?" Jess directed her question toward Mia's arm.

Mia cracked a smile as Zoe broke out in giggles.

"I think I heard your arm mumble something. Was it a yes, maybe? I think it was a yes."

Mia nodded.

"Are you sore, arm?"

Mia nodded, pointing towards the outside of her elbow. "It's sore here."

Compared to her other arm, the right one was swollen, as if something was trying to break free.

Jess looked closer without touching Mia's arm. There was lump across the side, throwing the shape of her elbow out. It looked like it could be broken or dislocated.

"Okay. Can you still move and bend and stretch?" asked

Jess, directing her question to the crook of Mia's elbow.

Mia tried to move her elbow, crying out with the effort.

"That's okay. Maybe we won't try to move too much yet," said Jess quickly. "Can you tell me what happened?"

Mia shook her head.

"Zoe, can you check on Aiden for me? Mia'll be out soon."

"Sure," said Zoe, springing up and out of the room.

"Mia, what happened, honey? Did you fall over?"

Mia shook her head. "No."

"Did you have an accident?" asked Jess.

With downcast eyes, Mia shook her head. "Mommy got mad."

"What do you mean?"

"She pushed me and I landed on my arm."

"Did she take you to a doctor? I think your arm might need a cast or a sling to help it get better."

Mia sucked her lip in. "It hurts."

"Did your mom give you something to make it hurt less?"

"No."

What was she supposed to do? Was Mia telling the truth?

The way Mia acted around Holly, meek and uncertain, suggested she was afraid. Jess had seen firsthand what Holly was capable of, but letting your child suffer with a broken arm was next level.

Sometimes Zoe dragged her feet and Jess gave her a push along, or moved her out of the way to avoid a collision on the street. Was that what happened—had Holly accidentally pulled Mia's arm too hard? She could see it now, a guiding hand leading Mia on a path she wasn't prepared for, her foot catching and crumpling beneath her as she landed wrong.

"She yelled at me because I left my crayons on the floor.

Then she got really, really mad," said Mia.

"Maybe we should call her and see if we can get you to a doctor," said Jess gently.

"NO! Please don't tell her I told you," said Mia desperately.

"We should get this looked at."

"You could take me," said Mia sheepishly.

"Honey, I can't take you to the doctor without saying something to your mom. And we can't lie to the doctor."

Mia looked like she was about to cry. She shot off, racing to the door, ambling awkwardly with her injury. Jess ran outside in time to find her slamming the car door closed behind her.

She was hiding in the back seat, lying curled on her side, hair tangled around her head.

"Mia, why don't you come in and we can talk about it?"

"No," said Mia. "Go away."

"Please?" said Jess, hesitant to open the door and upset Mia further. "We might find a treat."

Two eyes appeared in the window. "A treat?"

"Yeah."

"Like what?"

"Like... I don't know, but I'm sure we can find something in the pantry."

The door opened and Jess took the handle, opening it for Mia as if she were a chauffeur. "Miss," she said, bowing.

Mia giggled and got out of the car.

Once they were inside, Jess pushed past the cheese puffs and found some jelly beans. "Can I look at your arm now, honey? I'll be gentle, I promise."

Chewing on jellybeans, Mia nodded.

Jess rolled up Mia's t-shirt sleeve, looking for swelling around her shoulder, and noticed a blue bruise blossoming under her ribs like a stain.

"Oh my," said Jess under her breath.

While she was investigating the bruise, there was a knock at the door. It was probably Niki popping back to borrow some lip gloss—she never remembered her own.

Good. Maybe she'll know what to do about this.

"I'll be right back. We'll figure this out."

Jess fixed a pillow under Mia's arm and left.

For once, she was glad Niki was vain.

Jess threw open the door. "You can take your pick, but don't take the new lipstick. I'm saving it for—"

Jess stopped when she saw who was at the door.

Chapter 59

Now

Oscar stepped quickly beside the door as it swung in.

A nurse with searing green eyes and hair pulled tight at her neck burst inside. She looked from Jess to Oscar questioningly.

"Jessica, you have a visitor. He's waiting out front. He says he needs to speak to you urgently, but he wouldn't say why."

Oscar stood, motioning for Jess to go ahead.

"I told Clayton not to visit. Is Zoe here?" asked Jess, frown lines creasing her brow.

"It's not your husband," said the nurse. "Maybe you should see what he wants."

She shot Oscar a look. Thanks to Charles, half the hospital probably thought he and Jess were involved.

Jess brushed past Oscar as she left. "We can talk about Mia later," she said.

"We really can't be seen talking to each other. We can't be in here together again."

"Oh, please. You care what that woman thinks?"

"Jess, it's not just what she thinks. It's more than that."

What would Hayley think? She knew about the rumors, but

how long before she started wondering if they were true?

"I can write it down for you. Doesn't matter who sees it, they won't believe me anyway, right?"

"Jessica—"

"Don't," she said before leaving.

Oscar left behind her and saw Hayley watching him curiously.

Hayley crossed the room and spoke low, so no one could hear her "What were you doing in there, Oscar? If Charles saw..."

"I had to tell her myself why I can't be her doctor," he said.

"Maybe we can talk later, over a drink, or burgers?" he said.

"I—"

Hayley trailed off, watching Jess approach the foyer where her visitor waited.

"Can we have some privacy, please?" Jess asked nervously.

"Jess. I know you said not to come by, but there's something I have to tell you—" said the visitor.

"Don't say another word," said Jess, shooting a look at Oscar.

"Please," repeated Jess. "I'd like to talk to my visitor privately."

"You aren't allowed a visitor without supervision. I'm sorry," said a nurse.

"It's okay," said Hayley, stepping forward. "I can supervise. Come with me." She smiled at Jess encouragingly. "Talk later," she said, addressing Oscar over her shoulder.

"Hayley," he started.

"Later, Oscar."

Jess hesitated before following Hayley to the meeting room, ushering her visitor inside.

Hayley closed the door behind them and checked the venetian shade was closed, locking Oscar outside.

Chapter 60

Now

“What are you doing here?” asked Jess. “You should go.”

She cast a sideways look at Hayley, hoping that Ray got the message. *Don’t say something stupid in front of the psychiatrist.*

“I can’t do this anymore, Jess.”

“Don’t,” said Jess, her tone final.

“I have to. This has gone on long enough.”

Jess looked at Hayley, gauging her reaction.

“Just pretend I’m not here,” said Hayley. “This is your conversation. It’s none of my business.”

Ray pulled out a chair to sit.

“Don’t sit there,” said Hayley. She pointed at a chair. “Try this one.”

“Why?” He tested the back. “Is it broken?”

“Please,” said Hayley firmly.

“This is Hayley,” said Jess, suddenly aware they hadn’t been introduced. “She’s in charge of group therapy here.”

“I’m tired of all this,” said Ray, catching the toe of his boot on the wooden chair leg. “I know you didn’t take my daughter. You shouldn’t be here. I’m gonna get you out.”

"Ray, I don't need you to get me out of here. Don't be a hero. You'll get us both in trouble."

"Jess, Holly knows we've been talking. I mean, this time she really knows. I followed her to the park, but she saw me."

"What? How did you let her see you?"

"I was worried she was gonna hurt Zoe. I've been trying to keep her safe from Holly."

"Shit," said Jess, landing her fist on the table. "Is Zoe alright?"

"She's fine. I think I spooked Holly—she took off."

Hayley sat up straighter, looking at Jess's fist. "Are you okay? I wouldn't do that again." Hayley eyed the corner of the room.

Jess nodded. Hayley was warning her that there were cameras.

"Are they everywhere?"

"There's only one in this room, but it picks up most of the room. There's a blind spot, so one of the chairs is just out of view." Hayley glanced past Ray, her eyes moving on quickly. The camera footage wouldn't pick up that she was looking at someone.

"Ray, you need to get out of here. It'll look bad for you if someone tells the police you were here."

"But I know you didn't take her. You wouldn't."

Jess looked around, searching for the camera. She spotted it in the corner, angled toward the table. Hayley had told him to sit there on purpose.

"I get that you might not want to speak to me, given that you're in here," said Ray. "Do you trust anyone around here?"

"One person."

"Who?"

"My doctor—well, he used to be."

Hayley covered her mouth, pretending to scratch her top lip. "Go. I'll let him know. Meet him out the back of a place called Carnivals in thirty minutes. Whatever you have to say, you can tell him then."

Ray looked at Jess for confirmation before agreeing.

"Yeah," she said, hoping Hayley wasn't bluffing.

Ray looked at Jess one last time, apologizing for everything he couldn't say before he went.

Chapter 61

Then

"Ray! I thought you were Niki, coming back to borrow lip gloss. What are you doing here?"

"That's okay—I always carry my own gloss."

Jess narrowed her eyes. "I'm serious. What the hell are you doing at my house?"

"I think Holly's up to something. I saw her loading bags into her car."

"So?"

"I looked through them when she went inside to collect more. They were full of kids' stuff, but there was nothing of hers, so I don't think she's planning a holiday."

"Maybe she didn't load hers yet."

"No. When she finished, she closed the trunk. I think she's taking Mia somewhere. What if I never see her again?"

"Kids outgrow stuff. Maybe she's clearing out old junk."

"What if she's not?"

"We can talk about this later," said Jess. "I'm kinda busy at the moment."

"Um, my arm still feels sore," said a small voice behind Jess.

Recognition flashed across Ray's face. "She has my nose," he said.

"Go inside honey, I'll be there soon."

Ray waved at his daughter. "Hi. What's wrong with your arm?" he asked in a soothing voice.

Mia mumbled something and hid behind Jess.

"It's okay," said Ray, "you can talk to me."

"I don't think now's a good time for this," Jess said, trying to catch Ray's eye, but he was too busy taking in his daughter to notice.

"What happened to her arm?" he asked, stepping closer to see.

"Please, let me deal with this. You can't be here," said Jess, trying not to let Mia hear. "What'll happen if she says something to Holly?"

"I just want to talk to her. Isn't that understandable?"

"Yeah, it is. But that doesn't mean it should be now."

"We have to do something about her arm. She's crying," said Ray.

"I know," said Jess. "And the sooner you go, the sooner I can deal with it. Now would you please just go?"

"Hey, I hope you feel better soon, little lady," said Ray.

"Thank you," said Mia.

Jess's heart broke watching them. She couldn't imagine what it was like, being that close and not being able to tell your daughter who you were. She couldn't imagine taking that away from Clay, and she couldn't understand how Holly could take that from Ray.

"Did Holly do this?"

Jess looked away, unable to lie.

"Did she?"

"I don't know."

"Jessica, I'm not sending my daughter back to her. I'm not."

"Can we talk about this later, *please*?"

Ray moved closer, kneeling to check Mia's arm. "It's pretty swollen. Looks like it could be a pretty bad sprain. Can you bend your arm, princess?"

Mia shook her head as Ray used the back of his index finger to wipe away the line of tears streaking her cheek.

"Would you walk away if you were me?" Ray asked Jessica. "Wouldn't you do something?"

"I'm trying to do something," said Jess. "Please, let me take her to the hospital. They'll assess her and ask her what happened."

"When was your arm hurt?" asked Ray.

"A little while ago." Mia shook her head vehemently. "But we can't go to the hospital, or they'll take me away and put me with really bad people."

"No one should hurt you like this," said Ray, still kneeling beside Mia.

"It's okay, Mia," said Jess calmly. "We'll figure something out."

"I wanna go play," said Mia.

"Off you go," said Jess, smiling for Mia's sake and waiting until she was out of earshot before pulling Ray into the doorway.

"I'm not sending her back to Holly," said Ray. "I need to piss—where's your bathroom?"

Jess reluctantly showed him to the bathroom, pacing until he was out. What would she tell Clay if he came home? That she'd secretly been talking with Holly's ex because they both thought she was a psychopath?

Since the attack, Jess and Clay weren't exactly on good terms, and this would just complicate things more. He wouldn't say it, but Jess suspected that Clay still thought she attacked him.

"You can't be here," Jess said to Ray as he re-buckled his belt on the way out. "I want to help, but you need to go home so we can do this the right way."

"The right way? What the hell is the right way? Doing things the right way got Mia a broken arm. That's how useful the right way is."

"You're upset, and I get that. But this'll only make things worse."

"Let me take her with me."

"No."

"Why?" asked Ray, faux innocent. "I can't do any worse than Holly."

"Ray, if you take Mia out of here, do you think you'll ever be allowed to see her again?"

"Yeah," he relented. "It's just awful, seeing her arm like that. Are you taking her to the hospital?" asked Ray.

"If I wait until Holly gets back, I can say she fell and needs to go to hospital."

"You want to pretend she hurt herself while she was *here*?"

"If it means Mia's arm gets fixed, yeah. You need to focus on visitation. If you can't keep your temper in check, they'll believe everything Holly said."

"I'm trying."

"Look at that little girl out there. She has to mean more than just trying."

"Yeah. I guess," said Ray, walking toward the entrance. "Don't worry. I'll let myself out."

Chapter 62

Now

Hayley stood. The room they were in was used for supervised visits, but it felt too small for the three of them. "I'll see you out," Hayley said to Ray, leaving Jess with her head buried in her arms on the tabletop.

Luckily, Charles didn't work on Saturday, and no one else seemed to care much about the man with the beard and the baseball cap.

Ray looked different from the old photo the newspaper used. Ray was a by-line, the absent father. No one cared how he felt. Without someone to tell his story, Ray became the villain. Ray's new beard was thick at the sides and hid his features. Hayley wouldn't have recognized him if it wasn't for Jess's reaction when she saw him.

"Right this way," she said formally, showing Ray to the exit.

"Who was *that*?" asked a nurse, passing Hayley on her way back.

"Just an old friend of Ms. Green's I think," said Hayley smoothly.

"Where do I find a friend like that?" asked the nurse,

eliciting a few giggles.

Hayley chuckled and excused herself. She looked in on Jess, who was still in the meeting room. "You okay?" she asked.

Jess looked up from her arms. "Yeah. Thanks."

"Listen, I'm sorry things worked out how they did with Oscar. He's a great doctor, and I know he cares very much what happens to you."

"Yeah. I guess it's my own fault."

"I'll go find Oscar and let him know Ray will be waiting for him."

Oscar was usually in his office at this time of day. When Hayley reached his door, she rapped on the wood and went inside, closing the door behind her.

"Hayley," said Oscar. "How's Jess?"

"She's fine. I assume you know who that was?"

"Yeah. What's he doing here?"

"He left. He wanted to tell Jessica something."

"Did he want to ask her where Mia is?" asked Oscar.

Hayley shook her head. "I don't know, Oscar. Jess told him not to say anything, so I told him he should talk to you."

"You did?"

"Yeah."

"Why?"

"It's like you said. We should be open to finding out what happened to Mia, and Ray might know something that helps. Tell the front desk you're going out to work on research, and go get yourself a vegan burger at our spot." She looked at him meaningfully.

Oscar pushed his chair out from behind his desk and kissed her. "We'll talk later."

"Yeah," said Hayley, smiling. "Park in the back lot."

"Okay. Sure."

Oscar drove to Carnivals, the kiss still warm on his lips.

Ray was waiting in a gray sedan when Oscar arrived. It seemed like that's all anyone drove anymore. The windows were dark and closed, but Jess's visitor stepped out as Oscar approached. He looked different from the guy in the news article.

"Hey," said Oscar, offering his hand. "I'm Oscar."

Ray nodded and introduced himself. "Maybe we should talk in my car?"

"Right," said Oscar, hesitating as Ray climbed back inside the car, flicking the passenger door open. This man could be dangerous, but if Oscar wanted to know what he had to say, he'd have to get in.

The interior smelled like leather and air freshener.

"Jess said we can trust you," said Ray, watching Oscar carefully. "I hope she's right."

Oscar swallowed before speaking. "Coming from Jess that means a lot."

"Yeah," said Ray, an acknowledgment more than agreement.

"What did you want to tell her?"

"It feels weird telling you. What if Jess is wrong? I mean, I don't know you."

Oscar shrugged.

"How much do you know?" asked Ray, leaning back in his seat.

"About what?"

"About anything."

"You're Mia's dad, right?"

"Well, that you could've read in the news. Officially, I'm

not even her dad. Holly didn't put my name on Mia's birth certificate. She wouldn't like it if I had any say over what happened to Mia."

"Do you think Jess hurt your daughter?"

Ray studied Oscar out of the corner of his eye. "You think that's what I wanted to talk to Jess about? To see what she did with my daughter?"

Oscar shifted in the passenger seat. "I don't know. A lot of people think Jess kidnapped Mia, but I'm guessing you're not one of them, or you wouldn't be here?"

"I don't think Jess did it."

"Why not?"

"I just can't see it. I don't know her well, but I can't see her hurting Mia."

"So, if not Mia, what did you want to talk to her about?"

"I wanted to tell her I've been watching Zoe, making sure she's safe, but I think Holly's planning something."

"Why do you think that?"

"She's been following Zoe."

"Following her?"

"Yeah. I wanted to be sure before I told Jess. There's no point worrying her for no reason."

"What changed? Why are you telling her now?" said Oscar.

"I don't think I can keep Zoe safe anymore."

"Why not?"

Ray flicked the air freshener tied to the rearview mirror, sending it spinning around. "Holly's been visiting Jessica's house. I can't follow her in."

"What?"

"The first time, her and Clay just talked at the door. Then the next time, Holly went inside."

"Does Holly visit Clay much?"

"I don't know. She's visited a few times, I guess. I can't keep Zoe safe with Holly making home visits. I thought Jess should know."

"Yeah," said Oscar.

If Jess knew that staying out of Holly's way wouldn't protect her family, she'd have no reason to hide what happened to Mia.

"I'll let Jess know about the visits."

"Thanks."

"Is there anything else I should tell her?"

Ray hesitated. "No, it's okay."

"Ray, I'm a psychiatrist. We wrote the book on discretion."

"I'm not your patient, Oscar."

"I know. But your daughter's missing. That's gotta have an impact."

"I didn't know her. You're probably thinking I'm just another asshole. Truth is, Holly never told me about her."

"How did you find out?"

"Holly needed money. I told her she couldn't have any, so she said she needed it for Mia, that she came to me because Mia's my daughter. The timing checked out. I wanted to see her, but Holly wouldn't let me. I gave her a couple of hundred, then a couple more. Eventually, she asked me for a grand. She agreed to give me a photo of our daughter if I gave her the money, so I did."

Ray gave a half-smile. "She looks mostly like her ma, but I can see she's mine."

"Holly wouldn't let you see Mia?"

"She said my name wasn't on the certificate because she couldn't be sure. Truth is, I think she didn't want me to see her because Holly's a control freak. She's got a temper—I bet Mia's seen it too."

"Did you tell the police you're concerned about Holly's temper?"

Ray gave a wry laugh. "The cops wouldn't listen because of what Holly told them."

"What'd she say?"

"She made it seem like I hurt her while we were together. She had the bruises, and she was convincing. But it wasn't me. It was probably the other guy she was seeing. Then one day she left, and I never saw her again. Until I did."

"Did the police talk to you about Mia?"

"Why would they? I'm not listed as her father. I haven't been in contact with Holly, other than to collect my photo of Mia."

"Surely Holly told them? You would've been a suspect."

"Do you think Holly really gives a shit about Mia? Mia's a pawn for Holly to get what she wants."

Hadn't Jessica said almost the same thing?

"What do you think Holly wants?"

"Sympathy. Attention. With Holly, it depends on the day."

"But the police didn't talk to you?"

"Of course they talked to me. Jesus. But I don't know where she is. I don't think Jess knows either."

Oscar searched Ray for clues, but he couldn't tell. Why would Ray visit Jess and risk getting caught if he was guilty? In Oscar's experience, people rarely put themselves on the line like that—unless it was for love. As far as he could tell, Ray had nothing to gain from coming here to tell Jess that Zoe was in trouble.

Maybe he really was afraid of what Holly would do.

Chapter 63

Then

Jess sat with her elbows propped on the kitchen bench, a mug of warm green tea in her hand, listening to the kids playing outside. Zoe was laughing, the loud, squeaky one that meant she was really having fun. How much would it be worth if you could bottle that sound?

She took her mug and slid out the back door onto the deck.

"We're playing hide and seek," said Zoe matter-of-factly. "Mia and I are hiding."

"Okay. Well, don't run with that," said Jess, gesturing at Zoe's iPad.

Zoe nodded and set it down carefully for her mother's benefit. "Can we have juice?"

"Sure. Do you want to drink it out here?"

"I'll get them," said Zoe, racing to the fridge and grabbing out three juice boxes.

Trailing close behind, Jess went with Zoe, still contemplating what she should do about Mia's arm. So far, the best option was telling Holly that Mia fell over while the kids were playing, and offering to pay for treatment.

Jess was contemplating a third mug of tea when she heard her sister's car in the driveway. She opened the door silently this time, her face hot with embarrassment when she remembered how she greeted Ray earlier.

"Hey," called Jess, inviting Niki and Holly inside. "Mia had a fall. I think she landed on her arm. I'm worried it's sprained or something. I think she might need to go to the hospital."

"What? I'm sure it's nothing," said Holly dismissively.

"Oh my god," said Niki, pushing the door wide open and walking through. "Is she okay? Mia honey," she called.

"They're out the back," said Jess, gesturing for Holly to go through.

"She's fine, but it might be sprained or something," said Jess, downplaying Mia's injury. "I'm so sorry. I'll pay for any treatment, of course."

"How did she fall?" asked Holly.

"The kids were running around paying and Mia slipped on the deck."

"Mia, honey, come let me look at your arm," called Niki.

Jess shot her a look—they didn't want to scare Mia.

Aiden crawled out from the branches of a maple tree. "Aww," he said, disappointed to see Niki back. "We're playing hide and seek and Mia's in a really good spot. Can we stay and find her?"

Holly shot Jess a warning look. "Mia complains a lot about things. If she told you she fell and hurt her arm to the point of needing to go to hospital, it's probably just a scrape."

"Time to come inside, guys," called Jess, ignoring Holly's comment.

Zoe ambled past, weaving through the clustered adults.

"Put your stuff away please, Zoo," said Jess.

Zoe sighed and went back for her iPad, scooping it up in her arms.

"Mia," called Holly. "It's time to go. Let's move!"

Jess searched the yard, looking in the hedge and behind the pool.

"Come here now, Mia. You can come back another time and play," said Holly.

Zoe dove back onto the deck.

"Zoo, do you think you can help me look for Mia?" said Jess.

"Okay," said Zoe.

They looked around the trampoline, beside the garden shed, but found no sign of Mia.

"Mia, answer me!" said Holly warningly.

Aiden peeked outside from his post at the sliding door.

Jess caught his eye. "Aiden, do you know where Mia's hiding?"

"She's in a good spot," said Aiden, sounding impressed. He turned and ran, dodging more questions.

"Sorry," said Niki. "He gets shy when he's the center of attention. Don't know where he got that shyness from."

Jess smiled weakly and chased after her nephew. "Are you good?" she asked the bundle she found curled up against the couch.

Aiden nodded.

"Do you know where Mia's hiding?"

Aiden looked up and shook his head. "I couldn't find her," he said. "She's gone."

"Jessie, get your butt out here. We've looked everywhere. We can't find her," called Niki, her voice shrill.

Jess raced out, spurred by Niki's tone.

"We've checked everywhere," said Holly. "Maybe she got

out of the yard. How did she get out?"

"She was just here. She can't have gone far," said Jess.

"Maybe she went back inside to hide?" said Holly.

"I was at the bench the whole time. She would've walked right past me," said Jess, gesturing to the bench overlooking the yard.

They searched the house, looking under the beds and in the bathrooms, but Mia wasn't in any of the rooms.

"I'll check the car. Maybe she's hiding there. Niki, you stay here with the kids," said Jess.

"She's not. I already found her hiding in the car last round," said Zoe proudly. "You never hide in the same place if you don't wanna get caught," she said.

"Should we call the police?" asked Niki, eyebrows raised. "Oh my god. What if someone's taken her? Would Ray do that? You said he hit you—what if he's out of control?" she said, her voice gaining momentum.

"I don't know," said Holly. "Mia, you need to come here RIGHT NOW if you can hear me. This isn't funny."

"I'll call the police," said Jess, her stomach lurching. She grabbed her phone and searched *who to call for a missing child.* She dialed and waited for a response. "Hi. I'd like to report a missing child."

Chapter 64

Now

"What do you think of the char sui?" asked Oscar.

Hayley finished her mouthful and wiped her mouth on a napkin. "It's great, but I'm kinda missing burgers. They seem like our dish now."

Oscar laughed. "I know. I thought about making burgers, but then I realized..."

Setting her napkin down, Hayley picked up her chopsticks. "What? That stir fry's pretty good too?"

Oscar laughed again. "That too, but no. I realized that Carnival's would put my burgers to shame, unless you want a steak sandwich? My steak sandwiches are world famous in these parts, but you'll never know."

"This is pretty good," said Hayley, a piece of broccoli between her chopsticks. "But you didn't make anywhere near enough."

"We could get burgers," said Oscar. "If you're still hungry."

"That's okay, this is great. I wanted to talk anyway, where no one can hear us," she said.

"Okay. What is it?" said Oscar tentatively.

"Jess gave me a letter to give to you. I think she was hoping it'd explain a few things."

"Like what?"

"Maybe you should read it," said Hayley, sifting through her purse for an envelope.

"Did you read it?" he asked.

She handed him an unopened envelope, the corners pressed smoothly together. "Excuse me, I need the bathroom," she said, moving her chair back from the table. "Open it."

Oscar turned the envelope over in his hands. Printed neatly on the front was his name. He tore the edges away, working his finger under the binding, retrieving the letter inside.

Dear Oscar,

I wanted to thank you for sticking with me. I know I haven't been the easiest person to treat. I haven't talked as freely as I should have. I felt lost inside of myself, punishing myself for things I couldn't change.

The truth is, I lied to you, and I lied to myself. About Clay, and about Mia. If things were working, he wouldn't have thought that I tried to kill him.

I told you I killed Mia, and in a sense, I did. She didn't die by my hand, but she was in my care when she disappeared. The kids were playing happily when I checked on them, but by the time Holly and Niki got back, Mia was already gone. Niki told me Holly disappeared into the bathroom for a long time while they were out. I thought maybe Holly came back to my house and took her somewhere, but by the end of the week, everyone thought I'd abducted Mia. Even Niki didn't look at me the same. She wanted to believe me, but there was always some doubt. People who I thought knew me well looked at me like I was a tidal wave, ready to drown them with my turbulence.

Mia's disappearance drowned us all slowly.

Anyway, I thought you should know the truth. I've learned that not knowing is the worst thing, so here it is...

I don't know what happened to Mia, but I hope she's somewhere better than she was.

Sincerely,

Jess

Oscar heard Hayley slide across from him, back into her chair. He handed her the paper and loaded the dishwasher while she read Jess's letter.

Hayley folded the pages carefully on the table once she finished. "Do you believe her? I mean, how does a child disappear from an unplanned playdate? How would anyone know she was there, unless Jess told them?"

"I don't know. Kids are loud when they're playing. Maybe it was an opportunistic kidnapping."

Hayley looked doubtful, her upper lip curling inwards.

"You knew what the letter said before you gave it to me, didn't you?" He didn't wait for a response. "How?"

"I asked Jessica what was in the letter. She told me."

"Okay. Did what she say match up with what you read?"

"Pretty much."

"I know Jessica Green didn't kill Mia Edwards," said Oscar.

"How can you know that?"

"Because I spoke to Raymond Loxburg, and I think he knows where Mia is."

"Come on, Oscar. Don't you think the police would know if he took his daughter? He would've been their first suspect."

"All I know is, if my son went missing on a play date, I

wouldn't be as understanding as he is, unless I knew my kid was alright. We won't know if Jess is telling the truth until she's out of there."

"You think she'll go to Mia?"

"Maybe. There have been cases where kidnappers have been caught going to see their hostage."

Hayley reached for Oscar's hand. "Then let's get her out and see."

Chapter 65

Now

The common room was empty except for Jess, curled in a ball on the sofa, her chin on her knees, resting against her yoga pants.

"Did you try the yoga class?" Hayley asked hopefully.

"No."

"Maybe next time then. Jessica, I hope you don't think this is too forward, but I've offered to be your new doctor. You have a say, of course, but at this point you're looking at me or Charles."

"Oh, okay," said Jess. "Tell them I choose you."

"Did you give him the letter?" said Jess.

"Yeah."

"And?"

Hayley perched on the armrest, lowering her voice. "Did you mean what you said in the letter? You don't know what happened to Mia?"

Jess shook her head.

"Oscar believes you. For what it's worth, I believe you too. I want to help you get out of here."

"Can you do that?" asked Jess skeptically.

"Maybe. With the help of a lawyer, probably."

Jess sat up and crossed her legs. "I don't need to get out. I just need someone to check on my daughter. Can someone make sure she's alright?"

"Jessica, listen to me. I can send someone to check on Zoe, but it won't stop you from worrying. If you're out, you can be there with her and know she's safe all the time."

"Her father takes care of her."

"But her father didn't believe you. When you said you were worried about Zoe, he acted like you were the one with the problem, didn't he?"

Jess looked away. "He's doing the best he can. He just—He doesn't know."

"But you do. That's why Zoe needs you."

"Can you just send someone, please? I need to know."

"Sure."

"Listen, I'm not being completely honest with you."

"What?"

"I already put the request in, after my lawyer friend looked over it. I think they're going to approve it."

"Why? They could just throw it out and keep me here."

"They've already held you here for too long, treating you like you're guilty, when there's no evidence to prove you did anything they're accusing you of."

Jess shrugged, but looked at Hayley curiously. "What about Clay? I stabbed him in the leg."

"You reacted under stress, but there's no reason to think it will happen again. For the most part, you've really tried while you've been at Whitner. You've attended all of your therapy sessions."

Jess bit the edge of her thumbnail. "Thanks, I think."

"There's more reason than ever to get out now, Jess."

"What do you mean?"

"Holly's been visiting Clay, at your house. That's what Ray came to tell you."

"What? How did she get in?"

Hayley looked away. "Clay let her in."

Jess nodded. "I've blamed myself for this since it happened. I felt like I didn't deserve freedom. Mia was in my care." She shifted her weight. "You hear about people going missing, and it always seems like someone should've been able to stop it. I keep asking myself what I could've done."

"Maybe this is a second chance," Hayley said gently.

"Maybe. I don't want the other parents to look at Zoe and wonder if she's as crazy as her mother."

"Jessica, their opinions are none of your business. Ignore them. Take Zoe to school. Heck, move if you need to, but don't give up because of some misinformed opinions," said Hayley vehemently.

"Yeah. If only they didn't decide, right?"

"It might feel like they do. It's not fair, and it'll hurt when it seems like it's affecting Zoe, but fuck them."

"What?"

"Yeah, that's right. Fuck them. They're like the flu—and who wants to be friends with the flu? It probably just means you'll catch it."

"Right," said Jess, confused but amused by Hayley's analogy.

"Don't give them that power."

"It doesn't matter what I give them or don't give them. They'll take it anyway." Jess excused herself, cushions buckling under her as she stood.

"Jessica," called Hayley. "I'm not saying it's easy. What I'm saying is, I think you can do it."

Jess scratched her arm, uncomfortable in her own skin, uncomfortable with herself. "Mia went missing from my house while she was playing in the yard and I didn't notice. That's the truth, and I have to live with it."

"What if I can get you back to Zoe? You can stop Holly from getting that close to her again. You can keep her safe."

She considered her options. How could Clay let Holly visit their home when he knew how Jess felt about her?

"You're right," said Jess eventually. "What do I need to do?"

"Let them process the request. They'll ask why you want to leave Whitner. When they do, answer their questions. No more silence. Tell them you want to see your daughter, and that you don't know what happened to Mia."

"I *don't* know what happened to Mia."

"Then make them believe you."

Chapter 66

Later

Jess watched Zoe color from the sofa where she and Clay used to cuddle, fighting the feeling that someone was watching her from outside. It was just her imagination; when she looked out the window, there wasn't anyone there.

She'd been released from Whitner Psychiatric Hospital for just under three weeks and somehow everything about her old life still felt new. The only thing that seemed to have stayed the same was Mia's absence. Oscar had chosen to believe her despite having no proof, and perhaps that was the ultimate test of letting go—being able to let go without needing a solid answer. Choosing to put your trust in something, and having that be enough.

Jess knew once she was home, things between her and Clay couldn't stay the same. Maybe part of her wanted to stay at Whitner, to avoid finding out just how much had changed. She hadn't known she was truly ready to end her marriage until she was free.

"Hey Zoo, are you ready for bed?" asked Jess.

Zoe spun around in her pink pajamas.

"Did you brush your teeth?"

"Yes. Can I call Daddy? I want to say goodnight."

"Maybe tomorrow. It's bed time Zoo."

"He said I can call whenever I want."

"Tomorrow," said Jess, leading Zoe by the hand and pulling the covers back.

Zoe slid into bed, one arm wrapped around her rag doll, her toes peeking out of the covers. Jess tucked them in and slid in beside her, stroking the side of Zoe's face. She'd grown so much over the last months. Her hair was longer and a little darker. There were new drawings on her wall.

Jess waited until Zoe fell asleep and went to her closet, searching the top shelves for the old drawings that used to cover her walls—Clay wouldn't have moved them far. She searched deeper, right to the back, finding something she didn't expect.

She pulled a rubber case holding Zoe's old iPad from the closet. She used to love taking photos and playing games on it. Jess remembered the hundreds of photos they'd taken together, giggling as they applied funny filters to distort their faces.

Jess padded to the kitchen, rustling around in the drawers for a charger, hoping the photos were still there. She plugged it in and waited. It powered up after a few minutes, and she scrolled through the images. Zoe mustn't have used it after Jess went to the remand center; all the pictures were dated before Jess left.

Jess's stomach nose-dived when she saw a thumbnail for a video. Three little faces smiled into the camera—Zoe, Aiden, and Mia.

Tapping play, Jess watched them come to life in her backyard. She turned up the volume.

"This is hide and seek. I can find everyone," said Aiden gleefully to the camera.

"I'm going to hide in the best place ever," squealed Mia as the two girls went to find hiding places.

Zoe's giggles veered to the left, while Mia headed in the other direction, clutching her arm.

Aiden zoomed out and propped the iPad on its stand, the footage still rolling. He had a wide view of the yard, as he began counting in a loud voice, watching where Zoe and Mia ran through the gaps his fingers made.

Chewing a knuckle, Jess waited as Aiden finished counting.

"Ready or not, here I come," he said, running in the direction Zoe was hiding as Mia disappeared behind the pool.

Jess watched as someone jumped the fence in the background, just behind Mia.

Jess zoomed in and watched the abduction in horror, expecting to see Ray taking his daughter away from her house—she'd always thought that he'd came back to take Mia somewhere that Holly couldn't hurt her. The image was distorted, probably the result of grubby little hands dirtying the lens, but it didn't look like Ray bobbing back up with a hand over Mia's mouth.

The figure wore a black puffer jacket and loose-fitting pants, but it was clearly a woman. Jess thought she could make out a loose thread of dark hair as the figure propped Mia over her shoulder.

Mia didn't scream.

Jess had wondered why she never heard Mia scream, assuming Ray might've found a way to convince her to leave, but now she knew.

Mia knew her kidnapper.

It was Holly.

Chapter 67

Later

In the video, Holly leaned in and whispered something as Mia cowered. Was Holly telling her to be quiet, threatening what might happen if she didn't listen?

Was Mia scared of her mother?

Jess felt sick. Her stomach told her to stop watching as Holly disappeared over the fence, holding Mia, a cap cleverly drawn over her brow to hide her face.

Holly set me up. She had Mia all along.

All this time, Jess had believed that Ray took Mia. She thought it was an unspoken rule between them not to discuss it, a way to keep Mia safe; the less Jess knew, the better.

But she was wrong. Mia was kidnapped by her own mother, wearing a baseball cap to hide her identity. What had Holly done with her?

Jess struggled to focus, more agitated by the minute. If Ray didn't take Mia, maybe Mia was really gone.

She needed to talk to Ray.

Jess dialed quickly, willing Ray to answer.

"Hello?"

Thank god.

"Ray! It's Jess."

"Jess," said Ray, sounding surprised. "Is everything alright?"

"Not really. I—Holly took Mia," she blurted.

"Jess, what do you mean?"

"I saw her, Ray. I saw her take Mia." The panic in Jess's voice grew.

Mia wasn't safe like she thought. Holly had taken her that day, and no one had seen Mia since.

"Jess, I'm coming over. I'll be there soon."

He hung up before she could protest.

∞

A thump came from the door, someone knocking. Ray couldn't have gotten there that quickly. It was probably Niki, who wasn't very time sensitive when it came to appropriate visiting hours.

Not now Niki.

Jess threw open the door, went to close it again as she saw the icy expression, the sliver of black hair brushed forward.

Holly.

Jess pressed harder against it, but Holly was already using her weight to push it open, wedging her foot in the jamb. The door gave in and Holly slid inside, closing it behind her.

"What the hell are you doing here?" said Jess.

"I heard Mia's voice," said Holly, her eyes darting around as if she expected to find her hiding in a corner somewhere. "Where is she?"

She must've been referring to the video on the iPad and the game of hide and seek. Surely Holly wouldn't try to pretend that she didn't know where Mia was.

"It was a recording. Mia's not here," said Jess. "I saw you take her."

Jess could feel Holly's anger as she advanced, forcing Jess to back up. She moved quickly around the kitchen bench, eager to put something solid between them.

If Holly heard Mia's voice, she must've been watching her. How long was she waiting outside for?

"I told you what would happen," said Holly, "if you ever came back here, you fucking psychopath."

Find out if she knows what you are. Kat's words came flooding back.

Jess's feet slid backward over the tiles, maintaining her distance from Holly.

Holly was wrong. Jess's emotions had always overwhelmed her. She felt other people's feelings as if they were her own. She couldn't be a psychopath. She'd needed medication when Zoe went to kindergarten just to manage how she felt about it, to stop the anxiety.

It was how she'd recognized what Holly was.

Holly moved forward like an insidious vapor, poisoning the air.

"How's Zoe?" said Holly.

Jess stopped moving backward. If she went any further, she'd leave a path free to Zoe's room.

Was it Jess's imagination, or was Holly looking past her, right at Zoe's door?

How does she know that's Zoe's room? Clay had let her inside the house. Maybe she'd seen it before.

Or maybe she knew from watching them from outside, concealed in the dark. All those nights that Jess felt someone watching, but told herself she was being paranoid. Maybe it was Holly all along.

"Leave Zoe out of this," said Jess, holding her ground.

Holly rushed towards Zoe's room as Jess scrabbled for something in the drawer. Her arm arced, striking Holly harder than she intended, the metal mallet she'd used to prepare dinner connecting with a crack.

Holly hit the floor, the thud sounding just like Clay had. The weapon fell from Jess's hand when she saw Holly's expression, her eyes vacant and fixed.

Jess pivoted to the other side of the bench, escaping what she'd done, her knees buckling, sliding until she was sitting on the cold, hard floor. She barely noticed as Ray called out to her from the entrance. He let himself in when she didn't reply.

What was she supposed to do now? Holly was dead.

She was supposed to feel sorry, but all she could feel was relief. Holly couldn't follow her now, couldn't come into her house unannounced ever again. She couldn't hurt Zoe.

"Jess?" said Ray gently.

Her eyes flicked toward him. Ray hadn't noticed Holly laying in the kitchen yet. What would he say when he found out Jess had killed her? What if he saw her lying behind the waterfall edge of the island bench?

"Are you okay?" asked Ray, lifting her to her feet.

Jess nodded numbly.

"I've gotta be honest," said Ray. "I didn't think we'd ever see each other again."

She found her voice, tested it slowly. "Neither did I."

"Why do you think Holly took Mia? Did she say something to you?"

"I always thought it was you," said Jess. "I didn't know for sure, but after you showed up at my house, it felt like too much of a coincidence for her to disappear that same day. That's why I never told the police you were there. I figured you'd get some heat anyway, being Mia's dad."

"Alright," said Ray tentatively.

"I thought you got Mia away from Holly. And then I saw her," continued Jess.

She retrieved the iPad and waited as Ray watched the footage of Holly taking Mia from the yard.

Ray handed it back to Jess, frowning.

"I figured, if you helped Mia, that was a good thing. And if Holly took her... well, I think I always told myself the happy ending version, where Mia was safe and didn't have to worry about broken arms and bruises. If I knew, I would've told the police you visited my house. Maybe they would've gone in another direction."

"Jess, you didn't know. You thought you were doing the right thing."

"But I was wrong," said Jess, tearing up.

Ray took Jess gently by the shoulders to steady her shaking.

"You should be angry at me," she said. "I'm so, so sorry."

"If the police could've found her, they would've. I'm thankful you'd do that for me. That's... well, not a lot of people would."

"She deserved better," said Jess, wrapping her arms around herself protectively. "We should take the video to the police."

"Yeah. Maybe they can use it to lock Holly away."

"I'm so sorry, I didn't know. I thought you got her out."

If she could just get Ray to leave, she might be able to figure out what to do about Holly lying there on the floor. Perhaps she wasn't really dead. Maybe she was just knocked unconscious. Jess felt ashamed for not checking, but the thought of laying a hand across Holly's neck, even to check for a pulse, made her arms coil further around her.

"Get some sleep. We can go to the police in the morning. I'll come with you," said Ray. "They won't be able to do anything now."

Jess knew he was right. They couldn't find Mia before, and the only new information they had was exactly what she'd tried to warn them before—that Holly took Mia.

"It's fine," said Jess. "I can go alone."

"You sure?" asked Ray, tilting her chin so he could read her expression.

Jess nodded. "Holly wouldn't hurt her, would she?" She searched Ray's face for an answer. "I mean, really hurt her."

Ray lifted his shoulders in a shrug, trying to pretend he didn't know if Holly would take it too far, but his expression told Jess a different story. Ray definitely thought Holly might hurt Mia.

"Watch it again, in case there's something we've missed. Some clue about where she took Mia."

Jess navigated the touch screen while Ray waited, nervously shifting his weight.

"Why can't I find it?" muttered Jess, scrolling through.

"It was here a second ago." She caught Ray's eye, and she knew. "You deleted it."

Chapter 68

Later

Why would Ray protect Holly now?

"Jess, no."

"You should go. I'm sorry I called." She backed up against the bench. Maybe Ray knew it was Holly all along and he'd played Jess. Maybe they were in on it together, and it was all just a sick game to them, a bit of fun to make Jess think she was crazy.

"Jess!"

Ray caught her wrist, constricting it like a snake. She lost her grip on the tablet, catching it in her other hand just before it fell.

Slowly, Ray moved her away from the bench.

"Just go home. I swear, I'll forget you ever came here," said Jess.

"I knew," said Ray, "that she was going to take Mia."

Why would he delete the video? Was he going to let her go to the police with a phantom claim and show them she was as unstable as they thought?

"Ray, you don't have to tell me anything else. I don't want to know," said Jess desperately.

"I didn't think anyone would be watching. I'm glad you brought me that video." His hand tightened around hers, holding her so she couldn't move.

It took Jess a moment to realize that Ray's hand wasn't constricting, wasn't trying to stop her from running; he was steadying her, to stop her from falling over her own feet.

"That's not Holly in the video," said Ray.

"What?"

"When I saw Mia's arm, I couldn't just ignore it. So, I hired someone to take Mia somewhere safe. Someone who looked like Holly. I thought, if anyone saw them, they'd just think Mia was with her mother."

"Who was she—the woman who took Mia?"

"I don't know her name," said Ray. "It's safer that way."

"How did you find someone so fast?" asked Jess.

Ray looked away, but it was already coming together in Jess's mind. The first time she met Ray. The photos she'd seen him purchasing just so he could see his daughter. Holly yelling at him, knowing she had the upper hand, that he'd pay more for another set of pictures if she demanded it.

"You already had it planned, didn't you? Even before you saw Mia. You were always going to take her."

"I was waiting for the right moment for months. I saw her a couple of times, at kindergarten or out with Holly. I wasn't following them, not really, but I had to know their movements... to make the pick up easier. When the right moment came, all I had to do was make the call." He shuffled his feet. "I'm sorry, Jess. It was the only way to keep her safe. I had no choice."

A silence grew as the night moved around them.

"Why didn't the police find that iPad when Mia went missing?" asked Ray.

"It was hidden in the top of Zoe's cupboard. I guess they didn't think it was worth checking." And why would they? It was virtually a kids' toy, made to look even more so with the rubber casing to stop it from being dropped.

Jess swallowed hard. "Is Mia... is she okay?"

"Yeah... at least, her arm is. I just hope it wasn't too late."

"What do you mean?" asked Jess, scared that Holly had already done too much damage that Mia mightn't recover from.

"Well, it's just a couple of things I noticed while I was observing her. Mia's calm. She doesn't react to things like a kid. She's..."

Jess remembered that first day of kinder, when Mia got Zoe in trouble for something Zoe hadn't done. That first time she saw Mia, something hadn't seemed right with her. Then there were the bruises over Zoe's arm, the reports of kids hitting her. Maybe Zoe didn't want to tell Ms. Liu it was Mia.

"She's a bit like Holly," said Jess.

"What if I got her out too late, and she's exactly like Holly?" said Ray.

Jess thought about Holly lying there and tried not to look over again. "Even if she is," she said, "Maybe being away from Holly, away from the violence, will show Mia a different way to live."

"I hope so," said Ray.

Now that Jess knew what'd happened, she wasn't sure how she felt. "Where's Mia?"

"I can't tell you that, Jess."

Jess nodded unconvincingly, hurt.

Ray noticed her expression. "It's not like that," he said. "It's difficult knowing something like that." He ran a hand through his hair. "You've been through enough because of me. Sorry I took so long to come see you, but I couldn't risk it. I had to wait until things cooled down."

"I thought you were going to tell them you took Mia when you visited me at Whitner."

"I was. Holly got too close to Zoe, and I thought she'd make good on her threat. I couldn't let that happen because of me, even for Mia."

"Thanks for looking out for Zoe." Jess smiled wanly.

"How's Zoe doing?"

"She's okay. I think she misses her dad."

"Well, she has her ma back. I know that means a lot to her."

"I guess this is goodbye," said Jess.

"I guess it is."

She went to the door to let Ray out. A hand on her wrist stopped her, but this time, she didn't jump. She turned, her eyes meeting Ray's.

She looked away as he cupped her chin in his hand and moved her face to his.

When the kiss was over, he looked over her face, taking it in. "Well, if your neighbors are nosy, now it just looks like an awkward date instead of a late-night drug deal," he joked. "Let's hope the people across the street don't gossip."

"Oh, believe me, they do," said Jess breathlessly.

He kissed her again, more urgently, moving close against her. "The trick is to make it embarrassing enough that your neighbors don't know what to say—it's your best chance of them saying nothing."

She was surprised to find that she didn't dislike the feeling of Ray's lips moving against hers. Under different circumstances, she might've enjoyed it, taken it further.

"You know, in a different life, I'd be asking you out on a date right about now," he said, his hand moving over her face, past her shoulder and across her arm, tracing the peaks and valleys across her skin.

"In another life, I might've said yes," said Jess. "But in this life, I have a sleepy girl who needs me to tuck her into bed."

It was a weak excuse, and if she hadn't glanced back at the kitchen, at what was beyond the bench, hiding out of sight, Ray might've left.

Chapter 69

Later

Ray followed Jess's gaze, moving around the bench to see what had her attention.

"She broke into my house," said Jess, hating that it sounded like she was trying to justify what she'd done. "I thought she was going to hurt Zoe, I swear."

Ray glanced at the make-shift weapon on the floor, and back at Holly, clearly trying to put together a replay of what had happened. "Is she dead?"

Jess looked at Holly, still staring into the distance. "Yes."

"I thought you were acting strange because of the video of Mia," he said.

Jess needed to deal with this alone. The fewer people involved, the better. "Just go, please," she said. "Let me handle it."

"What are you going to do?" asked Ray.

It was a good question; one she couldn't answer just yet. She suspected she had no choice—she'd have to call the police and try to explain what happened, how Holly had forced her way into the house, threatened Zoe.

Surely they'd see that Holly broke in, that she was dangerous.

Jess looked at the weapon on the floor—the same weapon Holly used to attack Clay. The weapon the police had thought Jess had tried to kill her husband with.

Even in death, it looked like Holly might still win.

Once she was sure Ray had left and wasn't coming back, Jess went to her phone and dialed Oscar's number.

He answered right away, his voice soothing enough to make her believe it might all turn out okay.

"Oscar, it's Jess," she said. "Something's happened and I'm not really sure what to do."

"Jess," he said warmly, the greeting in his tone.

"Holly came to my house. She forced her way inside. I think she was going to hurt Zoe like she said she would if I ever got out."

"Are you okay?" asked Oscar.

"Yeah," said Jess, realizing it was truer now than when she'd been falsely accused of taking Mia. She walked to Zoe's room, watching her daughter sleep peacefully. "Holly might still win, but this time, I'm not going to stay silent. I'm going to fight."

Chapter 70

Later

Oscar kissed Hayley on the forehead and rolled out of bed. Pulling on some clothes, he scooped up his phone and went outside, the fresh air readying him for the phone call he was about to make.

"Hello?" said an impatient voice, making him wonder which curse word she'd saved his name under.

"Prisha, it's me. I need you to meet me for coffee at ten o'clock."

"What? No, I'm busy—I can't do it."

"Whatever you're doing, do it later. I need to talk—it's about Riley."

"Fine."

Oscar named a café they'd frequented while they were married, knowing Prisha couldn't refuse them on merit.

He arrived first and sat at an industrial looking table that had replaced the old wooden ones he used to love. He tapped his foot, going over what he wanted to say. Somehow, when he was talking to Prisha, the words he planned never came out the way he wanted.

Prisha came in, raising an eyebrow disdainfully as she took a seat at his table. "I don't have much time. What's this about?" she said.

Oscar finished his sip of coffee, the hot liquid already cooling. "It's about Riley's tombstone," said Oscar.

"What? You brought me here to bring up my baby's tombstone?"

"I want my name on it," said Oscar. "I'll pay for it, but I want it on there."

"No, it's not an option. He's not here because of what you did and I won't have your name on it."

"Calm down. I just want to talk."

"You don't get to make demands," said Prisha, standing as if she had changed her mind.

"Sit down, Prisha," Oscar said firmly. "Riley was fine when I was home with him. I heard you get home early that night and go to his room. After he died, I couldn't think clearly. I couldn't tell what was real and what wasn't. It took me a long time to accept it, but I know what happened."

Oscar had Prisha's attention. She looked at him, brown eyes wide. "I don't know what you *think* you remember, but like you said, you can't tell what's real and what's not."

"You were in Riley's room for hours before you started crying. You knew he was dead, but you didn't make a sound."

"What are you accusing me of?" asked Prisha indignantly, unshed tears lining her eyes.

"There's nothing I can do to bring Riley back," said Oscar pointedly. "All I want is my name on my son's grave, where it belongs. I want him to know I loved him."

"Oscar, you just accused me—"

"I'm not accusing you. I know what happened; what you did. I always knew. Maybe I should've been more supportive, seen that you were struggling, but I didn't think you'd hurt him. I blame myself for not saying something earlier."

Prisha pulled her sunglasses over her eyes, hiding her tears. "It was my *job* to know something was wrong."

"You were always too busy with your patients to notice what was going on with your family," said Prisha. "I thought you'd help me, but I didn't know how to ask."

"I know. You're right. I should've been there when you needed me. But I still want my name on my son's grave, and I want you to promise you'll talk to someone."

"I've talked to someone about it, Oscar."

"You have?"

"I talked to Charles. It was a mistake, and he used it against me." She looked down and wiped at her cheek, catching more tears as they fell. "I thought I could trust him—he made me think I could."

"What happened?" asked Oscar.

"Nothing. It's not important. He wanted to get at you so badly. I was just a means to an end."

Oscar leaned across the table to hug her. "I'm sorry I wasn't there for you. You shouldn't have had to go through post-natal depression alone. You needed help to process everything. I'm going to get you that, okay?"

Prisha smiled weakly and pushed her chair away from the table. "I don't need your help anymore, Oscar. But thank you." She nodded, one quick gesture. "You can have your name engraved on Riley's stone," she said and left the cafe.

That was it. She'd agreed. Oscar had to visit Riley's grave and tell him the news.

Oscar messaged Hayley and ordered a coffee and two pumpkin bagels to go—Hayley's favorite brunch.

"I'll also add a serve of pancakes and syrup," Oscar said to the cashier.

"That's part of our kids' menu, sir," said the cashier. "I can't sell them to you."

"It's for my son."

The cashier nodded and added pancakes to the order.

Oscar took the food to the cemetery and sat with his back against Riley's stone. "Hey Ri. I'm sorry I haven't visited more. Truth is, I didn't think I deserved to. I'm sorry I let you down. I brought pancakes and syrup. You never got to try them, but I know you'd like them." He set the pancakes on the headstone and held up a bagged bagel. "The rest of it's just stuff grown-ups eat to be healthy," he said, scrunching up his nose. "But Hayley likes them for real, I think."

"Yes, she does," said a voice from behind Oscar.

"Hayley! I thought you were sleeping. I was going to bring bagels when I finished up here."

"I got your message. I hope you don't mind me barging in, but I haven't visited Riley yet, and I wanted to say hello."

"Take a seat." Oscar gestured to a spot next to him and handed her a bagel. "Riley, this is Hayley," he said. "Don't worry, I won't let her eat all the pancakes."

Epilogue

A little girl plays in the yard, the smell of dinner wafting through the garden. She's been practicing her somersaults in the long grass on the farm. Since her arm has felt better, she can do all kinds of things.

She brushed grass off her knees—somehow it always stuck to her. If her mother had seen her grubby clothes, she would've been in trouble, but her mother wasn't here and Nini said that dirty knees showed you were having fun. She missed her mother, but Nini always had a big hug and a story at bedtime.

"Ami," calls Nini from the door. "Are you ready to come in?"

At first, she doesn't answer—she isn't used to her new name yet.

"I can keep it warm for you if you like. Five more minutes?"

Ami's tummy rumbles and she smiles, and runs to Nini. Today's a special day.

Today, she's meeting her dad.

Acknowledgments

A lot goes into writing a book. While solitary at times, it's definitely not a one person job.

A huge thank you to *you*, the reader, for reading How to Spot a Psychopath. To a writer, your feedback is invaluable and so motivating. I hope you enjoyed it.

Thank you to everyone who worked on the book and read the early drafts. Thanks to Laura J. who did an amazing job editing the manuscript. Thanks to Donald, Angelle, Anna, Tam and Enza for reading early drafts. Thanks to my writing group for their candor.

Thanks to Oni, Zen, Quinn and Xari for your patience.

I look forward to sharing the next one with you.

MQ

xx

When You’re Dying…

… a sneak peek at book 2

Prologue

"Where are you going?"

It was him, his voice deep and insidious. Judging by how close he sounded, he was right behind her, moving across the rooftop tiles. If he reached out, he could almost touch her. The edge of the roof loomed high above the ground. If she fell, she probably wouldn't survive.

The thought made her dizzy, but she fought the vertigo. She had to be ready for his attack.

Up here, the smell of fresh rain overpowered the mildew on the rooftop tiles. There was no chimney, just a few solar panels that looked as if they'd give out if she grabbed onto them. If he decided to push her from the roof, there was nothing to stop her from falling to her death.

The woman looked out at the darkened sky, the rooftop gritty against her bare feet. The turbulent humidity of deep spring beat against her as the east coast sky threatened to open with electricity, warming her cheeks and filling her lungs with energy.

She had nowhere left to run, and without turning, she knew he was blocking the way behind her.

He'd grown quiet; the sudden silence didn't fool her. He was playing a game. When she turned, he'd catch her off-guard and attack. He stalked silently now, trying to elicit fear. She wouldn't give him what he wanted, no matter how far her heart rose in her throat.

The roof tiles were slicked with layers of rain. A peal of thunder took her by surprise as she approached the roof's edge.

As if spurred by the crack of a whip, the rain picked up, blinding her senses so that she lost the sound of his feet shifting on the tiles behind her. Afraid to look back, she realized she was out of time—her toes were almost over the edge and she needed to time her next move perfectly.

She'd have to rely on her own dexterity, which wasn't as reliable now that she knew she was probably going to die. The plan was to get just close enough to the edge, so that when he lunged, she could duck, sending him toppling off the roof. She imagined him meeting the ground like the forked lightning, dispersing across the dirt with a boom.

She worked hard to calm her breathing, willing the rushing in her ears to stop.

She felt him creeping closer.

Get ready.

"There's nowhere to run," he said. It's clear from his tone—he thinks he's won.

"Who's running?" she said, angling her feet sideways and bending her knees for balance.

He stopped beside her, lining up his next move.

"What're you going to do now? Jump?" he said.

"Maybe," she said.

He laughed; the sound breaking the hum of the rain. She was right to think he was crazy. Blanketed in the dark, she was thankful he couldn't see her face. She wanted him to think he'd won, that she was stupid enough to run to the roof and trap herself without a plan.

She curled her toes, ready to spring into action, remembering why she was up here to begin with. She hadn't come this far for nothing.

She could feel him smirking, even in the dark.

"It'd save me the trouble," he said.

She set her jaw. "Why won't you tell me?" she asked. He'd kidnapped her sister, she was sure of it, but she didn't know why, or where she was now.

"Where's the fun in that?"

"What did you do with her? Did you bury her somewhere?"

"You'll never know. You don't deserve to know."

"I'll make you wish you told me," she said, wiping rain from her face, ignoring the itch it caused on her skin.

He stepped forward, the heat of his skin closing in, the sharpness of his features captured by the shadows, ridding him of that clean-cut charm that she saw right through. "You won't get the chance."

Now.

With a primal scream, she ran at him, knocking him off balance so that he slid on the slippery tiles. He rolled toward the edge, looking up at her, reaching out to take her with him.

This close, she could just make out his face, the look in his eye strange and stunned, the look of someone who knew they were about to die. She wondered if everyone had that same look as they realized their last moment was upon them.

She saw his fingers twist and curl around her ankle. She tried to get out of the way, but the rain slicked roof slowed her. Was she being punished for trying to end his life?

Maybe this was retribution, and she'd go down with him.

About the Author

MQ Webb enjoys writing thrillers, suspense, mysteries and horror stories and has always believed in the transformational nature of words, and a medium to utilize them. A fascination with human behavior and motivation led them to study psychology and human behavior. They once worked in a building that was converted from a gaol into an office space and has worked for NFP's, universities, and the public sector.

How to Spot a Psychopath is the first book in the Oscar de la Nuit Psychological thriller series.

Don't forget to sign up for the newsletter. You will only ever receive book news, events, giveaways and recommendations relating to the author. Your data will not be shared with third parties.

If you enjoyed this book, please consider reviewing and sharing it with readers like yourself.

You can connect with me on:

- https://www.mqwebb.com
- https://twitter.com/marswebb1
- https://www.facebook.com/MQWebbAuthor
- https://www.instagram.com/bookreviewery

Subscribe to my newsletter:

- https://mqwebb.com

Also by MQ Webb

When You're Dying

A shock diagnosis forces Verity Casmere to consider how she wants to spend the time she has left.

The one question haunting Verity is what happened to her missing sister, Ashlee. Was she murdered, like the police suspect?

How far will Verity go to learn the truth?

Moved by her situation, Forensic Psychiatrist, Oscar de la Nuit, agrees to help Verity learn what happened, but he quickly finds himself in deeper than he intended, placing himself and the people closest to him in danger.

Can they resurface before a dark secret consumes them both?

Lightning Source UK Ltd.
Milton Keynes UK
UKHW011843100422
401365UK00001B/25

9 780645 352016